The Road to Newgate

"Moved me greatly and brought tears to my eyes. Gripping, moving, and brilliantly captures this tense and sometimes brutal episode in late seventeenth-century English history."
Andrea Zuvich, author of
A Year in the Life of Stuart Britain

"A real pleasure to read."
Denis Bock, author of *The Ash Garden* &
The Communist's Daughter

"Meticulously researched, vividly imagined, and deftly plotted. Rich, resonating and relevant."
Catherine Hokin, author of
*Blood and Roses, the story
of Margaret of Anjou.*

Kate Braithwaite

CROOKED
CAT

Discover us online:
www.crookedcatbooks.com

Join us on facebook:
www.facebook.com/crookedcat

Tweet a photo of yourself holding
this book to **@crookedcatbooks**
and something nice will happen.

To Jean Taylor, my mum, with love.

About the Author

Kate Braithwaite was born and grew up in Edinburgh, Scotland. Her first novel, Charlatan, was longlisted for the Mslexia New Novel Award and the Historical Novel Society Award. Kate lives in Pennsylvania with her husband and three children.

Acknowledgements

Jean Taylor, Trisha Causley, Kat Smith and Zoe Fairtlough: there are not enough words to thank you for your patient reading of the many versions of this novel. Your feedback and friendship are invaluable. Others I would like to thank for their support for my writing endeavours include Shannon Albert, Jen Blab, Maren Albans, Sarah Miller, my husband Chris and our kids, Dominic, Max and Maddie.

Thank you, also, to authors Dennis Bock and Lee Gowan from the Creative Writing Programme at Toronto University. I am very proud and grateful to have received the Marina Nemat Award for an early draft of this book.

And thank you, Steph and Laurence at Crooked Cat for picking up The Road to Newgate and bringing it to publication. Your time and expertise is invaluable. It is a pleasure to be a Crooked Cat.

The Road to Newgate

London, 1678

Chapter One

Nathaniel Thompson

"All the world has been to the Bartholomew Fair! What do you mean you've never been here?"

"What do you suppose I mean?" Anne says, arching two fine, black brush strokes – eyebrows in a more commonplace face.

It is a genuine surprise. My wife has lived all her life in London. I'm astonished that she has never experienced one of the most famous attractions in the city.

"Well, look about you, Nathaniel," she says, tucking her arm back into mine. "It is not exactly genteel. Why did you think I was so keen to come?"

She smiles, a dimple playing in her cheek, but I suppress a groan. Of course, her family would not have stooped to visit such a place. Various choice answers spring to mind, but I wind my fingers in hers and hold my tongue. This is our holiday; not to be spoiled by awkward thoughts of Anne's relations. Instead, I kiss her smooth dark hair.

She is right about the fair. It is a storm of activity, and much of it far from decorous. Thankfully, we're here in the late afternoon, not the evening, but even so, there are few families present. Instead, the fair attracts courting couples, scrubby urchins chasing rats, and saucy girls up for a lark during a few hours excused from sewing work or service. Working men, their bellies warm with ale, crowd around stalls to trade insults and roar out wagers. We pass a trio of buxom dames, glorious to behold in citrus satin stripes and sweating under their wigs. One drops her purse and bends to retrieve it. When she stands, we are treated to the sight of her ample flesh escaping the confines of her corset. Her friends squeal and point as Anne clutches my arm. She has to dip her head to hide her laughter.

After that, we take our time strolling past stalls selling lucky charms, playing cards, fans, dice, snuff boxes, trinkets, all manner of things. My wife is entranced. She stops to pick up goods, quizzes traders on their prices, gasps at a troupe of acrobats, and teases me to win her a prize. I keep a firm hand on my purse and an eye out for any pocket-pickers, otherwise content to watch her enjoy it all.

We have been married for just over four months. Without taking anything away from my love for Anne, I will admit that married life is rather trying. When contemplating the changes that matrimony would involve, I failed to anticipate that the wonderful physical freedom to be with her all night long would also impact on my comings and goings during daylight hours. Perhaps I came to this marriage business a little late. I was more set in my ways and routines than I knew.

At any rate, I am thirty and she is ten years younger. Anne has a young witch's smile, silken skin, and bright, challenging eyes. I saw her and wanted her. I let go years of cautious bachelorhood and sneaked Anne to the altar when her family was not looking. It goes without saying that I have never been happier. But I'm a busy man, and while she does not complain, I've this curious guilt – an unaccustomed itch of responsibility, you might say – when I think about her sitting quietly at home when I am at work. After a neglectful week when I'd been out in Sam's Coffee House until the small hours and quartered in my office above Henry's print shop as soon as light broke each morning, I promised her this outing.

"There! That's what I want." She stops before a stall draped with exotic silk purses and scarves. "Win me something. Something colourful."

How can I refuse? The vendor, a grinning Turk with a brace of broken teeth, gives me three hessian sacks to throw at a wooden wheel contraption at the back of his booth. On it stand ten gold and silver bottles, and as he turns the wheel with a handle, I try to knock them down. It looks simple, but it isn't.

Three throws bring me nothing. Whether the fellow has

such skill to see how to move his wheel just as I take aim, or whether he has somehow nailed those damned bottles down, I cannot say. I hand over more money and take another turn.

"Nat! I don't really need anything," says Anne, after the second attempt yields nothing.

"Oh, but you do."

On my third round, I'm sure I hit one bottle squarely, but it does not fall.

"Here!" I say. Several passers-by stop to see what the commotion is. "Let me see you lift those bottles."

But the Turk shakes his head. He cups a hand to his ear and shrugs as though he cannot understand.

"Come on, fellow!" calls someone behind me. "Surely you can knock one of that lot down. You're a pretty-looking lad, but the lady wants a prize. She needs to find herself a tougher squire than you, you noddypeak!"

That galls me. Anne tugs my sleeve, but I am already counting more coins into the stallholder's hand.

I suspect the Turk fears that he will have trouble if this nonsense carries on, because – wonder of wonders – this time, I have no difficulty. A cheer erupts as I knock over the bottles and the man gives Anne her choice of his wares. While she decides, I feel a light tap on my shoulder.

"Mr. Thompson?"

At my side is a skinny fellow that Henry sometimes employs to deliver our pamphlets about the coffee shops. His sort often has a nose for news and will know if an arrest has been made or a scandal is brewing. He knows something now. I smell it on him, read it in the eager nod of his head. God knows, there's gossip aplenty in the city, with talk of a missing magistrate and arrests of prominent Catholic Lords, so I turn my back on Anne, anxious for news. My conscience may creak as I listen to the young lad's tale, but that's easily ignored. Easily that is, until the sound of an altercation causes us both to twist round.

A woman, tall and sharp-featured, her lips pulled back from her teeth in bare anger, has her hand on Anne's arm and is screeching at her. For a moment, I'm dumbfounded. I step towards them, but not quickly enough. In that split second, the woman tilts back her head and hurls a plume of spit right into my wife's face.

No-one moves. Then the woman disappears into the crowd and Anne does her best to make light of it. She wipes her face, shows me her new bag, and insists on continuing about the fair as if nothing has happened. All she will say is that the woman was obviously deranged, some Bedlamite; quite a sorry case, in fact. I squeeze her hand, proud that my young wife can be so composed. And then I put it out of my mind.

In my defence, there is little enough time to remember it or question Anne further in the days that follow. The rumour whispered to me at the fair is the main news on everyone's lips by the next morning. A man has been found dead in a ditch on Primrose Hill. He is identified as the missing magistrate, Sir Edmund Godfrey.

Chapter Two

Anne Thompson

All my pleasure in the fair is gone. I try not to make a fuss, but my happiness in the day has vanished. It was certainly a first. Accosted by a stranger, shouted at, spat on. I add these to the long list of new experiences I have encountered since we married. Many have been good, but some have not been so welcome.

We walk home soon afterwards. Nat is pre-occupied, his face serious in the half-light of early evening. His long jaw curls slightly at his chin, as if he's scraping his bottom teeth against the top. His brow is pulled low, his brown eyes narrowed in thought. I shiver. Something about this man catches my heart.

"Are you cold?" He turns and smiles down at me. The terrible things that the madwoman said about him disappear from my mind. My lips smile back.

"A little," I say.

"I'll warm you up when we get home."

Will he stay, though? Or will he disappear into the night, off to his office, to his publisher, Henry Broome, or to the coffee shops to catch up on the news of the day? Nat's London never sleeps. I've learned to read the signs.

"What is it, love?" I ask. "What did you hear?"

"Godfrey's been found."

"Dead?"

"Dead."

As a modestly brought up young lady from a very good family, I'm supposed to know nothing and look decorous. My childhood was luxurious, full of long days practising dancing, music, and learning to sew. But I also had a younger brother with a tutor who was kind to me, and I learned far more than my parents ever realised. My life may have been sheltered but I'm not ignorant about the world we live in. King Charles has no legitimate children. Many people are horrified at the prospect of his brother, James, Duke of York – a Catholic – on the English throne. My father says the Catholics will stop at nothing. Everyone knows that Godfrey, a prominent Protestant magistrate, vanished several days ago. There has been talk of little else.

"Murdered?" I ask.

Nat nods. "That's what I heard just now. Run through with his own sword. Already it's been said that Catholics are behind his disappearance."

"Will you have to go out again?"

"Probably." He puts his arm around my shoulders and pulls me close.

"You have a difficult job. Impossible, perhaps."

Five years ago, with rumours of treason proliferating, the Privy Council appointed my husband as His Majesty King Charles II's Licenser of the Presses. It was a great honour, he told me, for such a young man, with no family behind him. What it means is that beyond the authorised work of academics, lawyers, and the Church of England, nothing – *nothing* – is supposed to be written in the city without his permission. No-one should print or sell a word unless Nathaniel sees it first. All books must cross his table and bear his stamp.

It doesn't pay well, but I knew that when I married him. He maintains a cramped office above the printing house of Henry Broome, and supplements his income by writing articles for the *London Gazette* and producing diverse pamphlets of his own, concerning news from Parliament, the courts, and so on. The woman at the fair said such terrible, wicked things about him. A mistake, I think. Or just plain lies.

"I'll come home for a few hours," he says. "But then I'll have to catch up with developments. Henry will have the press ready, I'm sure."

We cross Iron Monger Lane. Nearly home.

"I love to walk," I say.

"That is a very good thing, Mistress Thompson, because we can't afford to be hiring a carriage and horses anytime soon."

"We don't need them."

"*I* don't need them. But one day, I hope to provide better for you."

"I don't miss all those things," I say.

***

When I wake the following morning, he has already left. Last night, he was out chasing information about Sir Edmund Godfrey until the Lord knows when. I stirred in the night and felt the weight of his arm across mine. Hints of coffee and tobacco linger in the air. But this morning he has slipped out without disturbing me. He means to be considerate, but I would rather not wake up alone.

Our house, on the corner of Thames Street and Love Lane, is a simple one, but like all the houses recently built in the area close to Pudding Lane, its brick walls are well enough made that the wind does not rattle our bones all the night as it can in some older dwellings. We have three rooms, stacked upon each other like boxes, and a basement kitchen with a cupboard for Kitty, our serving girl.

She has everything well in hand today. Together, we wash and fold linen, but the hours pass slowly. I wonder about the dead magistrate and how busy Nat must be. The house is very quiet. Too quiet. So, when Kitty asks if she may go and visit her sister, I do the same. My older sister Sarah is always at home in the morning. If her husband is there, I might ask him about the accusations made by that woman at the fair. As the son of a former Lord Mayor and now an Alderman himself, there is little that happens in London without James's knowledge.

It is a long-ish walk to their house on the north end of Chancery Lane and the autumn air is cool. Near Snow Hill, a small boy runs toward me and stumbles. A woman plucks him

11

from the gutter. Another second and a carriage wheel would have crushed his legs. She slaps him across the cheek, only to pull him into a crushing embrace and burst into tears. The sight of it makes my eyes sting. For the rest of my walk to Sarah's, I imagine little boys with soft brown hair and sharp brown eyes, just like Nat's.

James and my sister are both at home, but they also have another visitor that I am not prepared for.

Sarah rushes down the stairs towards me, pointing at James's study door with one hand and shushing me with her fingers to her lips with the other. She pulls me into their morning room and leans back against the door.

"Papa is here!" she says. "He has only just arrived. Five minutes earlier and you might have met on the street outside. Imagine!"

I blanch at the thought, to be honest. He would have looked straight through me.

"Why is he here? This is not a normal time for him to visit."

"No, but you have heard that Godfrey's body has been found? I'm sure your Nat knows all about it. Papa is most upset. You know how he is. About Catholics particularly."

"I should go."

"What? No. He will leave soon enough."

"But when he comes to take his leave of you?"

"Then he will see you, and perhaps this nonsense will come to an end."

I shake my head. "Or perhaps it won't. No, Sarah, I must go. I will come again another day. Maybe, in time, he will change his view of Nat. Until then, it is better he doesn't know I was here."

She is sorry to agree, but agree she must. My father swore to have nothing more to do with me when I ran away with Nat, and he's a stubborn man. My mother will always side with him, and she is likely far too busy worrying about her own health and entertaining the parade of quacks whose company she so enjoys, to even miss me. I have the idea that when children come, my father might soften, but my current hopes on that subject are too new and personal to voice, even to my sister.

"All right, but wait here." Sarah whisks out of the room. While I wait, raised voices can be heard coming from James's study across the hall. My father is truly agitated. There could not be a worse time to see him. I pick up an embroidery from Sarah's basket by the fireplace and examine it by the window. This is a lovely, light room looking out onto a walled garden. Someone has been piling up leaves and cutting back dead blooms. Sarah finds such work tedious, but I would love to have a garden to tend.

"What would Miss Frankham say about this stitching?" I ask with a smile, when she returns.

"Yes, yes, it's terrible," she laughs. "But it's what we are supposed to do, so I do it. You know how it is. Now here, look at this."

On the table by the window, she unfolds a bolt of pale, blue cloth. "Don't even think about refusing me," she says. "It is not my colour and I don't know why I let the woman talk me into it. But because I did, I simply can't face up to returning it. You must take it. Every time I look at it, I'm reminded of my weakness in buying it in the first place. Say you will take it home with you."

This is so like Sarah. My older sister is kind and generous to a fault. It would be rude to refuse her, and the colour is truly pretty. I take the cloth, kiss her on both cheeks, and slip out of the house before my father discovers my presence.

On the way home, I imagine the charming dress I will make. At some point I remember I had wanted to talk to James about that woman, but it is too late to turn back now. On Fish Street Hill, more people than usual are gathered around the new monument to the Great Fire. They are pointing. An addition has been made to the Latin inscription on its northern side. I've read the stone panel many times. It describes the fire that ravaged this part of the city, day and night, in 1666. On the third day, it reads, the fatal fire died out. But a new line has been added, indicating the rising tide of concern felt all across London.

One man translates, calling others to hear that it reads, "But

Popish frenzy, which wrought such horrors, is not yet quenched." Around him, people grumble their agreement. On the east side there is another addition, this one in Latin and English. I join the people peering at it and read, "The City of London was burnt and consumed with fire by the treachery and malice of the papists in September in the year of Our Lord 1666."

"Those Catholic bastards," one woman shouts. "They're the ones that should burn!"

I hurry home.

Chapter Three

Nat

Edmund Godfrey had lived in Westminster, just off The Strand by Charing Cross, on Hartshorn Lane – a muddled street leading up from the river, where grand houses jostle next to stables and storehouses.

Henry and I identify the dead man's house from a way off. It's shrouded in darkness, but two light-boys stand outside swinging bright lanterns back and forth. The magistrate was also a successful wood and coal-monger, but unmarried and childless. I presume his brothers will inherit his wealth. Since Godfrey was found dead with ligature marks on his neck and his own sword sticking out of his chest, there has been talk of little else. Within hours it was rumoured that papists had murdered him as part of a complex plot against the Crown. It takes little enough to make Protestant London flutter and fear. Godfrey's death is a public event, and we are not the only ones taking the opportunity to view the corpse. A steady trickle of men and women come and go from the house as we approach.

"And how is Mistress Thompson?" Henry asks.

"She is well."

"Settled?"

"Very."

For ten years, Henry Broome has been my publisher and business partner, my closest friend and ally. Unfortunately, he has doubts about my hasty marriage. Doubts that I don't care to hear expressed.

"What do you know of this Titus Oates?" I ask, to change the subject.

No more is required. Henry embarks upon a steady stream

of observations about this young parson I've heard about. Titus Oates has risen to prominence by revealing a plot to murder the King. Oates has been given lodgings in Whitehall, Henry says, and hailed as a hero. Oates claims he infiltrated a network of Jesuits, uncovered an assassination plot, and risked his own life to reveal it. While Henry explains, I say little, watching the smoke of his breath on the cold air spiral and disappear.

An old servant stands beside the open front door, scrutinising every visitor. The house is of modest size, and while Godfrey was not one to flaunt his riches, I have no trouble reading his success in the thick drapes at every window, the panelled walls, the silver plate, and the waxy white candles that burn so merrily. These are the details I need for the newssheets tomorrow morning. It is a fine property. I would very much like to see Anne in such a house.

William has arrived before us and we fall into step with him. He is a quiet fellow, my friend William Smith – a schoolteacher, very reserved – but he has a sharp eye for detail and a dry sense of humour. Anne likes him. She is certainly more comfortable with William than she is with Henry.

"Did you see that?" William whispers in my ear.

"What?"

"The housekeeper. Look how she glares at the old fellow at the door."

I've missed the exchange. Behind the scenes, the household is likely in some state. "Many questions must have been asked of them these last few days," I say.

We join the slow stream of people entering the room where Godfrey lies, and circle the open coffin. In life, Godfrey was a thin, whey-faced man. In death, his face is swollen and distorted. I hardly recognise him.

"Godfrey would not want all this," say Henry. "Not one for attention. And it does not help your position."

"What does this have to do with Nat's work?" asks William.

"He means the Licensing Act," I say. "It must be renewed by Parliament in the New Year or my post will disappear. I can ill afford that. Especially now."

"Why wouldn't it be renewed?"

"Because of this Titus Oates and his Popish plot. Parliament is in uproar. All normal business suspended," says Henry.

"Titus Oates?" William frowns. He looks from me to Henry and back again, but we have reached the hallway and must exchange a few words with Godfrey's brothers on our way out. I mutter the normal condolences, but Henry is more familiar.

"Dear sirs," he says, clasping each man's hand in his bear-paws one after another. "What news of the investigation? Has the King's reward prompted anyone to come forward?"

Benjamin Godfrey frowns, a peevish contraction of brows, but remains silent. The older brother, Michael, speaks for them both. A ruddy, fleshier version of the dead magistrate, he shakes his head. "Nothing at all, Mr. Broome, sadly. In my day, five hundred pounds was a lot of money." It is on my lips to say that five hundred pounds would be very welcome to me – in his day, my day, or any day – but I don't think they are too interested in my troubles. "My brother and I," he continues, "have concluded that poor Edmund was murdered for political reasons. I fear that those involved will not be tempted by money. They are indoctrinated in hate, these Catholics."

***

"A poor pair," says Henry, as we leave. "Godfrey was nothing like them. Very quiet and private, although he had some surprising friends."

"Yes?" I say.

"Edward Coleman, for one. Valentine Greatrakes is another."

"Surprising indeed." Edward Coleman is a Catholic, and secretary to the King's brother and heir, James, Duke of York. Valentine Greatrakes, on the other hand, is an Irish faith healer, of all things. The idea of Godfrey – a famously dour Protestant magistrate – consorting with either man, stretches credulity. William's chin is on his chest and he remains silent so I don't know what he thinks. As we stroll down the Strand past Somerset House, there are noticeably more soldiers

17

abroad, erecting and lighting braziers, lifting the customary gloom of London at night. The streets are busy with pedlars eking out pence where they can and young men gathering courage to sample the flesh-pots of Covent Garden. Ragged children and stray dogs nip in and out between carriages and horses like darting fish.

"Titus Oates," says William. "I know him."

We are only a step from Sam's Coffee House. Henry tips his head towards the door.

Until I met Anne, this was my very favourite place in London. In Sam's, the fires burn bright. The coffee boy checks that the water is boiling and sniffs to see how long until a fresh infusion is required. It's steamy hot. Men huddle on long benches, smoking, drinking coffee, brandy or ale; talking in low voices so that there is a constant throaty hubbub, broken by the odd crack of laughter and the clatter of dishes, or the swing of the door. It is always the same, day or night. I promise myself that I will not stay long.

As soon we are seated with drinks in our hands, Henry leans forward.

"Well? What do you know of Oates?"

"More than I want to, and more than enough," says William. "I was his teacher once."

"You were?" I'm surprised. William is older than me, but still.

"I was a young man then, of course. In my early twenties. And Titus is not so old now as you may imagine. He's not yet thirty, and I am only his senior by ten years."

"And where? Where was this?" asks Henry.

"At the Merchant Taylors' School. Years ago. In '64, or thereabouts."

"What do you remember of him? How would you describe him?"

William takes a breath. "He was backward, unpleasant, and untrustworthy. There. Is that what you wanted to hear?"

Henry and I exchange a speaking glance. He's as surprised as I am by William's vehemence. I have not known William long, truth be told. We met quite by chance, strolling through

18

Covent Garden Market one day last spring. Anne and I, not yet married, were there together, taking advantage of a lazy maid who was more interested in flirting with a young man from the barber's shop than watching who her mistress met in the market. We were buying herbs when a scrubby boy hurtled past and almost knocked Anne over. He had pinched an apple and was making a break for it. It was the boy that ended up in the dirt, however, and he would have been in the hands of the law had not William stepped in the way, blocking the path of the outraged stallholder while the boy escaped. Anne and I observed the whole pantomime. William pretended he had no notion of what was afoot, but Anne was sure his intervention was deliberate. She insisted we congratulate him on his kindness, and William and I struck up a friendship. He's an interesting chap who likes to talk politics, and I enjoy his company. He often visits us, and I have great respect for his opinion.

"In what way untrustworthy?" asks Henry.

"Oh, the usual. Stealing from other boys. Cheating. Blaming others for his failure to complete tasks. He was expelled in the end."

"I see. And his school work?"

"A struggle. I met his mother once. She told me he was much later to develop than any of his siblings." William's expression is grave. "She said he frightened her. For years she wondered if something was wrong with him. He had trouble learning to speak, he drooled, and had constant colds and dirty habits. She said that Titus's father couldn't stand him and would beat him as soon as look at him, yet the boy had always craved his father's attention. She was adamant that Titus had hated the sight of her."

"And you described him as unpleasant. How?"

"Crude. Angry. Prone to sudden outbursts."

"I suppose a man may change as he grows older," says Henry.

"No!" William swallows, as if trying to keep his emotions in check. "He is not much changed from the boy I've described. He frequents the Fuller's Rent Tavern. I have seen him there."

The Fuller's Rent Tavern has a certain reputation. I make sure not to glance at Henry.

"He is not liked there," says William. "But he is tolerated. Because Matthew had a kindness for him."

"Matthew?" I ask.

William's dark eyes are fixed on the table. "Matthew Medbourne, the actor."

"Where have I heard that name?" mutters Henry.

"Medbourne is in Newgate Prison."

***

An hour or two later, I walk home in the rain. There is no moon to help me see where to put my feet on the narrow runs between leaning houses. William's story about Medbourne weighs on me.

Medbourne and William had been at the Fuller's Rent one night when Titus Oates approached them. Oates had recognised his old teacher and William felt obliged to acknowledge him.

Henry had kept his gaze on his coffee cup while William pulled his fingers. Several times he'd lifted his chin as if to speak and then changed his mind. Finally, he had said, "Some things are not easily explained."

I consider that as I make my way down Grace Church Street, but the behaviour of Titus Oates worries me more. William described a man who had befriended another man only to use him. Medbourne had found this Oates a job in the household of the Duke of Norfolk. Without it, William said, the fellow would have been destitute. But as soon as he was settled, Oates turned on Matthew Medbourne. He dropped him, ignored him, and tried to turn the other fellows at the Fuller's Rent Tavern against him, too. Then Oates had lost his post. William didn't know why but suggested theft, drunkenness, or some lewd act most likely played a part.

At home, all is silent and dark. I have stayed out too late and let Anne down. But I needed to hear what William had to say. It is well that I did.

"Oates is vindictive. With power and influence he is dangerous," William had said. "Matthew Medbourne is a Catholic. He is in Newgate, charged with involvement in a Popish Plot that Titus Oates has exposed. Just the suggestion that Matthew could be involved in such a business is preposterous. But he has been in Newgate for weeks, and Oates will speak to Parliament in the House of Commons in a few days' time."

I pull off my boots as quietly as possible and rest for a moment on our narrow stairs. Perhaps Anne will stir when I climb into bed. I need her warmth and might find rest for my thoughts in her arms, if she wakes. For now, Henry's concerns occupy me. He does not like what is happening. Not the death of Justice Godfrey, not the mood on the streets, not what William just told us about Titus Oates, and certainly not the prospects for my future employment given all this upheaval.

To be brutally honest, neither do I.

Chapter Four

Anne

He swings his long legs out of the bed and rests his feet on the cool wooden floor. The bed ropes creak as I sit up next to him. I run my fingers through his cropped brown hair.

"Shall I cut it later?"

"Yes, if you think it needs it. Did you see the chains go up in the streets?"

"The length of King Street and the Strand, I was told." I pull on a long linen shift and go to the basin to wash. A giggle catches my throat as Nat, who declares he prefers to feel the air about himself, stands up. He is stark naked, surely tingling with cold. Perhaps when I am an old married woman such sights will be commonplace, but not any time soon, I hope. I like looking at my husband. He stretches his arms out wide and upwards until his fingertips brush the grainy plaster on the ceiling.

"If you ask me, the whole of London has run mad," he says.

Our bedroom is a cramped, close-quartered room, wood-panelled to its hips with white plaster walls above. It was the barest cell when he first brought me home, but I made it merry with some faded red tapestries. Even now, there is nothing in the room beyond a press for our clothes, a dresser for the basin and jug, and our bed. It is a far cry from my parents' house, but I am not regretful about that. As I straighten the bedclothes and tie the thick damask hangings – our single luxury – Nat pulls on his shirt and leans out of the window. I imagine a cradle in the corner, but have said nothing of my suspicions to Nat just yet.

"It reeks down there," he says. "But up here I catch a hint of the river."

"Well, that's not much to be thankful for!"

It's true. The Thames stinks; muck from the tanneries and rot from the markets sluice into it every day. It's become a regular scandal. Billingsgate Fish Market is very close by. I'm not sure my stomach will ever get used to it.

"No. That's not what I mean," he says. "I mean the river as it should be. Or maybe I mean the sea. It's fresher up here. You see if it isn't." With a grin, he reaches for me, trying to pull me to the window, and I know where that will end. It is not that I am not tempted, but a woman has work to do so he must settle for a kiss. I turn to my brushes and pins.

"I enjoy watching you pin your hair," he says, and my eyes meet his in my looking glass. He curls his shoulders like a shy boy. "I like the turn of your neck."

It is high time my husband's mind was taken out of the bedroom and into the day. "Are you going to the funeral?" I say.

"Wouldn't miss it for the world." Nat reaches for his breeches. "Why don't you come with me? I'm meeting William on Ludgate Hill."

I am absurdly pleased that he has asked. I rush to see that the fire is lit downstairs. I want to be ready in time.

***

We do not talk much. The warm thickness of his arm underneath mine contents me, and besides, I doubt we could hear each other over the rattle of coach wheels and the shrill cries of a street-hawker, selling oysters by the peck. I'm happy to see William smiling when he finds I am to join them. He has a long, thin face, very sombre when still, but a sweet boyish smile. I used to think he must be too shy to be a schoolteacher, but I have learned that he is the kind of man to use humour and patience as his brand of strength.

The Strand, when we get there, is even busier than usual. Men and women are gathered, stern-faced and grim, with arms folded across chests. Some whisper of conspiracy while others discuss the murder in outraged tones. Several makeshift trestles have been set out in front of closed and shuttered shops. They are crowded with customers. It takes us a few moments to worm our way in and see what all the fuss is about.

"Good grief!" Nat reacts quickly. I only see rows of silver medals, but when I pick one up I understand. On one side, there is a rough image of a man – obviously intended to be Godfrey – with a noose around his neck and a sword in his chest. And on the other side? Only the Pope himself, giving his blessing to Godfrey's murderers.

"And look here!" I drop the medal and pull him along to the next stall. "What do you think of these, Nathaniel?" It is a small iron blade with the words *'Remember the murder of Edmund Godfrey. Remember religion'* engraved on the side.

"You mean, apart from my awed admiration of the quick wit and entrepreneurial skill of our fellow men?"

His sarcasm I expect, but William and I are both surprised when Nat buys one. He puts it into my hands as we step back into the flow of people.

"A Godfrey dagger," he says.

"Why buy it? I thought you hated such things."

"I do. When I heard they were the most popular souvenirs on the streets in the last few days, I didn't really believe it. I had to buy one just to appreciate that they're real."

Not for the first time, I'm anxious about what is happening in the city. My thoughts go to my father. He is probably here somewhere, as worked up as anyone about the Catholic threat.

"Is it true, Nat? Is what people are saying true?"

"That depends what you've heard. And who you speak to."

We walk on in silence. Nat's face is gloomier than I like it. When he worries, he looks older; his brows shade the normal brightness of his eyes, his cheeks look gaunt, and his wide, generous mouth thins to a line. I squeeze his hand and wait. I have seen the clouds come down around his head before. There is certainly something going on in London, that's why there's such a fuss over the funeral of poor Justice Godfrey. All the talk is of Catholic plots. It's hard to believe, but with so much concern, it's hard not to believe it either.

Finally, Nat says, "There is talk of a Popish plot but information is thin on the ground. There is a man, Titus Oates. He will speak to Parliament tomorrow and I'll go and listen. It is probably all just bluster and flummery. Look about us. Most people are simply taking advantage of a change from the everyday routine, drinking too much, and stuffing their bellies with hot pies and chestnuts. Nothing to worry about."

I am not so sure.

Soon enough, the funeral procession begins. The crowd shuffles back, and truly it is a sight to behold. The coffin, carried by six men, is draped in a fine cloth, decorated with armorial bearings. Upwards of seventy Church of England divines and hundreds of mourners respectfully follow its progress. We lose sight of William in the swell of humanity, and just when it seems we cannot possibly find him, he reappears at Nat's shoulder. We melt into the congregation inside the church of St Martin-in-the-Fields, ready for Dr. William Lloyd's eulogy.

I am no expert on funeral oration. I could count the number of funerals I have attended on the fingers of one hand, and none were as prestigious as this. But to my mind, Lloyd gives a tremendous performance. He's a bull-necked, heavy-jowled, glowering preacher. He stomps into the wooden pulpit flanked by two thick-set clergymen who glare at the congregation, silently daring any man to make a move against their colleague. There is no time to ask Nat or William what they think of it all. My eyes are riveted on Lloyd. His scowl swoops and plunges over his audience as he leans forward and slowly raises his arms. His gaze withers us, drying up words, sealing lips. When we are all hushed and ready, he thunders.

This must be what it is like to stand outside during a storm. His invective whips like the wind, his anger rains down until his outrage saturates my skin. He describes the death of a good, even a great man. His words conjure the clearest vision of a loyal servant to justice and his king, whose life has been stolen, ended in tragic murder.

Godfrey was stabbed through with his own sword.

25

Garrotted. Beaten. His body was thrown in a ditch. He declares that a heinous act of butchery has been committed on the streets of London. The ignominy and violence of Godfrey's end is already a sensation. Spitting out every detail, here, in this church, Lloyd turns it into a cataclysm. If this can happen to such a man, the rest of us have much to fear. That fear is mirrored in the eyes of people all around me.

Then Lloyd points the finger. There is no doubt about whom we must blame, despise, and now hunt down. Godfrey's death is laid at the door of the Jesuits. Once again, those Catholic devils are plotting against our king and country, against our rights and freedoms, against our security in our streets and in our homes. But we can join together. Together, we mourn the loss of a man who represented all that was good in the City of London, a man murdered by those devils incarnate, the Catholics. If we stand together, they will not defeat us.

The crowd sucks it in. People shuffle and nod. They clench their fists and thrust forward their jaws. Godfrey's brothers and sisters nod fervently behind their handkerchiefs. William bites his lip. But not Nat. Nat has one eyebrow raised and his arms folded over his chest. He leans back on his heels and closes his eyes.

The three of us are quiet as we walk back home across the city. Near Somerset House, we come upon another crowd. We halt, separate from the angry gangs of men and women who mill around beneath all those splendid windows. Many in the crowd wear silver medals or clutch Godfrey daggers. Their voices are raised, hot suspicions spiralling up, swirling around the Queen's residence. Something cuts through the air above us. There's a crash, the crackle of breaking glass, and the crowd sways back. Instead of frightening them, though, it brings a cheer. As quickly as they've moved away, the crowd presses forward again and a chant goes up: "Give us your priests! Give us your priests!"

"This is what I hate," Nat mutters. "Ignorant fools."

"They're afraid," I say.

"Of what? A barren Catholic queen and her gaggle of

26

clucking priests?"

William says nothing. He's looking around, not listening to us.

"Well, no. But they have a point, don't they? All Catholics have been ordered from the city, and yet everyone knows the Queen's priests are still in there."

"Let's keep walking." Nat grips my elbow and steers. "It sounds like you've been listening to your father."

"And what if I had?" I yank my arm from his grasp and we glare at each other. I'm aware of what he thinks of my family, that the difference between their world and his – ours – is vast. I can only imagine the range of insults he has in mind. "Well?"

"I simply don't believe that all these people – people we've shared our city with for years, in toleration if not in trust – have suddenly put their heads together and decided to overthrow the King."

"But there are cannons outside Whitehall, Nat. They searched Parliament for gunpowder the other day. How can that be? Only a fool would think there was no truth in it."

"So now you're calling me a fool?"

"No! I didn't mean it like that."

"But if I don't agree with you, that's what you'll be thinking." His face is transformed. The way he's looking at me is hateful.

"I—" The breath is locked in my chest.

"Well, that's just wonderful." He steps away. "Bloody wonderful."

"Nat—" I stretch out a hand. Tears smart at my eyes.

"No, don't bother," he says, stepping back from me. "But ask yourself, what do we know, what does anyone actually know about this threat? Little enough. Yet suddenly, half the population is baying for the blood of the other half. Stones are being thrown. Thrown by neighbours, thrown at people they've lived beside quite happily for years, speaking to, buying goods from, nodding and waving as they passed each other in the street. I am not the one being fooled. Do you hear?"

This is a new Nat. This Nat is loud. He jabs a finger at me, his face is twisted, he is openly scornful. Then he turns his back and walks away, leaving me standing alone in the street, with tears sliding down my cheeks. The face of that woman at the fair fills my mind. She said her name was Mary Twyn. She told me that Nat had killed her husband.

I whip out a handkerchief and sniff hard, clamping my teeth together, dragging up some composure. I'm about to leave – not to follow Nat. No, I'm going as far as possible in the opposite direction, but when Nat yells William's name I turn back.

Soldiers surround William. Orders are shouted. His arms are pulled behind his back and a sword is levelled at his chest. A broad, ugly man in uniform reads something in a loud voice, but the words don't make sense. Nat pushes his way into the group around William, only to be shoved back. The soldiers manhandle William and take him away. I step toward Nat, who shakes his head. William is dragged from my sight and Nat disappears after him.

For a few moments, I just stand and stare. Then I go to find Henry.

Chapter Five

Nat

The next morning, I wake with my head on my desk and my lip spit-tacked to an open book. I think first of William, and then of Anne. William was taken to Newgate and charged with sedition. There is no man *less* likely than William Smith to be involved in an attempt to launch a rebellion, but that does not help him any. We must play a waiting game. Henry will be in touch with his contacts in Whitehall again today, to see what can be done; which leaves me with Anne to think about.

I stayed out all night and drank way too much. I don't even remember coming up to my office instead of crawling home. I could head there now. It is early enough that she will still be asleep, and I see myself slipping under the covers, letting the heat from her skin warm mine. The prospect is sweetly tempting – assuming we are on speaking terms, that is. But as I sit up and blink in my surroundings, I'm overwhelmed by the work I need to do. With my livelihood in danger, I need to make money while I still can.

My office is a square, whitewashed room lined with bookcases. Once it was orderly, but I have taken up the hoarder's habit of never throwing anything away. Now my shelves are crammed with letters trussed up in ribbon, fistfuls of crinkled old broadsheets, folded pamphlets and stacks of books, bound, unbound, read and – all too frequently – unread. A large desk squats in the middle of this chaos, piled with all my current manuscripts and letters. There is only a bare hollow left clear at the centre where I work on my own writing or, as in the current case, sleep.

No. I don't have time to go home. I certainly don't have

time for another pointless argument. Instead, I send a boy with a bland message. Then I read, make notes, and read some more. In all, I shuffle papers for five solid hours. When I finally head out, the cold assaults me. It is a typical, squally November afternoon. I make my way through narrow streets, munching on a hot pie and minding my feet for turds and turnips. My destination is Parliament. Dr. Titus Oates is due to edify the Members with his terrific tales of treason today. William – William, of all people – has been arrested on this man's say-so. I need to take his measure.

The chamber of the House of Commons, viewed from the public gallery above, resembles nothing so much as a stew-pot bubbling and turning; a human soup. Noise rises up like steam, and little of what is said has any real substance. Tempers flare, men spark with anger and then subside in their turn as debate flows back and forth across the floor. Attendance is irregular, but on this occasion, there's nowhere else to be. Bewigged, be-robed, befuddled, bemused, belligerent, and bellicose: all our great men are spread out before us.

I stretch forward in my seat and catch my first glimpse of Titus Oates. He's swathed in clergyman's silks and sports a gloriously rich russet periwig that falls to his shoulders in two soft, spaniel's ears. He's a tall, broad-shouldered man who, at least from this perspective, appears to tower over the Members of Parliament tightly packed into seats on both sides of the Commons chamber. Oates's face is not unknown to me. It has been impossible to be alive in London and not see the strange features of this self-proclaimed 'Saviour of the Nation' flapping on the newspapers and engravings that hang from bookstalls across the city. Nor is it a face easily forgotten. He has a notably short brow – barely two fingers' width of flesh separate his hairline and eyebrows – and his eyes are deep-set, hard for me even to see at such a distance. He has a large nose over a surprisingly small mouth, but it is the chin that draws all eyes. Like a fat toad on a lily pad, Oates's chin squats on his white surplice, absorbing whatever neck he might once have possessed. His puffed-up cheeks are red (with the good living of Whitehall, I suspect), and surely his head is swollen with his new-found prominence in the world. He stands, head bowed with apparent humility, until the rabble falls silent.

"I have been instructed," Oates declares, "to lay out a little of my own history to you, so that you can understand how I have been able to uncover a most horrifying litany of treachery and rebellion."

He is an ugly man and he has an ugly way of speaking; his voice is almost as extraordinary as the face from which it issues. It is nasal and surprisingly soft, with a hint of a lisp. There is a feminine quality to it, quite at odds with his large frame and ox-like demeanour. And there is something peculiar in his pronunciation. When Oates produces a vowel, it's pulled out of him, almost unwillingly. Somewhere between a stammer and a hesitation, he holds onto each vowel for just a second too long, lengthening his words. At times he must have been ridiculed for his strange looks and absurd speech, but no-one is laughing now.

"I am, as my garb declares, a clergyman. I am a Doctor of Divinity, having gained my degree from the University of Salamanca in Spain. Returning to England, I spent some years in a good living in Sittingbourne, but in time I felt a young man's urge for a more exciting existence. I became a chaplain at sea and saw out some of the fiercest battles of our Dutch wars. I had the honour of voyaging with men of real worth; Sir Richard Routh, to name but one."

It appears that the Members can forgive Oates his ugliness and attune their ears to his bizarre nasal delivery. Many are nodding. I think of William and grit my teeth.

"Throughout my voyages and adventures," Oates says, "I met many men and heard many whispers that began to cause me great concern." He frowns as if the memory leaves a bitter taste on his tongue. "I heard," – here he sucks in an audible breath – "the whisperings of the Catholics."

From both sides of the House comes an answering rustle, a flapping of wings.

"Over time, my dear sirs, I became persuaded that it was my duty, my destiny even, to pursue these hints of treason, these murmurs of rebellion and revolt. In brief, I determined to get at the truth. I risked my own person for my country and for my King. I decided, to convert." Oates pauses and raises both hands as though warding off an assault. Very dramatic.

"In my heart and in private I have remained a true Anglican," he says. "I tell you this exactly as I told the King and Privy Council, under oath. But to all outward appearances, I became a Catholic and devoted myself to infiltrating their most ardent and extreme membership. I refer, of course, to the Society of Jesus."

He nods sagely, his chin bulging against his clerical collar, and folds his hands over his chest.

"Of my early trials – the difficulties of carrying out such a masquerade; of suppressing my own true beliefs; of participating in practices which are naturally offensive to me – I will say little. Suffice to say that I was true to my purpose and soon in the position of being asked to carry letters for Thomas Whitbread."

As he says the name, Oates looks studiously off into the distance. The Members stir again, more noisily than before. Whitbread is the Jesuit Provincial, probably the most prominent Catholic in England. I scribble down his name.

"Carrying letters was the most efficient way of obtaining information without being suspected, and I have reported my discoveries in a series of eighty-one articles. This is the evidence I presented to the Privy Council, evidence originally held by that poor martyr, Sir Edmund Godfrey. There is no doubt in my mind that the day I took what I knew to Godfrey, he became a marked man."

Again, Oates pauses, letting the connection between himself and the murdered man settle in the Members' minds.

"Did you copy the letters you read?" One Member half-rises to his feet to call out the question.

"Very few. I was rarely alone with the correspondence for long enough. I wanted to do everything in my power to discover the terrible danger facing our nation. Had I been found copying letters, my opportunity to gather information would have been lost."

Several friendly nods and a murmur of approbation clearly

please him. He clears his throat and thrusts out his barrel of a chest.

"And so now," booms Oates, "I will tell you all that I have learned, as well as I am able. First, rebellion in Scotland."

***

"I had to admire his fluency." Henry and I are at the table in our little dining room, spooning warm broth from two bowls squeezed into the gaps between the piles of paper I deposited there when I got home.

Anne is perched on a high-backed chair over by the window, bent like a lily, toward the light as she sews. We're acting like strangers. She has not asked me anything and Henry was here when I arrived, so I assume she knows that William is still in Newgate. At least they are in charity with one another. I take another mouthful of soup and plough on.

"First, he explained about various plots in Scotland, Ireland, England, and France. He said he'd opened letters detailing a plan to promote a Catholic uprising in Scotland; a country, in his words, well-recognised as a haven for violent, intemperate plotting. He explained that as part of his so-called conversion, he was sent abroad to study his new faith at Valladolid – the English college in Spain – but instead he devoted himself to uncovering treason. He says he read of a plot to poison the King unless Charles agreed to restore the Catholic faith in England. More, should Charles's brother James fail to fall in with Jesuit plans, he would be similarly dealt with. Never mind that's he's one of their own."

"It's incredible," says Henry.

"So you might think, but you should hear him. Hear how glibly he recalls dates and quotes from his written articles. He constantly referred the Members to the deposition lodged with Godfrey. He said Father Whitbread was promised large sums of money by the Spanish if he would arrange the murder of Charles II. Apparently, they've already made repeated attempts upon the King's life and have assassins preparing to shoot him as he walks in St James's Park, or stab him at Windsor. This

Father Whitbread has numerous accomplices. And Oates is not afraid to name names."

"He learned all of this in Valladolid?"

"No. Oates said he also spent some months in the Catholic college, St Omer's in Flanders. While he was there, he read letters revealing French willingness to finance Jesuits working to destroy Protestantism, root and branch. Oates claims he learned of significant French support for an uprising in Ireland, with the threat of an army landing to support the Irish cause. He says there is a plot to muster an army of 20,000 French and Irishmen, and five thousand horses. They could invade England with only ten days' warning."

"And what was the response?"

"What do you imagine? The place was in uproar. Several times the shouting and cursing at Catholics interrupted him, and he had to wait for calm before he continued. It was as if he swelled in stature and confidence before our eyes."

"So, you admit Oates is convincing?" Anne puts down her embroidery. I squint but cannot read her expression; the light from the window hides her features.

"Oh yes. There's no doubt about that. But then it's easy to convince, when everyone is hearing their worst fears brought to life. And he has a talent for delivery. He mixes up his evidence, interchanging broad plots of uprising with overheard slander against the King, misfired assassination attempts, and vast sums of money amassed by fanatic Jesuits across four countries. Many a sensible fellow might not see through it."

"Like you do?" she asks.

I still cannot see her face properly. "If you like."

I turn my back – probably not the wisest choice – but I am anxious to give Henry the full picture of all I have heard. "It just went on and on. Eight thousand Catholics wait north of the border, ready to rise up against the English King, with money provided by the French. Here, in London, Oates has seen Tewkesbury mustard balls that could destroy Westminster, sparking a second Great Fire. He mentioned the Fuller's Rent, where William said he met him. Oates said that men may be found there, on almost any evening, abusing His

Majesty's name and threatening treason."

"That's not good," said Henry.

"Let's hope it got lost in the crowd of his accusations. He even said that if the assassins failed, there were Catholic plotters who had bought the services of the Queen's own physician, Sir George Wakeman. For ten thousand pounds, he'll poison the King. You may believe that that claim got a reaction. It was a full five minutes before order was restored. They screamed for Wakeman's arrest. All I could do was stare at Oates. I wish you might have seen him."

"How did he look?" Anne speaks up again but without looking at me, still bent over her stitching. She is angry. I knew when I woke in my office and not at home in our bed that there would be consequences, but she needs to consider what is happening here.

"He was calm." I say. "Almost serene, while disorder – near hysteria – ranged around him. He was feeding on it. I'm sure of that."

"So now we understand why the Privy Council dared not disbelieve him," says Henry.

Sick with it all, I push back my chair and pace the room. There is so much to consider, and then there are words that Henry and I are not saying. With Parliament in chaos, I'm almost certain that my post will not be renewed. My income will be cut in half. It's a problem I must solve. Daylight has disappeared. We are all sitting in a gloom only alleviated by the flickers of the fire. I rattle around looking for the tinderbox and thump two heavy candlesticks down onto the table.

"I wish you would calm down." Anne's voice is shrill.

"Calm down, did you say? That's the last thing I want to do."

"Nat," Henry's tone urges caution, but I don't heed him.

"This is not the time to be calm, Anne," I say. "Do you have any idea of just how serious this has become? Who *is* this man? Why do we all rush to believe in him and his plot? Think of Parliament. My God, if you could have seen how those self-serving, power-seeking reprobates whipped themselves up to a frenzy as he spoke to them. If you had heard them crying that

35

the Privy Council was at fault, how our government was impotent, how only they, the Members, would be able to protect the nation. Do you see it? Do you? Don't tell me you are fool enough to think that they're there for the good of the people? Of course not. The people's latent bigotry and hatred of Catholics is being used. Oates and those politicians are equally to blame. They're all there for the good of themselves, by which I mean more power to Parliament and less to the King. And what happened the last time Parliament became too powerful in this country? Tell me. Eh? What happened then?"

There is silence. Anne turns her back and gazes into the blue-black windowpane. Henry looks at me, his eyes full of pity, mirroring my loss, thinking of my father, his friend, who died in the Civil War.

"But if you don't like that argument, then let me give you another," I say. "Think about what has happened. Think. How many men, how many priests, has this Titus Oates already had dragged off to prison? Ten? Twenty? And how many more will follow? William! Our own friend William is in Newgate Prison. Have you any idea of the conditions there? Of course you do not. This Titus Oates has brought chaos and panic, he has stirred up the crowd until it must turn ugly. He has spoken to the worst fears and doubts of the people and fanned their deep-seated mistrust of Catholicism. You can see that, can't you? You can see how he has worked them. But will you go to the hangings, Anne? Shall I take you to Tyburn, buy you a souvenir, and drink chocolate while we watch these men die? Because that's what will happen. Men will die on his say-so. On the word of this, this, *nobody*. It is not right."

I sit down deflated, the anger hissed out of me, my head empty of thought. Henry's hands are on the arms of his chair. He looks poised to move, but not sure how to take his departure. And then she clears her throat and speaks.

"But that was all right for you, wasn't it, Nat?"

In the candlelight she appears jaundiced, her skin taut and thin.

"You," she says, "can shout about Oates causing men to lose their lives: men you think, but don't know, are innocent.

36

But you have not applied such scruples to yourself, have you?"

She stands.

"And don't answer that. Just don't. Because whatever you say, we will all still know that it is the truth."

She crosses to Henry, bends and kisses his cheek.

"I don't suppose you remember it, Nat. Why would you? But that woman who spat in my face at the fair? Her name was Mary Twyn."

Henry is poking in his pockets and will not meet my eye.

"She told me you murdered her husband, Nat. That he was tried and hanged on your evidence, just as you say people will be hanged on the word of Titus Oates."

"John Twyn was guilty—" I begin, but Anne has already turned her back on me.

She walks out of the room, and her footsteps echo as she climbs the wooden stairs.

***

"He was guilty," I say a few minutes later, as Henry shrugs on his coat and picks up his stick.

"I believe you thought so at the time, Nat. I will tell her so if you would like. But she may need to hear it from you."

Henry heads out into the night and I am left to sit in front of the dying fire and consider. Not straight away, but slowly, a little nugget of resentment hardens somewhere in the middle of my chest. Anne is my wife, not my conscience. I decide to wait downstairs until she is asleep. I'm not used to answering to anyone for my actions. I've no intention of talking to her about John Twyn.

Chapter Six

Anne

Upstairs, I get undressed and brush out my hair with firm strokes. Pent-up anger cracks in my limbs. Twice I go to the door, ready to march back downstairs and demand we discuss it, but each time I pull back. Doubt grips me. His confidence in his own opinion grated. To come home finally, only to rant about this conspiracy and this Oates character: how could I not react badly? But what have I done, throwing out an accusation about the Twyns when I've no real information beyond what his wife said at the fair? Henry and Nat are probably shaking their heads over my outburst. They may even be laughing at me. I turn and crawl into bed. My outrage is replaced by anxiety.

I don't know how much time has passed when Nat comes to the bedroom. I feign sleep as he sets his candle on the dresser and shrugs off his clothes. Then, candle snuffed, he climbs into bed next to me. I make sure to breathe in and out steadily. I wait for his breath on my neck. I wait for his fingers in my hair. But he shifts away and settles down. I lie awake for hours.

***

Yesterday, after they took William, I ran straight to Henry's shop, The Star, in Little Britain. In this cluster of streets, south of Smithfield and north of St Paul's, many booksellers run their businesses. Henry sells books at the front of his property and prints pamphlets in the back, while Nat does his work as the Licenser upstairs. Outside each shop are tables piled with a profusion of books, maps, and papers. I had only been there once before and thought myself lost until I caught sight a faded yellow star against a blue background on a sign swaying up ahead. Henry was working in his shirt-sleeves, wiping the sweat from his brow. A sheaf of paper slid from a table as I rushed in. Before he could grumble, I told him the news.

"William has been arrested. Nat followed them, but I don't know where they have taken him or what the charge can be."

"You are out of breath. Take a seat." Henry pointed to a chair by the fireplace.

"No! You need to go. You need to help them."

"And I will. See? I am getting my coat on. But take a seat and compose yourself. Where were you? Where was he arrested?"

Reassured by the sight of him pulling his apron over his head, I subsided into the chair. "Outside Somerset House."

"And how many took him?"

"At least six men."

"Armed?"

"Yes. It happened so quickly."

Henry shovelled his arms into the sleeves of his coat. "My best guess is Newgate. We can assume that Nat will do his best to speak to the Warden. I'll go to Sir Robert."

"Surely it can be nothing so serious?" Robert Southwell is a member of the King's Privy Council and a crony of Henry's. "What crime could William have committed?"

"I cannot imagine. But this is the quickest route to find out." He crossed the room and put a hand on my shoulder. "You did the right thing coming to me," he said, and then he was gone.

I sat back and pressed my hands to my cheeks. The argument with Nat, followed by William's arrest and now Henry's unexpected kindness, brought tears to my eyes.

"Miss?"

I dropped my hands as the blood rushed to my face. A small boy, perhaps no more than ten years old, stood awkwardly before me, chewing on a fingernail of one ink-stained hand. Of course, there were apprentices working in the printshop. I pulled myself together.

"I'm sorry. What's your name? Do you need some help?"

"Yes, Miss. It might be burning."

"Burning?" I followed his eyes and the smell reached me. How had I not noticed? In a moment the boy put a cloth in my hand and I lifted the pot that was hanging in the fireplace.

In this manner, I found myself feeding four young boys and eating with them, all the while promising myself that if grisly stew was the best Henry could do for himself and his boys, then Kitty and I would intervene. When our poor meal was over, I resolved to go home and wait for news, but the boys looked at me expectantly.

"What should we do?" asked Jim, the one who had approached me first. "The master isn't back yet and the paper is drying out." He pointed to a pile of creamy sheets above a large basin of greasy water. "Everything is ready," he said. The others nodded.

"Do you know what to do?" I asked. "What would your master do if he were here?"

Another boy stepped forward. He was older, perhaps thirteen, with a boyish face still, but taller than me and broad across the shoulders. Nearly a man. "Tom here is the beater. He uses those inkballs to prepare the forme."

"The forme?"

"This." He showed me a frame filled with tiny metal letters.

"Perhaps we should wait?" To be honest, I was not sure Henry would like this, not one bit.

"He said this job was urgent, miss. We was in a rush to get started when you came in, and now he's gone. If we don't do nothing, he'll sack us."

"You mean he'll sack you, John," said Jim. "You're the pressman."

"Pressman?" They smiled at my poor questions, but what would I know about a printshop of all things?

"He runs the press. The only one of us allowed to touch that." Jim pointed to one of the three presses, and for the first time I took in the scope of the enterprise that Henry runs. Each press is large, as big as a cart, and I saw in the centre where the forme of type would sit. There was already paper pinned flat on a hinged surface, ready to be positioned over the type. John, the pressman, would pull the lever that lowered heavy block and pressed paper and ink together.

"Why would he sack you? Why don't you just go ahead? Surely he will be pleased with you?"

But the boys did not agree. They shuffled and muttered, and eventually Jim took the role of spokesman. "Mister Broome hasn't checked the forme, yet. He left too soon. It needs checking."

They looked at me in expectation.

"I don't want to interfere."

"I just need you to read it over. Only the first one. To check for mistakes." Jim would not look me in the eye. None of them would. These boys cannot read.

And so I stayed. I stayed all afternoon. I checked the type, and took a turn at rubbing the leather inkballs together, smelling the linseed oil, and lifting and lowering drying sheets of printed paper until my arms ached. The boys were organised but inclined to bicker and criticise one another. I saw the pecking order they operate under and how Henry has trained them to take on more responsibility as they grow older and stronger.

Dusk was falling when Henry returned. I scanned his face for news of William but also feared his reaction to my still being in his printshop, in his territory, a place he had never invited me to be.

If he was surprised, he hid it well. "William is in Newgate, charged with sedition. He was named by Titus Oates in his written deposition to Parliament. Oates claims he overheard Smith and others talking treasonably in a tavern. Nat is looking for character witnesses for him. He went to the school, but fears William may lose his teaching post. The Merchant Taylors' School has a reputation it is anxious to protect."

"Did you see Sir Robert Southwell?"

"I did, but he did not offer much hope. If Titus Oates can produce a witness to corroborate his claim against William, then the case is dire."

"I can't believe it!"

"Do not panic entirely. William's friend Matthew Medbourne has been in Newgate for several weeks and Oates has not supplied any witnesses as yet."

"Then why has he not been released?"

Henry let out a tired sigh. "Medbourne is a Catholic. William, however, is not. Nat will go next to obtain evidence of William's Protestantism. If he supplies that and Oates doesn't supply his proof, then we will secure William's release within the week."

"Thank God. Is it so very terrible inside Newgate?"

"Every bit as bad as you may imagine." He turned from me and looked around. "Now, boys. Show me what you have done." I gathered up my things and prepared to leave. My hand was on the worn doorknob when he called me back.

"Anne." His face was softer than I had ever seen it. "Thank you for helping them."

"It was nothing," I said.

"More than nothing." He took my hands in his large warm grip. "It has been an anxious, shocking day, but you have been calm. More than calm. You have been helpful. I am grateful."

"You are my husband's closest friend. I want nothing more than to help." His smile encouraged me. "Might Kitty and I send over some food for you all tomorrow?"

Henry nodded, and I left with my heart full.

But then the hours ticked by and Nat did not come home.

It took me some time to grow angry. All afternoon, I regretted my words before William's arrest. I longed to see Nat and put the foolish argument out of my mind with kind words and apologies. All evening, I regretted my sharp tongue, and jumped at every creak and whisper in the house or the street outside. Thoughts of the child I believe I'm carrying make me alternately happy and anxious. I do not want to be at odds with my husband at such a time. I settled at nothing, hoping for good news for William; longing to see my husband. But he did not come. In the morning, I woke to a cold and empty place beside me on the bed.

All day today my temper has been on the rise. Shopping,

sewing, helping Kitty make sauce in the kitchen: through all, I've been on tenterhooks. When his note came, it told me nothing but that William was still in Newgate and that he, Nat, had work that could not wait. I played solitaire at the sitting room window, looking down every second or so for his familiar hat and wig coming down the cobbles. Solitaire! Kitty took lunch to the print shop, but I ought to have gone myself. With no-one to talk to and nothing to do, my mood swung from fearful to indignant like a rising tide.

Still, more than anything I wanted to put yesterday's cross words behind us. But when he did arrive home, Nat talked of nothing but Titus Oates. Not for the first time I thought that this husband of mine might be arrogant. How can he be so sure there is no Catholic plot? What makes him so much better than everyone else? John Twyn's wife did not think so. Far from it.

My temper got the better of me.

I may be the greatest fool in London accusing my husband in that manner. But why did he stay downstairs? Why not come upstairs and talk things out? When sleep finally comes, it only does so fitfully. I do not like my dreams.

Chapter Seven

William Smith

No-one will tell me what charges I face, but they are serious enough that the Keeper of Newgate raises an eyebrow and whistles when he looks at the paperwork the soldiers give him. He tells me I may send no messages and will receive no visitors. I'm manhandled into a large dark room and sold a candle that costs me nearly every shilling I have on my person. Then I'm left to find a space for myself in the gloom. Men, little more than bundles of misery and rags, huddle on the floor or on narrow boards fixed to the wall. The smell of excrement is overpowering. I find a gap in a far corner and lean into it as my stomach heaves and sweat breaks out on my forehead. This is the condemned hold.

Mercifully, I do not spend many hours here. Someone – Nat, I assume – visits the Keeper and pays for my swift removal and elevation to a cell upstairs on the Masters' side of the prison. At first, I chafe at the irons at my wrists and respond to any sound of movement outside my cell, expecting release at any second. I pray fervently, but in vain. No-one comes, and my optimism that this was a mistake soon to be rectified, bleeds away. By evening, my mood is as dark as the patch of sky visible through the window above my head.

Three days and nights pass like this. Fear turns my bowels to water. I barely sleep, tormented by skittering beetles and the lice I imagine creeping across my skin, into my mouth, my eyes. I try to steel myself and bear this trial with patience and fortitude, but the injustice, the indignity, and above all the fear of the unknown, infects my thoughts. My heart hurts in my chest. Weak tears and snot warm my cheeks. My mind is in chaos and I can't rein in my despair.

And then suddenly the cell door opens. I am taken to a larger, cleaner, lighter room, furnished with only a table and two chairs. I'm told I have a visitor.

It is Titus Oates.

I'll admit that the first thing I feel is relief.

"By the stars, William," he declares, striding in. I think he's about to embrace me, but at the last moment he shrinks back. Instead, his eyes widen, and he fumbles for a handkerchief. "Good God, man. What's that smell?"

"Me, I suspect. Titus, thank you for coming—"

"Indeed, you ought to thank me!" he says, settling himself in a chair and indicating that I should sit across the table from him. "It is not everyone who can visit prisoners such as yourself without considerable outlay, or indeed risk to their own reputation."

"Risk? I don't even know what I'm charged with."

"Sedition, Schoolmaster. Although after this—"

"What are you saying? *Sedition?* I've done nothing."

"Of course not, William. Of course not. No-one who knows you could think otherwise. And doubtless, in a few months when no evidence is found—"

"Months?"

"—then you will be released. But I doubt the Merchant Taylors' School will look favourably on such an episode."

His voice trails off.

"My God, Titus. What are you saying? My whole life is tied up in my work, in that school."

"I suppose it must be." He walks to the door so his expression is hidden, but when he turns he is laughing. "Oh, you poor man. Would that I had a glass so you could look at your own face. You know, I never liked you. You know that, don't you?" He goes to peer out of the narrow window.

"You were a woeful teacher," he says, casting me that sly grin I remember all too well. "Always choosing favourites. Soft when you should have been strict. Criticising when you should have been helping. Unfair."

"Really?" Tired and terrified as I am, there is something

remarkably familiar about this. Titus is a bully. And as a teacher, I have met my fair share of those. His insults won't touch me. But I am beginning to wonder what he wants.

"None of the boys liked you. Oh, some would pretend, but that was only because they wanted to please their parents with your good report. We would talk about you after school, you know. The boys you liked particularly. They would laugh about you. They would say how you would—"

"Enough!"

Titus doesn't like that. He turns and walks back to the table. Leaning down, he spreads his fat fingers on the wood, and his large face looms toward mine. Beer has soured his breath.

"You don't tell me, 'enough'. Not any more. Do you hear me? You need to know who I am these days. Who I've become."

Tiredness washes over me. "Tell me," I say. He will not be satisfied otherwise, I am certain.

"I have lodgings in Whitehall. Did you know that?" He steps away from the table and paces the room as he talks. "Fine rooms, and a rather handsome young boy to light my fire and bring me whatever meat or drink I might desire. My days are busy. Almost intolerably so. Those Members of Parliament are all so keen to discuss this terrible Catholic threat. And so grateful to me for bringing it to light. I am invited to dine and welcomed to their homes."

He breaks off to take my measure. I will look impassive if it kills me.

"The Earl of Shaftesbury. I imagine you have heard of him," Titus says. "When I speak, he takes notes. Notes! And I have been furnished with my own guard, did I mention that? Then there is a matter of the death of that poor magistrate, Godfrey. It was an ill day for him when the old man Tonge and I took our deposition to him. Godfrey was so superior toward us; I disliked him quite particularly. But knowing our secrets cost him his life. He should have had more respect."

"The man is dead, Titus."

"What, so now I must lie and pretend I liked the fellow?" He takes the seat opposite me and lounges back, almost as if

46

we are two old friends enjoying a gossip. "Oh, in some places perhaps, but we know each other well, William. And between these four walls we may speak openly. Sir Edmund Godfrey was as pompous a man as you could hope to meet. He barely gave me the time of day. Of course, my dress was not quite so fine then." Titus runs his fingers down the cloth of his surplice and touches at his periwig. "But if the magistrate was as clever as everyone said he was, then he should have recognised our significance and behaved accordingly. If a man is rude to me, am I expected to shed tears when he is found dead in a ditch, strangled by some Catholic assassin? I think not."

"Have his murderers been apprehended?"

"I believe they have. Three of them, I'm told. They may even be somewhere in this stinking hole. And they, old fellow, have even less chance of release than you do. Although sedition, as I say, is a serious, serious crime."

He has found his way, despite his vain meanderings, back to me.

"Why are you here, Titus? If your only aim is to gloat, then we can agree you have succeeded."

"Gloating? Or simply stating the facts?" With his elbows on the table, he leans in and lowers his voice. "I won't split hairs with you, schoolmaster. The point is that I am someone in this city these days. Whereas you, William, are a nobody. You are nothing. Look at what you're facing. Living in this filth. Co-existing with these beasts. Trying to sleep amongst the noise and the stench, trying to survive until you're put on trial, and then strung up by the neck until you're dead. How can you escape your fate? Isn't that what you want to hear?"

"I'm not guilty." I try to speak normally but my voice cracks.

"And you think that matters?"

"What are you saying?"

"I'm saying that you are a fool. I'm saying that you will do as I tell you and say what I want, or you will sink and suffer in this shit-hole until you're pulling the rope around your neck yourself and begging them to let you swing."

I concentrate on breathing. I am still sitting at the same

table. My feet are flat on the floor, my hands clasped in my lap. Anyone looking in through the square grille at the door would see us in normal conversation, but the tension is palpable, and his eyes are locked on mine. I disliked Titus Oates when he was my pupil. I despised him when I met him again as an adult. Now he terrifies me.

"Do what?" I hate my own words. I don't want to open the door to his evil or suggest that I might be an accomplice to his malice. But I am afraid. I am cold, tired, hungry, and I am weak. I have always been weak. And he knows it.

"There is someone else in here, accused of similar crimes to yourself. Accused of railing against the monarchy and wishing to see the Catholic Church restored to power in the nation. Accused of raising money to support an assassination attempt."

"And?"

"And I want to you to be a witness to his crimes."

"I can't."

"You not only can, but you will. In return, I will secure your release. The charges against you will vanish into the air. There is a witness to your crimes expected to attend the courts in the coming days. He will not materialise. But only if you do as I say."

"But...but who is this man I'm supposed to condemn? Who will believe me – giving evidence against someone I don't even know?"

Titus smacks his hand on the table against the table and smiles. "But that's exactly why it will work so beautifully. You do know him. You know him very well."

A horrible thought yawns open in my mind: Matthew Medbourne, my friend for years, one of my closest friends, and latterly someone who befriended Titus, even though he showed him nothing but contempt in return.

"You are not serious?"

"Whyever not?" Titus is relaxed now, disgustingly so, as he lays out the information he wishes me to put forward. "Medbourne is a Catholic; he has never hidden it. All you need to do is say that you have seen him talking with priests at the

Fuller's Rent Tavern. That you have heard him talk openly about his support for the King's brother. That he has denigrated the memory of Queen Elizabeth and praised her sister Mary. That he calls on others to toast the Pope. That you have seen money exchanged between himself and some priests. You don't need to name them. Just say what you have seen."

"But I have seen nothing! Matthew has no interest in such matters. We both know that. Why do such a thing? Why would you? Why would I?"

"For the very same reason," he says, the smirk back on his ugly face.

"I don't understand."

"Then you are even more of a fool than I have always taken you for, schoolteacher. Matthew called himself my friend, but all he did for me was find me a post with the Duke of Norfolk. The pay was poor, and the man's arrogance was insufferable. I have nothing to thank Matthew Medbourne for. His help was an insult. And he insulted you – don't try and pretend that he didn't. You thought you were special to him, but the day I walked into the Fuller's Rent Tavern, Matthew Medbourne dropped you like a hot turd. Here is your chance to get your own back. And you will save your own miserable skin into the bargain."

"No!"

Titus rocks back in surprise. He hears the determination in my voice. To be honest, it surprises us both.

"I will not do it, Titus," I say. "Not to Matthew. Not to anyone. I am innocent and will take my chances. You think I'm a weak man, and God knows you are right. But I will not damn another man to help myself. I am not worth it. My miserable skin – you are right about that – is not worthy of the sacrifice of someone else's. I will not do it."

He snorts. "You will change your mind."

"No. No, you will find that I will not." I am very hot. If I lifted my hand, it would tremble. A tremor starts in my calf. If he does not leave I'm afraid my whole body will begin to rattle. "I'd like you to go now."

He takes his time about it. He rubs at his chin. He straightens his robes. He smiles and shakes his head at me. I do not drop my eyes. I cannot stand, but I hold my head high.

At the door he turns. "I will hear from you. When you change your mind, let me know."

I do not reply.

**

Two days later, I'm taken from my cell once again. My skin is slick with dirt, my scalp itches, and sharp pains grip my bowels. As they lead me down into the yard, I muster the strength to tell him no again. Nothing will make me put my life before that of an innocent man. There is a light rain falling and the sky is a solid mass of grey.

They take me to the gate. There is someone waiting. A man. It is not Titus Oates. When his face resolves itself into the features of my friend Nathaniel Thompson, the rain on my cheeks mixes with stinging tears. I am a weak man, but I have not been weak. And now I'm free.

Chapter Eight

Nathaniel

Henry rests a shoulder against the doorframe, recovering his breath. "Are you ready?" he asks.

I lift my eyes from my papers. "Find a seat. I just need a few more minutes."

I have spent all afternoon in my office. For once I am on top of my required reading and have been writing something new. Titus Oates has been the talk of London since he appeared before Parliament two weeks ago. It is time for a few doubts to be expressed.

"Here." I thrust a few pages into Henry's hands. He steps over one pile of leather volumes and clears another from the chair on the other side of the desk. Tilting the paper towards the window in the fading light, he purses his lips and reads. He has hardly begun before he speaks.

"It won't do."

"What? Why not?"

"Because there is nothing here that people want to read."

My eyes drop away and I gaze at the ink on my fingers. The nails of my right hand are stained black around the cuticles. When I look up, Henry's mouth is set in a line, his head turned slightly to one side.

"Why the hell not?"

"Because there's no appetite for your point of view. The public has gorged itself on fear of papists, fire, French invasion, Jesuit murderers and duplicitous kings. They have swallowed Oates's story. They believe in it and won't hear anything else. I'm not saying you're wrong, Nat." He slides back in his chair. "But being right won't serve, not now."

My shoulders drop. I pick up a cloth to scrub the ink from my hands.

"So, you're saying it's pointless? That I shouldn't even try to expose the inconsistencies in Oates's evidence, or ask who this man actually is and where he comes from? You are saying that these things shouldn't be done?"

"Not like this, Nat. At least, not now."

"Not now?" I echo. "Do you believe in it then?"

"In what?"

"In these plots, of course. In the threat of invasion. In the plots to murder the King. That the Queen would sanction her doctor poisoning her husband. That those three poor bastards they've arrested really murdered Godfrey. That there are Jesuits ready to stab, shoot or murder anyone who would stop them making England a Catholic country again."

"No. But almost everyone else in London does." He steps across and squeezes my shoulder. It is a gesture of friendship, but I feel like a schoolboy being patted on the head. "And how is Anne?"

"She's fine." My irritation seeps out. He has been asking after Anne every day since that ridiculous scene he witnessed over John Twyn.

"She is young, Nat. From a different world than ours. You must talk more. And be patient—"

But I am on my feet, grabbing my coat, unwilling to discuss Anne with Henry. She made up her mind, without the proper information, and put me on a par with Oates, just like that. There is much I could say to both Henry and Anne on the subject. I could ask them, for example, if it is too much for a husband to hope that his wife should have some faith in him. Instead, I've said nothing, and Anne has not mentioned it either. It is almost as if the conversation never happened. Almost.

Of course, I'm in a thoroughly bad mood now. "We don't have time for this," I say. "Come on. Otherwise we'll be late."

***

Henry and I meet Sir Robert Southwell over at Clerkenwell. It is a crisp, chilly evening and already dark, but at least it is not raining. William was to join us, but he has cried off. That week in Newgate hit him hard. At least Southwell will distract Henry from his interest in my marriage, and he's always a useful source for me. As Clerk to the Privy Council, he is frequently in the company of the King and his closest advisors. He looks rather displeased when we arrive, but Henry affects not to notice his friend's reserve, and even Sir Robert can't maintain his irritation in the face of Henry's wholehearted enthusiasm for the entertainment ahead. We join the stream of men walking up Cow Cross and Turnmill Street towards Hockley-in-the-Hole; a rabble of men of all trades and stations, talking loudly and anticipating the main event of the evening. I don't share their excitement. Henry's dismissal of my work has left me bristling, but I trail after them anyway. Sir Robert is a great man for the dogs and wants to see how they fare against a hundred and fifty butcher's stones of live bull. I have newssheets to fill, and if I want the latest gossip from the Court, I must go, too.

Our destination is a large circle dug into the ground, open to the elements above but fenced on its innards with a sturdy wooden wall that rises up to about my waist. At four points there are small gates and steps through which the dogs and their owners can enter and leave. Southwell leads us to a point directly opposite another wider gate, from which a slope extends, to enable the bull to be led into the pit. The ring is bare but brightly lit by high braziers and torches fastened to the pit walls. A thick iron hoop, with a long coil of rope tied to it at one end, is fixed in the ground at the centre of the ring. The whole place hums of wet hay, damp fur, and sweat.

The crowd is lively; raucous, even. These are common working men, noisy and expectant, shouting and stamping to keep their feet warm. The dogs are not in view, but their harsh barks and yelps stir up the audience until a sudden hush falls and the beast is led into the ring.

It is so damned ugly, it's almost beautiful. The bull's meaty shoulders roll and ripple with grease, shiny against sleek black hair. Its head swings ponderously from side to side and forward of its body, so that it appears low to the ground, yet its horns are as high as the chests of its handlers. Its nostrils flare and smoke. Two small eyes twist and circle as the creature tries to make sense of its surroundings. Its handlers tie it to the rope and flee the ring, as the animal strains and stomps, looking for a way out. In contrast to its bulky chest and neck, the bull's rear quarters look vulnerable, its legs thinning to neat ankles. I imagine the dogs flinging themselves at those fine tendons, piercing the skin with sharp white teeth, and glance at Southwell. It is surprising what some outwardly civilised men like to do in their spare time. I would prefer to be at home with a glass of wine and the *London Gazette*.

The crowd begins to clamour for the dogs. A bottle is thrown at the bull, smashing into its flank and bringing it skipping round. From another side, a bucket of slops is thrown at the beast, and it shakes its great head, showing the sharp points of its horns.

Southwell and Henry talk loudly to be heard over the vociferous crowd. I listen to them exchange the news. It is clear that there is much concern amongst the Privy Council about the arrest of three Catholic men for the murder of Edmund Godfrey.

"Shaftesbury is having a field day," admits Southwell. "The more Catholics implicated in this disastrous plot, the more he can mutter against the King's brother. He has set up a committee in Parliament to investigate Oates's popish plot, and swears only the will and drive of the elected members will get the results the public demands."

"Next he will be hinting that the Crown has a reason to be lax in its attempts to solve the murder," says Henry.

"You think so?" I have to lean forward and twist across Southwell to make sure they can both hear me over the shouting. The Earl of Shaftesbury is the strongest opponent to the Crown and the King. Oates's plot might smell rotten to me, but it sings of sweet opportunity to a politician like Shaftesbury.

Henry shrugs. "It is what I would do, were I in his shoes.

His wish is to deny James the succession. Shaftesbury doesn't want to see a Catholic on the throne. That lies behind all his actions. If I were him, I'd be suggesting that the reason it took so long to find the Catholics who killed Godfrey is because they were protected by James, perhaps even by Charles. Why not?"

Southwell purses his lips and sucks his cheeks as if testing the idea on his teeth. "He may try it. But tomorrow the King will increase the reward for more witnesses in the case. That may bring something out of the woodwork."

"Other than more damned worms," I say.

"You will gather that Nathaniel here is not an admirer of Dr. Oates," says Henry. "But I have told him he will do himself few favours by making his views public."

Southwell opens his mouth to respond but pauses. The first of the dogs is flung though its gate and into the ring. All eyes follow it as it circles the bull, keeping close to the floor and out of reach of those lethal horns.

"I'm not sure you are entirely right in that, Henry," he says. Southwell has the long, sombre face of an academic, but his eyes are gleeful, riveted on the spectacle below. "And besides," he says, "our young friend here has worries of his own. With this storm, there will be no renewal of the Licensing Act in the New Year."

We all keep silent then, our eyes fixed on the ring. The noise, the movement all around carries on, but the certainty with which Southwell speaks freezes me. So, there is no hope. The Licensing Act will not be renewed, and my post will cease to exist. At least half of my income will be gone in an instant. My first thought is of Anne. I should never have married her. A man does not marry a woman and then fail to provide for her. I am sickened. Ashamed. Nor is it just about the money. Without my position, what will I be? Little more than the newsmonger Anne's parents have always said I am. My thoughts swirl and I have trouble keeping my ear on their conversation. I cannot look at Henry.

Southwell is far from finished. "And yes, Henry, the public believes in Oates and might well turn in anger on anyone who crosses him. Yet there are those who have their doubts and have begun to express them, if only in private."

"Who?" Henry demands. Somehow, I must put my panic to one side and listen.

"The King for one," said Southwell. "Wait—"

Before he can say more, we're thrust into the fencing by the swell of men behind us. The dog, at a sharp instruction from its master, darts forward and snaps at the soft, wet nose of the bull. It misses, and the bull kicks the dog away. It spins, skids on its side into the wall of the pit, and yelps in pain, but it's instantly up on its feet and circling the ring again.

"Another, another!" calls the heaving crowd. "More dogs. Send in more dogs!"

"The King?" I say.

"In a moment." Southwell bends far over the fence as a second dog runs barking and frisking around the bull directly beneath us. It forces the beast to twist first one way and then back, making it snort with exertion. Still, the bull proves nimbler than expected. The little dog whisks in and stumbles. The bull lowers its head, thrusts forward its horns, and tosses the dog high in the air. It twists and arcs over our heads, then crashes to the floor of the ring. I hear its skull crack, I swear. My stomach turns over. I want desperately to walk away but need my question answered.

The crowd erupts and Southwell sniffs in apparent satisfaction. "I was present while the King interviewed Dr. Oates," he says. "Mostly, His Majesty spoke little, but when Oates talked of having been in the presence of Don John of Austria during a discussion about funding the physician Wakeman to poison Charles, the King took an interest. He asked Oates to describe Don John."

"And?"

"Oates said he was tall, of spare frame, and dark-skinned. But the King pointed out that Don John is, in fact, short and unusually fair."

"See Henry!" I say. "The man is a liar. An opportunist at best."

"You'll enjoy this also," says Southwell. "The King next

asked him where he'd met Louis' confessor, Père La Chaise. Oates said the meeting took place in a Jesuit house, near the Louvre."

"And?"

"Well, the King said promptly that there was no Jesuit house within a mile of the Louvre."

"There! The King knows the man is a liar. He must be got rid of—"

"Ah!" Southwell interrupts me and gives a knowing smile. "But Oates is no fool. If nothing else, he's a quick study. For he turned to the King and glibly pointed out that the Jesuits are so deep in their plots and underhand ways that, of course, they have a house near the Louvre, but one so secret that no-one else knows of it."

"But that's nonsense! Why, by that reasoning the man can say anything and no-one can argue!"

"Exactly."

"Such audacity," says Henry, folding his arms across his chest. "To talk in such a manner to the King. Has he offered any written evidence, Robert?"

Again, the crowd presses forward and I'm forced up against the wooden fencing. Southwell holds up a hand, waiting for the noise to abate. "Some letters between senior Jesuits and Thomas Bedingfield. Bedingfield is the confessor to the King's brother," he explains. "Oates was the only man there who claimed to recognise the handwriting, but anyone could have written the damn things."

"In Parliament, he said he had been able to copy only a few."

"Quite. And what's to say he did not make those up entirely? But even if we could prove that letters he showed us were forged, this plot has assumed a life of its own."

"What was the King's response?" asks Henry.

"He made no visible response. But he left the chamber shortly afterward. The whisper is that Charles is desperate to have Oates whipped from Aldgate to Newgate, but believes it would be impolitic to do so."

"So, he'll let these arrests continue—"

"Watch your words, Nat," says Henry.

"—and allow panic and rumour to rule the streets?"

"Until the time is right," says Southwell. "Yes, that's exactly what he'll do. But I believe he will reward well anyone who can turn the tide of public opinion against Oates. Now. Watch this."

This is very typical of Southwell. He drops his message and then directs our attention back to the animals while his words sink in. Through every gate, dogs are being despatched into the ring. There are at least ten angry, barking little bulldogs goading the beast, snapping at it from all sides. The bull still looks strong to my eyes, though. What might such diminutive opponents actually achieve here, beyond exhausting it? They yelp, growl, and run about the giant's hooves. The bull's chest heaves, and steam rises from its flanks. Suddenly, one of the new dogs lunges forward and clamps the fleshy nose of the bull in its jaws. The bull bellows in pain. It lurches backwards as blood spurts, covering the dog's head, pouring into its eyes and then running down the ugly wrinkles of skin on its flat muzzle. The dog will not let go. Southwell sees the disgust on my face.

"Remarkable, isn't it? Note how clever that is, Thompson," he says. "The bulldog has been designed for this sport, bred to it. The wrinkles allow the blood to flow off the dog's face. Its character keeps it on the bull's muzzle until the bull tires and collapses from the pain. The dog is tenacious and has only one purpose. It will serve its master and take down the bull. I have seen dogs lamed, maimed, crushed, and half dead, who will keep attacking a bull or die in the attempt."

It's as if he is speaking from a distance. I'm caught in the moment, trying to balance the mixture of sorrow and disgust that the sight of the bull staggering towards submission conjures up. Its knees buckle. Its strength is crushed by the pain. Henry appears unmoved. Two men with long knives enter the ring. They slit the creature's throat, catching its steamy blood in a large metal pail. Finally, the dog is pulled off, amidst great shouts and cheering.

"So, Robert?" Henry asks, as we turn and the crowd begins

to quickly disperse. "The King seeks a champion to combat Oates for him. These are indeed interesting times. That would be a brave fellow, mind you. Perhaps even a foolhardy one."

"Needs must," Southwell says. "And the King's approbation can be worth much."

I have had enough of their thinly-veiled commentary. The King wants Oates attacked, and I am about to have time on my hands and a driving need for funds. The point has been made. "What's the next act in the drama?" I say. "Where should we be looking next for news?"

"Well, to Edward Coleman, of course," says Southwell. He pulls his cloak about his shoulders as if stung by the cold night air. "His treason trial concludes tomorrow. Face it, gentlemen. With Godfrey murdered and – as it looks like – Coleman convicted, Oates's plot is made real. The Jesuit priests he named are under arrest. Godfrey's murderers also. But, friends, I have to go. I promised Lady Southwell that I'd secure some of the meat of that bull. Nothing compares with baited meat for flavour."

Chapter Nine

Anne

At first, I don't mind all the people. Crowds are London, and London is a crowd. We live elbow-to-elbow and bustle together in the shops and markets and up and down our narrow thoroughfares. Everywhere is noisy. There are shouts and cracks of laughter. There's a piercing brawl between two women over a sack of I don't know what. An angry driver loses a wheel and blocks the road. He is roundly cursed and spat at by the farmer stuck behind him. I mind my feet. The streets run wet with housewives' washing water, animal dirt, and worse. This is probably a terrible idea. But I'm determined to see it through nonetheless.

Will you go to the hangings? That's what he asked me, that night. Weeks have passed since our argument over John Twyn, but we act like nothing occurred. We woke the following morning with his body curled snug around mine. Whatever thoughts or ideas might separate us, our bodies tell a different, happier tale. The argument faded away. We took pleasure in each other as we always have.

But I have spent many hours alone this past month. Apart from my now daily visits to Henry and the boys at the print shop, I have been lonely. Nat is always at out at work somewhere, and William has all but disappeared since those few days in Newgate. Nat says he is miserable and won't say a word about his time there. Losing his teaching licence hit William hard. With time on my hands, I brooded on this matter of the Tywns until I decided to find my own answers. It irks me that Nat has not spoken about it and I've no wish to start another disagreement, but it is a shadow on my back, darkening all my new hopes. Sarah has promised to question James about John Twyn's death, and I expect her to visit this evening. I pray that what she learns will put my fears to rest.

Will you go to the hangings? There was haughtiness in his voice when he said that. Almost a sneer. He thinks that I am some weak woman, unused to the world, and oblivious to its harsh realities. I am determined to show him I am neither.

I arrive at the print shop, determined to insist they take me with them to Coleman's execution, but none of the usual tables cluttered with books and papers are set out in front of the shops. Shutters, red, green – blue in Henry's case – are closed and latched. I knock several times on the door in case they're both up in Nat's office, but I already know I've missed them. I should turn back. Instead, I set my feet to the task and quickly find High Holborn is a much longer road than I imagined.

It takes me nearly an hour, but at length I arrive within sight of the gallows. People are gathering. I pass one group laughing at a picture of the Pope with the words 'avarice', 'lust', and 'pride' around his head. Edward Coleman will be brought here on a hurdle, a kind of crude sleigh, as traitors are denied the dignity of travelling upright in a cart. Beyond that, I'm not sure what I expect. One minute I'm part of a walking crowd, the next we've stopped. Beside me, two men are discussing a play that one saw the night before. I've heard of it but not seen it. *The Coronation of Queen Elizabeth*, it's called. Henry told me it shows the Pope seducing a nun.

The man I'm listening to thinks it is a disgrace, but he believes that the story is true. Hate is in the air. The blessed relief that my walk is over is quickly forgotten as my back begins to ache. Our progress grinds to a halt but, twisting my head along with everyone else, I see that this man's last journey from Newgate to the Tyburn Tree is nearly at an end. Two horses plod slowly. I can't see what they're pulling, but there is the priest walking behind, and the crowd folding in and following in its wake. The horses snort and their breath steams up against the harsh December chill. Here is the traitor.

He is middle-aged and has a smooth, thoughtful face. People jeer, spit, and curse at him. A stone cuts the air as it flies by my cheek. A red cut opens up under Coleman's right eye. His face is white with fear. Then he is past me. Bodies shuffle into mine. Caught in the crowd, I follow, pressing on towards Tyburn to see a man die. My plan was to make a point to my husband. To show him that I am not a child and not naïve. But if I am honest, I wish I had not come.

Under the triple tree – the triangular gallows where eight men and women can be hanged simultaneously – the lace is cut from Coleman's throat and his hands are unbound. His coat is stripped from his back. His hat and wig are thrown into the crowd and fought over so fiercely that both are surely ruined. He's allowed to stand while a rope is placed about his neck and tied fast to the beam above. Prayers are said. The wait is interminable. Finally, the driver of the hurdle shakes the reins and the horse pulls away. Coleman swings.

He doesn't fight it. I've heard that victims of the hangman struggle: legs kicking and veins bulging as they fight for breath, but not if they want to die quickly. If his neck snaps at the first drop, he won't know what follows. After a few minutes, the hangman climbs up and cuts the rope. Coleman drops to the ground. My heart drops to my stomach as his body plunges down. Next, he is manhandled up onto a wide wooden pallet, the noose still tied around his neck. The crowd presses forward. He may be dead. I don't want to look. I turn away, but people push forward on all sides. Coleman's shirt is ripped away. A knife is raised. His belly is sliced open and his steaming innards slide out. He screams.

The crowd loosens, and I stumble away, sickened and retching.

"Anne? What on earth are you doing here?"

"Thank God, Nat." I whisper. My stomach heaves.

"She may faint," Henry says. "Get her away from this. Don't let her see the blood."

Relief washes over me. Blinding tears save me from witnessing anything more.

***

62

"It's hard to believe that anyone deserves such an end," I say later.

"It's a traitor's death. You couldn't have chosen an everyday hanging for your first taste of death, could you? You have seen justice at its most visceral today."

I shift the pillows up higher behind my head. They have brought me home in a hired carriage, and Nat has helped me upstairs. The drapes are drawn around us in our bed. I have slept through most of the afternoon, he tells me, and it grows dark in the city very early at this time of year. Both the darkness and his voice are comforts.

"The evidence against Edward Coleman was damning," Nat says. "His house was searched. They found letters, written in Coleman's hand, which proved unequivocally that he was asking the French to support James becoming the King of England in his brother's place. In return for French funds, Coleman told them James would make the country Catholic again."

"And so, Oates's plot stories are true?"

"It would seem so."

We are silent a few moments.

"Only seem so?" I ask.

He shifts his body down the bed and plants a kiss on my shoulder.

"Titus Oates named Edward Coleman as part of the Catholic conspiracy, and the evidence supports him. Oates lodged his statements with the magistrate Godfrey, and Justice Godfrey is dead. You might say only a fool would not believe it."

I wince as he repeats my own words to me. At least his voice is gentle. Perhaps I might bring up the subject of John Twyn. Yet, when I remember my collapse at Tyburn, courage deserts me. I could not have failed in my attempt to be taken seriously any more spectacularly. I want to hold onto this moment of intimacy. "But you still have your doubts?" I say.

"Most certainly."

"What can you do about it?"

"Ask questions. Look for holes in his story. Find out more

63

about him. I've asked Kineally to find out what he can about Oates."

"Kineally?"

"John Kineally. He works for me sometimes. Finds people. Or information. That kind of thing." There is a pause, and I sense his hesitation. "In fact, I should really go out now to meet him." Nat squeezes my hand. I'm glad he can't see the disappointment on my face. "Anyway, your sister sent a note. She wants to see you and will arrive any moment. So, you won't mind if I'm out – just for an hour or two – will you?"

"Not in the least," I say with as much cheer as I can muster. "Happily, there is one member of my family we can always be glad to see."

He gives a short laugh and, to be honest, I am glad, both that Sarah is on her way and that Nat will not be here when she arrives. We have much to discuss.

***

I let her deliver her news first.

"John Twyn. Don't give him or his wife another thought."

"No?" My memory of Mistress Twyn's twisted face when she accosted me at the Bartholomew Fair is all too clear. I would love to put her out of my mind.

"No. James knew all about the case. He says Nat's part in it was to make the arrest and nothing more. Twyn was running an illegal press, printing seditious pamphlets for some extreme group or other. Your husband is simply being stubborn by not explaining this to you. He was the Licenser and he was only doing his job."

Relieved as I am, there's something in the way she speaks that gives me pause.

"*Was* the Licenser?" I say.

Sarah shifts and looks a little uncomfortable. "James thinks that Nat's post may not be renewed in the New Year."

"Whyever not?"

"Because Parliament is in uproar with the Catholic threat. All normal business has been suspended."

"Nat will find something else." She had better not disagree with me.

"I am sure he will." She pats down her skirts and doesn't meet my eye. "Anyway," she says, "your note said you had something particular to discuss. Unless it was just this Twyn nonsense."

My sister's resilience is one of her best qualities. Her open heart is another. That heart is on full display when I take her hands in mine. I whisper my suspicions and a smile, as broad as the Thames, lights up her gentle face.

* * *

Hours later, with Sarah long gone, the house is quiet. Logs split and crunch in the fire. There are dull echoes of movement next door, the cry of our neighbour's infant son struggling for sleep and the bark of a dog in the street outside, nothing more. I take up a volume of poems but haven't the patience for them. I should not have doubted Nat about John Twyn. I need to have faith in him now. I have to. Especially now. This question of his employment must wait for another day. I will him to come home. Anticipation makes my mouth run dry.

We will want wine. We will want to talk and to celebrate, and I'm suddenly re-composing the scene I've been planning. This morning, before I made a fool of myself at the hanging, I went to Leadenham Market. It was bitterly cold, the sun slung low, and a damp mist hanging about the streets. Before I married Nat, I bought things; of course I did. But now I *shop*. I have learned about prices, about measures and weights, about cuts of meat, about firm flesh and ripe scents, and so much more. I carry my own money and count out my own coins into the rough hands of men in greasy aprons with yellow rinds for nails. I relish the weight of my purchases on my arms and the hardness of the streets through the soles of my shoes as I carry everything home myself. This morning, I bought tongue, cheese, and two sacks of dried peas, one of which I must take to William.

I jump to my feet and pick my way down to the kitchen. It

smells good. There is a pipkin cooling on the stove, and the warm scents of stewed tongue, vegetables and thyme are very satisfying.

I take the wine and a plate of cheese and some bread that Kitty slid from the oven just before she went home to her mother for a visit. I carry everything up the stairs and set it out on our dresser.

I hang up my dress and climb into bed in my shift, hugging my knees. Imaginary conversations play in my mind. After a minute or two, I slip back out of bed and run down the stairs barefoot to find that book of poems I tried and failed to read earlier.

I am just back under the covers and finding my page when the scrape of the door and the shuffle of Nat pulling off his boots tell me he is home. Sarah agreed with me. It is time to share my news.

Chapter Ten

Nat

After a brief meeting with Kineally, I head straight back home. It's not late, only a little after nine, but the lower floors of our house are in darkness. I pull off my boots, coat and hat. Then I climb the stairs, twirling my wig on my balled fist. Candlelight trims the cracks around our door. Anne is propped up in bed with the drapes still pulled back, reading a book.

"Poetry?" I ask.

"Yes."

I busy myself pulling off my shirt and washing my face in the pitcher.

"Well, I hope it's not Andrew bloody Marvell."

"No. It's not Andrew *bloody* Marvell – although just because you don't like his politics, I don't see why I can't enjoy his poetry."

I cross to the bed and look down at her. "I've heard some wives are submissive to their husbands' views and—"

"Is that really the kind of wife you want?"

We smile, but I'm aware that my answer is important. "No," I say. "There is only one kind of wife I want. And it's you."

"Good."

She pulls me into the bed with her, and her lips find my ear.

"Because I have two things to tell you, Nat."

"And what may they be?"

"First, I want to apologise. About what I said about John Twyn."

"I did nothing wrong."

"I know that now. I should always have known it."

"Or asked me."

"Or asked you."

"And the other thing? You said two things." She is smiling at me. My wife looks highly kissable.

"I am with child."

***

Two hours later, I'm in the Fuller's Rent Tavern.

We have talked, as husbands and wives do, about her news and what it will mean. But when Anne fell asleep, I found that I could not. I stared at the ceiling until my eyeballs felt they might crack. All I could think of was the Licensing Act. It won't be renewed, and I will lose my position – precisely when I need it most. I crept from the bedroom carrying my clothes and tiptoed down the stairs. I needed a drink.

I suppose curiosity brought me here. Oates, whose appearance is certainly to blame for my current employment woes, met William and Matthew Medbourne in this tavern. He even mentioned the place in his deposition to Parliament. I need some time to think things over, away from my usual haunts. I've no doubt that Southwell was pushing me in the direction of attacking Oates, hinting that rewards would follow. But do I have time to work towards rewards that might be as thin as the breath that whispered of them? I am going to be a father. The thought fills me with as much dread as it does joy.

The Fuller's Rent is hardly the den of treason that Oates described. It's hot and airless. Tobacco smoke pricks my eyes and throat, and almost every seat is taken. I squeeze into a dark booth near the door and order a brandy. The men here are young and certainly less serious than my normal companions in Sam's Coffee House. Laughter spikes the air, and a group near the fire sing lustily, undeterred by the cat-calls of some, bowing before the applause of others. There are working men: ostlers, still in their leathers; farriers with thick arms and strong necks; but also a mix of more languid-looking fellows with quantities of lace at their throats and cuffs, wearing colourful garters and costly wigs. That's the kind of men this place has a reputation for, not for traitors. The atmosphere's convivial, the clientèle more interested in banter than debate. They are also intent on drinking heavily, as testified to by a loud choking sound, mingled with cries of horror and disgust from somewhere near the far corner of the room. It suits my mood. I down the brandy and call for another, with a pint of ale.

I wanted time to think, but suddenly there is nothing I want to do less. I tip back my head, open my throat, bloat myself with ale, and straight away call for more. I brood upon recent events. Southwell disgusts me. He is so passionless, so cold and analytical. At that bull fight, he was more concerned about the flavour of his beef than the state of the capital. The King doesn't believe in Oates but will take no action to stop him. This madness will run unchecked. And meanwhile, the Licensing Act will lapse.

Anne picks her way into my thoughts then, like a child at a scab, itching, tugging away. How on earth will I support her when I am not the Licenser? How will I support our child? Asking her to leave her home to be the wife of the Licenser was one thing. Expecting her to remain with a nobody, with a man struggling to scratch a basic living? That won't do. I need income. Henry has been reticent, but he wishes I would not write against Oates, notwithstanding the fact that his influential friend suggested I should. I knock back another shot of brandy. It is a task I could take on with relish, I'll admit. Doesn't someone have a duty not to let Oates's conspiracies dominate the public consciousness, completely unopposed?

I drink some more. Anne and I are happy, I believe. Our only true argument in all these months of matrimony was about John Twyn and that can be set to rest now, as least far as Anne is concerned. As I said to Henry, my conscience is clear. I didn't pass judgement on John Twyn. I didn't write the laws that he broke. I didn't place the noose around his neck or go to gloat as his legs kicked into the void. But since Anne's accusation, I have felt uneasy. I drink some more, dredging up the truth about my actions over John Twyn, bowing my head and rubbing one finger and thumb against my eyelids.

My difficulty is not that I arrested the man and caused him to lose his life. That's not the guilt that bites. No. The truth is that I never paused to think about it at all. Twyn was a printer, a man not unlike Henry, but a printer of seditious material for the Fifth Monarchists. Henry would never do work for a group like that. But Twyn did. I caught him in the act of it and gave no thought to what would happen to him after the arrest. I thought about nothing but making my own name and earning sufficient funds to support my mother and brother back in Sussex. Nothing more. Not of the life of a man, of the loss borne by his wife, not of the fatherless children left to struggle in the wake of my progress.

What kind of a man does that make me? I even enjoyed it. That night. The arrest. Summoning those guards. Was that what Oates felt when the Privy Council took him seriously, installed him in Whitehall, sent him out into the streets at the head of an armed guard to arrests those priests and prominent Catholics? I revelled in the attention that Twyn's death brought me. I imagine Oates is doing the same right now.

Fear grips my guts. I've spent ten years in London working to create a career that's about to disappear. I have a beautiful wife who put her faith in me, abandoning her family and a life of comfort. Now she is going to have a child. What can be done?

I've finished another drink by the time I reach this point of self-loathing, and lean back against the wooden panelling, gazing around for some distraction.

I'm about to get much more of a distraction than I wanted.

The double doors of the tavern are thrown wide open. Two smug-looking fellows, puffing for breath, hold them ajar without a care for the chill wind and spots of rain that blow in as they wait.

'Shut the bleeding door!' howls a young lad at a nearby table, only to find a stick under his nose. He's told to mind who he's bloody speaking to and, before anyone can say anything more, a group of six or seven men, heads bent and heavily cloaked, march into the tavern. The two from the door have no difficulty clearing a table for themselves and their companions. As the group settles and they remove their low black hats, I let out a gasp of surprise. Shrinking back into the shadows of the booth, I attempt to gather my somewhat pickled wits. And I'm not alone in my shocked reaction. Everyone recognises him, and he knows it. He smiles and nods like a visiting dignitary. It is the man of the hour, the Salamanca Doctor himself, Titus Oates.

The landlord of the Fuller's Rent falls over himself in his effusive welcome of Oates and his cronies. I'm caught somewhere between horror at seeing the man at such close quarters and delight at watching Oates at play. He appears friendly at first sight, but as the landlord retreats, Oates's lip curls into a sneer. He busies himself smoothing down his surplice and listening, after a fashion, to the whispers of one of his companions. Drinks are brought, and he sucks thirstily on a tankard of wine.

"Ugh!" With a loud cry, Oates spits his drink across the table. "Here, Thomas! Get your foul carcass over here," he shouts. The landlord returns, hands clasped, a concerned expression on his face.

"What piss is this?" Without warning, Oates grabs the landlord by the collar and pulls him down until there is barely an inch of air between them. "Thought to serve me piss, did you, Thomas?" Oates speaks quietly, but the whole tavern is silent. "Thought you could piss in a pot and laugh while I drank it, did you?"

The landlord shakes his head. His eyes roll as he tries to look for support, but no-one's moving.

"People in this stinking hole have laughed at me in the past, haven't they?" says Oates. "They laughed at the holes in my clothes and let me sleep on the street, rather than help a fellow man in need. But how many of these filthy scoundrels would like to beg a hand from me these days? Eh? Eh?" He rises out of his seat, pulling the poor man up by the scruff like a stray mongrel. Anger has turned Oates's face crimson, but as he sees how rapt the whole tavern is, the colour fades. A crescent of a smile forms on his lips. "Well, we will laugh together now,

71

instead," he says. He raises his voice. "Drinks for everyone, I say. Whatever they have a fancy for. Fetch them out, Thomas, fetch them out! On the house."

Finally, Oates lets go of the snivelling Thomas. The poor man darts back to his bar and begins serving ale and wine. Oates, meantime, sits back down amongst his companions, who laugh and toast him in fine style. He lifts the very tankard he was so unhappy about and gulps down the wine.

The tension in the room ebbs as drinks are served and new conversations begin. The group around Oates are all sycophants, busy laughing at his jokes, assuring themselves of his comfort and satisfaction, no doubt hoping to profit through their fawning and petting of London's saviour. One in particular – a fat, watery-eyed young man with a double chin and a snout for a nose – butters Oates up most assiduously, pointing at other men in the tavern, doubtless whispering snide comments in the good doctor's ear. At any rate, his commentary prompts several bursts of immoderate laughter and more spitting of wine. They sicken me, but I can't take my eyes from them. At length, I stand, planning to slip out for a moment to relieve my bladder. But as I step past the fine company around Oates, the fat fellow sticks out a foot and trips me.

I crash to the floor like a felled tree. I'm drunk enough not to be hurt by the fall, but not so soused as to be oblivious to their sniggering. In a mounting rage, I raise myself on all fours, then with the aid of a chair, clamber up and glare at them, my fists tight at my sides. No-one helps me, but at least no-one else is laughing, only Oates's little flock.

"Is there a problem?" asks the pig-faced one, as Oates trills with laughter.

I sway a little on my feet.

"Oh, ignore him, Harry," says Oates, putting an arm around his friend's shoulders. "He's just some drunk, nothing for you to concern yourself with." His grip tightens, and he rubs a fleshy hand up and down Harry's knee. "I only hope this maltworm hasn't hurt your leg with his clumsiness. Thomas!" Oates calls across to the landlord. "There are some rather

72

undesirable characters in your tavern this evening. Get him out."

"What?" That wakes me up. I'm about to plant a fist on that pink face, ready to show Oates that though all of London might bow down before him, I, at least, am not afraid to speak my mind. But even as I bend, firm hands grip me by the arms and I'm whipped back like a dog on a leash.

Titus Oates gets to his feet and takes a step towards me. Recognition flickers in his eyes. Like him, I'm far from unknown in the city.

"Why, but you're the Licenser, aren't you?" he says, his breath warm on my face. "Or at least, you are for now. Here, Harry," he says, "this is Nathaniel Thompson. Have you heard of him?" I glare at Harry who looks back at me blankly.

"No. Should I have?"

Oates giggles. I swear he giggles like a girl at the fair. He turns his gaze on mine and looks me right in the eyes, but when he speaks it's as if he's still addressing his companion.

"No," he says. "And if you haven't heard of him yet, I'm sure you never shall." He blinks and speaks to the man holding me. "Chuck him out."

In another second, I'm out in the street. Of course, I try to push my way back in. I rattle and hammer on the door. I stamp and slosh in the gutter. I'm shouting, bringing forth an avalanche of invective, cursing about Oates and his poisonous little friends and their pathetic schoolboy bullying little ways.

I scour the street for a rock or a stone to throw at a window. "I'll smash you, you bastards," I bellow through the rain. "You'll see!" At last, I find a lump of wood and hurl it at the tavern. It bounces back at me off the wall.

Chapter Eleven

Anne

The Year of Our Lord, 1679, begins like no other I have ever known. First, it is so cold that the Thames freezes over. People skate across its silver crust and buy wares from impromptu stalls established on the ice. Nat and I only peer at them from the safety of firm ground. There is no ice-skating for me this year, and besides, I am less than light-hearted. Every day I wait for my husband to tell me that his post as the Licenser has disappeared, and every day he says nothing.

The early months of carrying this child are a struggle. The queasiness that began at Edward Coleman's execution plagues me for two full months. I sleep a great deal and Nat is in and out, working relentlessly, but to what end? Sarah tells me in January that the Licensing Act has lapsed, as James had suggested it would.

We are now in February and still my husband keeps his own counsel on the subject.

In the matter of Titus Oates, however, he cannot keep his views to himself.

Perhaps he has decided to court business through notoriety? Whatever his reasoning, he is about to issue a very public attack on Titus Oates, for I saw the pamphlets being set for printing with my own eyes. Henry is concerned. He says nothing, but I share his fear. Nat, these last two months, has fastened his energies upon Oates like a clam on a rock. Where Oates is, my husband goes. He has watched Oates hold public meetings, preach sermons, and speechify as if he was born to it. Everywhere Oates is, Nat says, he scatters the seeds of panic. His fame is unparalleled. And Nat is about to attack.

His pamphlet, *A Brief History of This Latest Conspiracy,* is ready to be distributed to every coffee shop in the capital. Scorn for Oates's plot laces every line of it. But Nat is nervous this morning.

"You're up early," I say, as he scrambles into his breeches and pulls a fresh linen shirt over his head.

"I am. The magistrate's murder trial begins today."

He has chosen today of all days to publish – the first day of the trial of three men for the murder of Sir Edmund Godfrey. Oates will be centre stage in Westminster Hall, his plot on everyone's mind. Nat could not throw his doubts and accusations out at a more inflammatory moment. I won't remain here quietly, waiting for Nat to come home and describe it all. It's time I saw Titus Oates for myself.

"Good," I say. "I am coming with you."

***

Westminster Hall is another new world to me, a huge cavern of activity where lawyers bustle past shoppers, sightseers, stray dogs, and men of business on their way to the court set up in the south east corner. The workings of the Court of the King's Bench are open for all to see. The Judge sits on a raised dais under the window, and Nat leads me up a short number of steps to a row of seating to the Judge's right. This gallery view makes the proceedings appear rather theatrical, but I quickly realise this is no light-hearted matter.

Fat old Justice Scroggs and Attorney General Jones waste no time. They use their opening remarks to batter home the point that Sir Edmund Godfrey was a devout Protestant. The jury nod and turn, as I do, to examine the men in the dock. At least two of them are Catholic. All three are employed, in varying capacities, by the Queen at Somerset House. In the current climate, that fact in itself will probably be enough to see them hanged.

Oates is called first. Beside me, Nat straightens up, pen in hand, ready to take down his testimony word for word. My first impression is that Oates is immensely sure of himself. I try to imagine William as his teacher and fail miserably. As we look on, Oates swaggers to the witness stand and reels off his oath as if these are words he has said many, many times. He declares that he has indeed known Sir Edmund Godfrey and that he and Israel Tonge – I glance at Nat; this is not a name I'm familiar with – visited Godfrey twice to make depositions about the infamous plot against King and country. Afterwards, Oates says, Godfrey also visited him. The magistrate expressed concern that his involvement with Oates and Tonge had made him unpopular in certain quarters and might even have put his life in danger.

As Oates's testimony concludes, Nat writes furiously. His mistrust of Titus Oates only grows. It is not what the public thinks, or what my father thinks, but Nat is certain that Oates is a liar. I don't know if I agree but, if he is right, then it is a sorry thing this trial, for there are three men fighting for their lives. With a deepening sense of concern, I listen as the court moves to the details of Edmund Godfrey's disappearance. A thin, slightly chinless, fellow named Thomas Robinson is called as a witness. Robinson describes himself as a long-standing friend to Godfrey, and says they last saw each other on Monday the 7th of October, five days before he disappeared.

"He was not himself," Robinson states. "Edmund was normally very calm, very precise. That night, he was confused. Often, he opened his mouth as if to speak, only to shut it again. He talked to me about the deposition he had taken. It was evidently praying on his mind. He said, 'I will get little thanks for my involvement in this matter, Thomas.' Those were his exact words."

"Did Sir Edmund Godfrey give you any reason to suppose he felt threatened or afraid?" asks Jones.

"Certainly. He said he feared he would be the first martyr – his words – but that he would not part easily with his life. I urged him to take a man about with him, to give him some protection and ease his fears, but he wouldn't listen."

"And did you gain any impression about which group or individual had made your friend so terrified?"

"No. I was struck by his choice of the word *martyr*, but he was very vague. I can't say any more."

"Just that he told you he would be the first martyr?"

"Yes. Just that."

Robinson leaves the witness box. My eyes linger on the accused men: Robert Green, Lawrence Hill, and Henry Berry. They don't inspire sympathy, although I pity them. Two are older, their weathered faces fat with worry. The other is younger. He has the set of a labourer about his shoulders, an unlined, pale face, and long yellow hair. He keeps his eyes down, but every minute or so he looks fleetingly across the courtroom toward a young woman, presumably his wife. Her eyes are rimmed red although the day's events have hardly begun. The way her dress swells across her belly tells a story. She has so much to be concerned about, yet still she manages to smile at her husband, albeit a thin crust of a smile, clamping anguished words behind tight lips and clenched teeth. Do they have children already, or will this be their first?

As the next witness is sworn in, I study her, ashamed by how little I've considered the realities of this event. I haven't distinguished enough between the three men in the dock to know if she is Mistress Green, or Berry, or Hill. I must pay better attention. The new witness is ready to begin. His name is Miles Prance.

My first impression is of a weak, limp sort of fellow. He is short and narrow-shouldered, with thinning gingery hair and too-large eyes, but he appears very composed in the witness box. He's a Catholic and a successful silversmith with a shop near Covent Garden. Prance speaks quietly but clearly. He is an educated man and the jurors take him seriously.

A few months previously, Prance says, he fell into company with some priests, and through them came to know Lawrence Hill, Robert Green, and Henry Berry. They stiffen as he names them. The blond, younger man reacts first, and I assume that he is Lawrence Hill. My eyes are drawn again to the frightened face of his wife. I am sick at heart for her. Meanwhile, the courtroom falls silent as Prance describes the murder.

Hill and Green, he says, followed Godfrey for at least a

week before his death. On the Saturday afternoon in question, Hill ran to Prance's house in Princess Street, not far from Somerset House, and begged him to help them. Prance glances across at the jury. He's nervous. It was the priests, he says. The priests convinced him that Godfrey was actively working against English Catholics.

"Priests?" I whisper to Nat.

"Jesuits. Three of them. Arrested by Oates."

Below us, Prance admits that he went with Hill. Mistress Hill hugs her arms around her chest.

"We followed Sir Godfrey for hours," says Prance. "And in the evening, when he returned from some business in a house near St Clement's Church, they murdered him. It was about seven or eight o'clock, quite dark. Lawrence Hill stopped Sir Edmund Godfrey just at the back-gate of Somerset House. He told him that a quarrel was taking place between two of the Queen's servants in the yard there. He said he was afraid they would kill each other, and needed help to pull them apart. Berry and I pretended to fight. But as soon as Godfrey was in the yard, Green lunged out of the shadows. Berry ran to block the lower water-gate entrance, Hill took the back-gate and I stood guard at the upper-gate."

Prance clears his throat and then points across at the accused. "It was Robert Green. He took a twisted handkerchief and drew it about the magistrate's neck. Then he called us back. The others fell on him, holding him down while Green choked the life from him."

A collective gasp breaks from the listening crowd. Nat squeezes my hand, but my eyes are fastened on Green, Berry, and Hill. There's no reaction. All three stand with their heads bent, gazing at their feet. Prance isn't finished, though.

"The old man was strong. I returned from the gate, but his body wasn't still. I saw his leg and an arm stirring. Robert Green went back, straddled the body, and grabbed the head in his hands. Then he twisted his neck round sharply and stamped on his chest." Prance's face twists. It's the first emotion I've observed from him. "They talked about stabbing him to make certain he was finished off, but Hill said they must not spill any blood. We set about concealing the body."

Poor, poor Mistress Hill. Her hand is over her mouth and her eyes are wet. Who will take her home when this is done?

Next, Prance describes how Hill directed them to take the corpse to a room within Somerset House. He says it lay there for two nights. There's a muttering through the crowd at this. Everyone remembers the week of Godfrey's disappearance. We all wondered and gossiped about what had happened to him. Inevitably, I remember Nat and Henry discussing it. No-one would have imagined Godfrey was lying dead for days in a room in the Queen's household. After two days, Prance says, the body was moved to a different room. By the Wednesday, they were ready to remove it altogether.

"We carried the body out of Somerset House in a sedan chair. Berry was a porter there. He opened the gate. We took it like that as far as the Greek Church in Soho. From there, we shovelled him up on a horse, and Hill led the horse and its load out to Primrose Hill." His face is flushed now. "That was my suggestion," he says. "I'm a member of a club at the Horseshoe Tavern nearby."

Prance says the murderers met up again a few days later. They told him that Hill had taken Godfrey's own sword and stabbed the dead man before leaving him in a ditch.

"Why did you meet?" asks Jones, the Attorney General.

"It was in the manner of a celebration."

"Did you dine together?"

"Yes. On a barrel of oysters and a dish of fish. I bought the fish myself." A snigger ripples around the crowd while Justice Scroggs scowls.

"And what were you all about there?" says Jones.

"Reading an account of the murder. And making merry about it."

"There were priests present?"

"Several."

Jones looks meaningfully at the Jurymen and the Judges.

"And now, I must ask you a question which is of great importance to the strength of the evidence we have to put before our jury. Do you know a Mr. Bedloe, Mr. Prance?"

Nat scribbles down the name.

"I do," says Prance.

"Had you ever had any discussion with him since you were imprisoned?"

"None."

"Inevitable," whispers Nat in my ear. "Oates could not remain a lone voice for long. Watch. This Bedloe is another scoundrel, just like Oates. Full of information of dubious provenance, especially when that information may lead to a reward."

The new witness slides into the witness box. Mr. Bedloe has a crooked smile. He runs his fingers through his hair and winks at some wench in the crowd, drawing whistles.

"It's rumoured that he has fortune-hunted all over Europe, blackmailing, seducing, and thieving as it suited him," says Nat, and it's not hard to believe. Bedloe is in his mid-twenties and looks to me to be good-humoured, light of heart, and entirely untrustworthy. "The five hundred-pound reward offered to help find Godfrey's murderers brought him up to London from Bristol like a rat up a drain," mutters Nat. "Since his arrival, Bedloe has made himself indispensable as a second witness to all of Oates's claims."

Like Oates, Bedloe is at ease in the courtroom, and he has a lot to say for himself. He reels off a list of priests who, he claims, tried to tempt him take part in this and other crimes.

"Did these priests explain why they wanted Justice Godfrey murdered?" he is asked.

Bedloe shrugs. "They told me he was an important man. Said he had all the information gathered by Titus Oates and Israel Tonge, and that they needed him dead and the papers taken from him. They said that there was money available to those who helped them; money made available by Lord Bellasis and Edward Coleman."

"Ah, the merry sound of the ring of truth," says my husband. He writes the word 'tenuous' in angry capital letters in his notes. "What a happy knack these witnesses have of picking on people who are already dead, like Coleman, hanged on the back of Oates's evidence; or disgraced, like Lord

Bellasis, who has been thrown in the Tower of London with no right of redress. It surely shames us that we call this justice."

Bedloe proves to be a slick witness. He speaks clearly and never hesitates. His testimony is scattered with little details and familiar asides that give his words an appearance of truth. He doesn't corroborate Prance's story closely or incriminate himself. But he does swear that he saw the body at Somerset House, and firmly identifies Prance, Hill, Berry, and Green as having all been present at a discussion about what to do with it.

"I was for tying weights to his hands and feet and throwing him in the Thames," Bedloe declares, "but they wouldn't have that." His grin makes my fingers twitch. If I were Hill's wife, I'd long to slap his handsome face.

"Tell us how you came to identify the witness, Miles Prance," asks Jones.

"I came across him again quite by chance," says Bedloe. "I was in the lobby of the House of Lords, awaiting their Lordship's pleasure, when Dr. Oates pointed out Mr. Prance. I recognised him at once. As he was already in custody, I told the guard to keep a firm hold of him while I laid out what I knew."

***

After Bedloe's evidence is over, the trial moves swiftly toward its inevitable conclusion. My eyes continue to be drawn to Mistress Hill. Can she see her husband's life slipping away from her as clearly as I do? Her mouth is set in a thin white line and her hand rubs at her back. She keeps her eyes fixed on her husband, but he looks to her less and less often. Beside me, Nat continues taking notes. A Constable Brown takes the stand and confirms that he recovered the body from a ditch on Primrose Hill. Godfrey's own sword had pierced right through his chest and they found another, slighter, stab wound, but there was no blood found in the ditch at all. There were bruises to the victim's chest, and his neck appeared to be broken. Godfrey's stick and gloves were found near his body, and there was plenty of gold and silver in his pockets, ruling out robbery as a motive. Then a surgeon, Zackary Skillard, is asked to give a cause of death. I know nothing about such matters and his testimony leaves me none the wiser.

"Are you sure his neck was broken?" asks the Attorney General.

"I am sure," says Skillard.

"Did it appear that he was strangled or hanged?"

He puffs out his chest. "I would say that there was more done to his neck than ordinary suffocation. And I would say that the sword wound through his heart would have produced some blood if it had been done quickly after his death."

"And what of the condition of the body?"

"He was a lean man," says the surgeon. "His muscles, if he had died of the sword wound, would have been turgid. Then again, all strangled people never swell, because there is a sudden deprivation of all the spirits and a hindering of the circulation of the blood."

Nat has written these words down verbatim while I study the jury. Their faces, as I am sure mine is, are as blank of understanding as white cotton bleaching in the sun.

"You examined the body at midday on Friday the 18th of October," continues Jones. "How many days dead do you believe he was?"

"Four or five days. Or they may have kept him a week," says Skillard. "He never swelled, being a lean man. Only when we cut him open, did putrefaction begin."

His evidence is confused, but on one thing Skillard's certain. He is adamant that Godfrey's injuries could not have been self-inflicted. The man was murdered. In this surgeon's view, Prance's story is plausible. There's a shuffling amongst the prisoners. It's becoming difficult to look at them.

More witnesses follow. Godfrey's maid, Elizabeth Curtis – a young, thin girl with a pretty but pinched expression – fixes her eyes on a space somewhere off in the distance, and swears firmly that she saw Hill and Berry at the house in Hartshorn Lane in the days just before Godfrey's disappearance. She's far from convincing – I've seen children of eight make better recitals from their prayer books – yet her evidence goes unchallenged. Nat shifts a little when Sir Robert Southwell takes the stand. He is becoming as prolific in these cases as Oates, but Henry says he hates the attention.

We learn that Southwell was responsible for testing Prance's veracity by asking him to point out where in Somerset House the body of Justice Godfrey was hidden.

"At His Majesty's suggestion, My Lord," says Southwell, "Mr. Prance showed the Duke of Monmouth and myself the actual places he has described."

"And was Mr. Prance clear and ready in showing you these areas?" asks Scroggs.

"Yes," says Southwell. "Although he did afterwards show some confusion."

"In what way?"

"When we asked to be shown the other room to which the body was moved, Mr. Prance undertook to do so, but although we followed him and at first he was sure of the way, he could not find out the room for certain."

"Excellent!" declares Scroggs. Nat and I exchange surprised glances as the Judge continues. "Mr. Prance's doubtfulness and his reluctance to commit himself falsely, speak directly to his honesty. The dishonest man lies brazenly, showing no signs of doubt or confusion. Only the honest man will not swear to facts of which he is uncertain."

Southwell gazes at Scroggs, his eyebrows just fractionally raised. Lawrence Hill stares open-mouthed up at the bench, and his wife has covered her face with both hands. Their child will be born without a father.

The man has spirit, which makes it even harder to watch. With his fists at his side and in a clear, brave voice, Hill asserts that he has several witnesses who will prove that he was always in the house from eight o'clock every evening and therefore could have taken no part in these terrible activities. It gets him nowhere. One sweet-faced young woman from Dr. Godwin's lodgings in Somerset House swears that there could never have been a body hidden there without the whole house knowing, but Scroggs is instantly wriggling in his seat, snorting his derision, making it very apparent to the jury that a pack of Catholics are not to be relied on one bit.

Hill is running out of witnesses. His voice cracks as he asks for some water. His wife pulls out a sheaf of papers and tries to get a clerk to take them, but she's roughly refused. Hill sinks back down, as crushed as Berry and Green beside him. Tears slide down his wife's cheeks.

Green fares even worse. His single witness is discredited as a lying Catholic before he can even begin, so it's only Berry who manages to produce anyone whose evidence is taken seriously. This hinges on the question of the removal of the body. Berry produces several soldiers who are adamant that although a sedan came into Somerset House, none could have got out without their knowing. The Attorney General looks frustrated, but it's only one small point against so many statements stacked against them.

"Mr. Prance?"

In a moment of hush in the courtroom, Mistress Hill speaks up and calls on Prance, sitting just to the right of the jury. The people around her step away. Scroggs opens his mouth to shout her down, but perhaps the sight of her condition gives him pause. She grasps her moment. "I wish you would tell the court, Mr. Prance, why you denied all this to the King." Her voice is not strong, but this is something out of the ordinary. The crowd leans in.

"It was because I was afraid to lose my livelihood from the Queen and other Catholics. I had not been given a pardon at that point."

"And will you swear that you were not tortured?" she says.

Prance's throat moves although his lips remain closed. He turns his head slightly and looks at a tall, determined-looking woman in the crowd. Mistress Prance, I presume.

"Answer the question," says Scroggs.

"I was not."

"But it was said widely around town that you were tortured," Mistress Hill persists. "Several people have said that they could hear your cries in the prison. Won't you say it?" She pushes forward, pleading with Prance with her eyes. "For it is all false, all this. It is as false as God is true. It will be shown to be false, I swear. But by then it will be too late!"

"Enough, Madam," calls down Scroggs. He shuffles his flesh round in his chair so he can address the jury with a wry smile. "Do you think Mr. Prance will swear these three men out of their lives for nothing? Let us hear no more of it. No more."

On his words, Mistress Hill faints clean away and has to be taken out to be revived.

Lawrence Hill puts his head in his hands and howls.

***

It is soon over. The Attorney General sums up the prosecution evidence and then Scroggs addresses the jury. His words will stay with me forever.

"Gentlemen," he says, "this is a murder set on by priests and conducted by men yoked to the power of the Pope like beasts of burden. Their faith depends on the doctrine of belief and absolute obedience, the freedom to do right is not in these men's hands. Indeed, all Roman Catholic gentlemen in England would do well to quit this kingdom. For they cannot be quiet in their religion unless they are disturbing us in ours. It is not possible for them to live amongst us without seeking to take away the religious freedoms we so enjoy.

"In short, there is monstrous evidence of the existence of the whole horrid plot in this one killing. Sir Edmund Godfrey was murdered because he knew something that the priests would not have him tell. I leave it to you men of the jury to look at the evidence and see if it satisfies you in your consciences that these men are guilty."

Nat is silent as the jurors leave the Hall to find their verdict. He truly believes they are innocent and, having witnessed this, I believe it, too. There is horror and despair in his eyes. In truth, the three defendants do not match their role in this drama. They are as inept as Quince and his fellows, but sadly, this is no dream.

When all three are found guilty and sentenced, Scroggs is

openly delighted.

"Gentlemen," he declares. "You have found the same verdict that I would have found if I had been one of you, and if it were the last word I were to speak in this world, I should have pronounced them guilty."

The crowd answers him with hoots and loud applause. In ten days' time, Mistress Hill will be a widow.

Chapter Twelve

William

The loss of my license to teach is a blow in the guts every morning when I wake up and remember that I have nowhere to go. Henry Broome tolerates me in his print shop but we both know that my heart is not in it. Something has been stripped out of me. Some days I don't get out of bed at all. Anne's gentle kindness is like a balm to my soul, but I do not want kindness. Instead, I torture myself by listening to Nat. My friend's talk is all of Titus Oates, and I have not even told him of how he threatened me. I don't want to relive that interview, and Nat is fired up enough about Oates without my poor story to feed on. His pamphlet pouring scorn on Oates's revelations is the talk of every tavern and coffee shop for a week. Nat rants for days about the trial of Godfrey's murderers, and when the time comes, I go with him to the hangings. He is concerned that Anne will insist on going. She can be deceptively stubborn, but she waves us off without a word. The sight of the pregnant wife of Lawrence Hill collapsing as the rope around his neck tears his life from him is not one I will quickly forget. "Thank God Anne stayed away," is all Nat says.

In the weeks that follow he continues his public pursuit of Titus and repeatedly asks me to take him to Newgate to meet Matthew Medbourne. I give in at last, although fearing no good will come of it. I should hold out, but I'm too exhausted. I don't see any other way to stop Nat's badgering.

Rebuilt since the Great Fire, Newgate's new exterior sits in stark contrast to the horrors inside. They retained the gatehouse front it always had, but now new columns, battlements, gargoyles, and stone statues of Justice, Mercy, and Truth provide an ornate facade. Inside, it assaults my senses. I'm seasick as a stowaway, trapped in the dark. I'm thankful though for every step that takes us from the lower regions of the prison. Matthew has not been well, and his friends – by which I mean his wealthy friends, a group that I was never a part of and have no hope of joining now – have paid for an improvement in his accommodation. But it is still Newgate.

To make matters worse, we are here on a Monday. Execution day. The fires in Ketch's Kitchen are out by now, but this morning the gaol woke to the sound of bells ringing for the condemned. They were taken from the hold across the press yard to the chapel. From there, their route to Tyburn is well known, but most people give little thought to their journey back, to the bodies returned to Newgate and delivered to the kitchen. That's where Jack Ketch completes his work; he is not only a hangman. He's also responsible for stripping the bodies, and poaching heads and limbs in his kettle to better make them last out on those spikes and gibbets, and to keep the birds away. As Nat and I make our way through the prison, the smell of bay and cumin turns my stomach; that, and the bouquet of boiling flesh.

In contrast, Matthew's room above the press yard is almost civilised. It's small, and although it's sparsely furnished, he has a sumptuous throw piled on his narrow bed and a quantity of drawing paper and good quality inks and pens stowed on a small table near the door.

It sickens to see him here, so completely out of place. He's a soft-featured, childish-looking man, with thin wispy hair and a weak chin. Always, his face puts me in mind of a sweet, chubby puppy with long, curling eyelashes and a dimple in each cheek. There's a youthful look about him, although he is older than me. His hand grasps mine. I try to will strength to him through my fingers.

"Mr. Thompson," he says, turning to Nat. "I'm very happy to make your acquaintance. Very happy indeed. These surroundings are ghastly, of course, but please take a seat."

"Thank you." The room has only one chair, which Nat takes, while Matthew sits on the bed and I station myself next to the narrow window.

"Have you had occasion to visit Newgate before?" Matthew asks.

"Sadly, yes. I've written about the prison and its inmates. I've been inside several times now," Nat says. "Although I am not sure I'll ever get used to the smell."

"The smell? Ah, if only I could say the same. I have been here, well, longer than I had anticipated, and it barely registers with me now." He shakes his head in mock dismay.

"Do you have any hopes of obtaining your freedom? Friends working on your behalf?"

"Some. I have many friends, and most have stood by me despite this setback. But many of them are Catholics and their influence currently is – how shall I put it? – a little limited. I was hoping that you might have come to join in their number." Matthew's eyes narrow and some of his smooth way of talking slips. "Have you come to be my friend?"

"Not as such, no," Nat says. "There is no reason why I might not become your friend, but I must be honest. I'm here because I want information from you, not because of anything I may be able to do for you. Do you see?"

"Yes." Matthew purses his lips and folds his arms across his chest, throwing me a glance. "Well, I shall have to think about that, shan't I?" he says.

"As you wish." Nat sits back in his chair and waits for Matthew to decide. He has told me he can offer Matthew nothing more than the chance to proclaim his innocence. Nat is an honest fellow. I've never heard him make a promise he cannot keep.

"Tell him about Titus," I say.

Matthew rubs his hand over his mouth and stares at me for a few moments. Then he begins.

"I first met Titus around Bartholomew-tide, back in '76. It was my birthday, so I remember it quite well. I was a different man then. I am an actor by trade, and a writer, a comic, and a member of the Duke of York's company. Perhaps you have seen my translation of *Tartuffe*, or seen me on the stage even? I had a pretty role in Otway's play, *Venice Preserv'd*, the other year. You didn't catch it? Well, no matter.

"I suppose I would say I was at the height of my powers when I met him. I was approaching forty, although no-one knew it. I had a good reputation, there was work whenever I wanted it, and my work was my life. I am a single man and have never been interested in finding a wife.

"I was with a band of fellows in the Fuller's Rent Tavern near High Holborn – my treat. As I said, I was doing well and celebrating. We were rather swollen with a good deal of claret, and while my friends laughed and broke into some ribald song, I sat back on my bench, just enjoying the warmth of the wine and their companionship. That was when I saw him. He was sitting several benches away, hunched over a tankard of ale that he sipped while he eyed our antics. He was an awkward-looking fellow, all chin and gloomy eyes. I thought him brooding and, in my rather luscious state, very interesting. Some idea of warmth and human friendship took hold of me, perhaps something about his way of sitting reminded me of a lonelier, younger version of myself – I don't know any more. But I approached him, that's what counts.

"I offered him a drink. He refused at first, mumbling about having no funds, but I was having none of it. I dragged him with me to join my circle. Even now, I can't explain it. There was something so unusual about him. I just wanted to have him near me. He said very little. I saw he took to the wine very easily, though. I hoped it would mellow him, and so it proved."

Matthew pauses in his tale and looks at me. All I can do is nod.

"Titus soon opened up," he says. 'What no-one understands,' I remember him saying particularly, 'is that I have a special knowledge of spiritual matters'—"

Matthew breaks off again. His imitation of Oates's drawl is quite perfect, and Nat bows his head in acknowledgement. Matthew loves the approbation. His cheeks pink for a moment but then he cuts back to his story.

"I hadn't the faintest idea what the boy was talking about," he says, "but I pressed up next to him to hear more.

"I remember his exact words. He said he knew about hypocrisy. He said he knew how hubris, avarice, and sanctimony dominated the priesthood. He said he'd been badly treated but that his enemies would regret their treatment of him.

"Now, William here will tell you that this shows you what a fool I am." Matthew's tone is light, but he doesn't look at me, only at Nat. He spreads his arms theatrically wide. "And you will probably think the same, Mr. Thompson. Or even worse. But I have little to lose by giving you the truth of myself, and you have asked for my story and will have it. You see, I liked Titus. I thrilled at his darkness. You may not understand it, but the more he swore and muttered and groaned, the more I was drawn to him. He was unusual. Damaged. I felt something for him."

Matthew's eyes fly towards me and away again. "Of course, I wish now that I had never laid eyes on him, but what is done, is done. I sat with him. I put my arm around him and we drank more wine. I bent my head to his as he told me some story of being unjustly accused of some crime he could not reveal. Still, it might have come to nothing."

"Matthew." I can't stop myself. "Are you really going to blame me?"

"What? Of course not!"

"But—"

"But nothing, William. I am merely telling Mr. Thompson that you arrived and Titus recognised you. Seeing you so far from delighted to meet him, made me even more intrigued. You see. All my fault. Mine."

Is that true? I dare not ask. What must Nat make of this? Of Matthew, and of me?

Matthew draws a breath and continues. "And so I came to know Titus Oates. He talked and I listened. He told me that he had been harshly treated by his father, although I could tell that he still sought his approval. He spoke of early beatings, of being ignored at school, of all the alienation that I could understand only too easily. He was less than charming about our dear William here, something that I found terribly amusing. I was all comfort. I patted his knee. I may have stroked his cheek. I let him indulge his anger and self-pity wholeheartedly."

"And then?" asks Nat.

"And then when he asked if I thought you, William, might be a friend to him now, having been less than kind – in his mind – when you were his teacher, I said I was sure you that would and furnished him with your address."

"You did what?" I start forward from the window and have to stop myself. "I always thought that he followed me." He lays his hand across his forehead. "*You* told him. Oh Matthew!"

"Well, I was drunk, William. And I had no idea of what he really was. No-one did. Not even you."

"But you gave him the means to find me, and thereby you, whenever he wanted!"

"Yes. If I am honest, that is what I intended."

Matthew looks from me to Nat and back again. If Matthew has regrets, it seems that he has come to terms with them. He has no fear of Nat's opinion. I wish I felt the same.

"Titus was adrift in London," he continues. "He had few friends and little money, and I enjoyed showing him my rather glamorous existence. I took him to the theatre. His eyes lit up when we stood in the Royal Box. I loved his contradiction. He was always so brooding and so self-contained, and then he'd simply burst out with some outrageous profanity. It was as though a whole swell of blackness was swimming about in his gut somewhere and every so often a bubble of bile would erupt.

"What his true beliefs were, or are, I couldn't begin to say. When I met him, he was disgruntled but firmly Protestant. As he became familiar with my friends at the Fuller's Rent Tavern, he became less so. It is a rule of our club that religion is never mentioned. Perhaps that was part of our attraction for Titus. Certainly, he did not come so often in search of little old me. Our friendship was – I see it now – always all on my side.

Please—" Matthew waves Nat away with his hand, although I see no sign of Nat interrupting him.

"Please," he says. "I have been vain all my life and have never put anyone first but myself. I'm a selfish creature and have indulged myself whenever I could. But I have never been a fool. Oates took up with me whenever he was short of funds, when there was no-one else to sponge from, because he knew I liked him. He told me he was drummed out of the Navy for sodomy, you know. I gave him the introduction to Norfolk and he gained a place in that household. He would have been sleeping on the streets if I had not. Still, within a week I found him imitating my voice and mannerisms to a crowd of fellows over a bowl of punch. Many a time he walked past me in the street without a greeting, without a nod, without a glance. Once or twice in the Fuller's Rent I approached him, but he just turned his back as though I wasn't even there. Yet when he came to me, I could not refuse him. Why? Oh, all the obvious reasons. You wouldn't like me to lay it out for you any more than that, would you?"

"No," Nat says. "I understand you."

Matthew almost smiles. "So, there you have my story with the famous Titus Oates. Through the years of his alleged evidence-gathering and assumed Catholicism, I saw him not regularly, but fairly often. Always, of course, when he was in need of money or a place to stay."

"But you must have had some rupture with him, some falling out?" Nat says.

"No. What makes you think that?"

"Because you're here. Because you are imprisoned on his say-so. You don't strike me as a dangerous traitor. It is hard to see you as a threat to King Charles, or as any kind of fanatic."

"I should hope not! All I am is a self-pleasing old ham. I'm a tired-out, lucked-out, randy old player, whose tastes have never been run of the mill but have never run to treason, not at all. You wonder why Titus named me?"

"Yes!"

"Well, obviously, because he could."

***

Nat is quiet when we leave the prison. I wait for the sign that he is repelled by all he has heard. I don't imagine he will be rude to my face, but I may see less of him after this. We trudge through the streets under a clear, spring evening sky, stepping in and out of the gutters, passing storekeepers pulling their shutters fast. Children fill the streets, chasing balls and shrieking at each other. Ahead of us, two lamplighters set a string of lanterns aglow, and by the time we reach Fleet Street darkness has descended. We pause at Temple Bar.

"I don't want to go home just yet," Nat says. "To be honest, Henry will be there, visiting Anne, and I have no desire to hear another homily on the perils of attacking Titus Oates. I might just call at the apothecary and then at Sam's to see if Kineally has left any messages for me. But you go on. She's expecting you."

Relief floods my veins. "She won't be too tired? Wasn't she out with her sister all morning?"

"She told me to insist on your attending her. Besides, she is stronger of late."

"About Matthew," I begin.

"I like him," Nat says quickly. He holds my gaze. "Neither you nor he have any need to explain yourselves to me."

"Thank you," I say.

He smiles. "So, I'll see you at home?"

"Yes." There is still more I need to say. "I am worried about Matthew. He is not discreet. He is what he is."

Nat grins, but his expression is quickly sombre again. "And?"

"He's changing. He's different."

"He has been alone too much, I expect," Nat says. "That's probably all. When he is released, you will see him back to his old self. I am sure of it. Now, go on. Tell Anne I will not be long. And try and tell Henry to spare her his worries about my new reputation as the thorn in the side of Titus Oates. At this point, it's not as if I have a choice."

Chapter Thirteen

Anne

The Royal Exchange at Cornhill is only a step away from Sam's Coffee House. Nat is in my thoughts as I pass the coffee house on my way to meet Sarah, even though he won't be there. He and William are visiting William's friend, Matthew, in Newgate. Nat does not often tell me how he spends his days, so when he does, I cherish it. As my belly has swelled over the last few months, I have settled for simply being glad that he is at home as much as he is, and not asking difficult questions. That he is working hard cannot be doubted. Whether it will end well is another matter altogether. Henry and I prepare Nat's pamphlets in the print shop. Nat is almost as famous as Titus Oates these days. Henry shakes his head but says nothing. William is still very quiet and I'm not sure how to help him.

Today Sarah and I are going shopping for fans. It's a frippery, a luxury item, exactly the kind of thing I turned my back on when I married Nat. But the child will not come until the summer, and Sarah insists that a fan will be useful as well as pretty. When she offered to buy me one as a gift, I weakened and said yes. If Nat even notices it, he will never have an idea of how much it cost. He would choke on it, probably, if he knew. In a few short months we will have a child. And if everything is not exactly as I would wish between Nat and myself, at least affection is not lacking. He may not share his worries with me, but at least he loves me. There are many women settling for a great deal less.

By the time I reach the Exchange, I've decided to enjoy myself. Downstairs, sombrely-dressed men meet to conduct their business. Tall Dutch merchants put their heads together and a crowd of Jews wave their arms. Voices are kept low, but there is such a busyness of buying and selling going on that the sound bubbles up to the floor above. Here, upwards of a hundred shops sell every manner of colourful gewgaw a girl with a longing for finery could desire. Not so very long ago, I couldn't walk here alone. I came with my mother and was bustled along, or had to put up with being trailed by a truculent maidservant, whose face tripped her at the sight of all the trinkets she might never afford. Now, as a married lady, I take all the time I want. I'm almost disappointed to see Sarah is there already, waiting for me by the statue of the King in the centre of the Exchange. But then the list of questions I have for her about childbirth and midwives come bubbling up, and I walk toward her as quickly as my changed body allows.

All goes well until we select the fan. Sarah is excited, and she is keen to buy me a slim tortoiseshell one, cool and smooth against my fingers, which opens to show a French pastoral scene. But a folding fan made with ivory struts is expensive; one made of tortoiseshell even more so, especially if the folds are hand-painted with any skill.

"No, no, Sarah," I say. "It is too much."

"Not at all. You deserve it. I want you to have it."

"Does James know?" It is difficult to imagine any husband agreeing to such wanton generosity, particularly not one as cautious as James.

Sarah's face turns pink and she says nothing.

"What is it?" I say. I take a long look at the fan and then hand it back to the shopkeeper. "Sarah?" I take her by the elbow and steer her along to a quiet corner. "What is going on?"

"It is a gift from Mother."

My eyebrows shoot up. "Truly? I am surprised."

"She wants you to have nice things. She is concerned that you and the child will be ill-supplied."

"Ill-supplied?"

Sarah throws me an anxious glance. Quite rightly, she does not like my tone. "Mother is afraid that Nathaniel will not be able to afford all that you will need for the baby, Anne. She is your mother. She loves you."

"She loves me enough to buy me a ridiculous fan but not to accept the man I have chosen to marry."

Sarah lays her arm on mine. "She just wants you to know that your family cares for you."

"Cares for me?" I throw off Sarah's arm and start walking toward the stairs. She rushes behind me, still trying to talk.

"She cannot approve of Nat, Anne. I thought you understood that? And especially now…" Her voice trails away and she follows me down the stairs in silence.

"Especially now?" I ask when we reach the bottom.

She does look uncomfortable. I love my sister. It pains me that she lets our mother do this to her. I have many things I could say to her about not doing our mother's bidding, but my argument is not with Sarah, so I bite my tongue and wait.

"Mother and Father are worried about your future," she says. "Since Nat lost his position as the Licenser, he has done nothing but cause trouble, writing pamphlets and stirring up distrust in the Government."

"In Titus Oates, I think you mean."

"And thereby the Government, Anne. Oates has many supporters. Good men that our father knows personally. Until Nat changes course, our parents will never visit you or receive you and Nat together. But Mother does hope you will visit her. With the child."

My hand goes to my belly. It will not be long now and if I could only forget or put aside certain matters, I would love to take my child to meet my parents. But when the certain matter is my husband? It is a visit I will never make.

"That will not happen, Sarah, and you may tell her so. You mean well, dearest, but a bribe from Mother? You should refuse to be party to such a thing."

She chews on her lip and looks at me sadly. "I miss our family," she says.

***

97

In the evening, Henry and William discuss *The Weekly Pacquet* while we wait for Nat to arrive. It's a pamphlet by Harry Care, a man who despises Nat for questioning the veracity of Oates's Popish Plot. Care has commissioned a drawing of Nat's face on the body of a small terrier dog dancing at the ankles of a sombre and sensible-looking Titus Oates.

"All Nat does is gain notoriety," mutters Henry.

"But his cause is just."

"A just cause will not pay his bills."

William, since the loss of his teaching post, has been relying on working at the print shop to pay his own bills. He has the sense to be quiet.

"It may cost him more than any of us have imagined," says Henry.

There is no answer to that, and I'm immensely glad when Nat comes in a moment later. Without him, my fears and doubts are undeniable. When he is here, that all fades away.

Tonight, he is lively. He kisses me on both cheeks and pats Henry and William across the back. We eat quickly because, Nat says, his man Kineally left a message that he would call here this evening with news of his investigation into Oates's past.

"I want to hear what he has to say," I whisper to Nat as we leave the room briefly – Nat to change his coat, and me to remove the plates. He frowns but does not demur.

When Kineally knocks on the door, Nat, William, and I all jump to answer it. Only Henry remains still, brooding by the fire.

"Well?" Nat barely lets the man take off his hat and sit down. He's a short, thick-set fellow, and plainly dressed. To me, he looks like a tradesman or someone's grandfather, not a person of intrigue in any way. We all wait while he puts on a pair of spectacles and organises his papers on the table.

"Five years ago," he begins, "Titus Oates was living in Hastings. It's a fishing community on the south coast. He worked there at All Saints' Church, as curate to his father, Samuel Oates."

"And?" Nat's impatience doesn't ruffle Kineally, but his eyes slide in my direction once or twice.

"My representative reports that Oates's father was far from popular with his congregation but was tolerated. His son was a different matter. They still talk of him in the Sun Tavern. He was known as a drunk and as a liar. It was said that he set neighbours quarrelling and spoke in a way wholly inappropriate to his position in the Church."

"There!" Nat slaps his hand on the table. He glances over at Henry, but Henry's eyes are closed and his chin is down on his chest, although I don't believe for a moment that he's asleep.

"I like it, Kineally," says Nat. "But you have more, I am sure. Come on, man. Spit it out."

Kineally looks directly at me now. "I am not sure," he says. "I am not sure that the information I have is entirely suitable for the company."

I turn to Nat. I have absolutely no intention of leaving the room and am glad to see he reads my determination. His lips twitch, and he leans back and folds his arms across his chest.

"My wife is made of strong stuff, Kineally. Go ahead."

Kineally still looks uneasy. "If you are sure," he mutters. Then he clears his throat. "Captain John Parker was the first to complain formally about Oates's conduct. He wrote a letter to the Parish Council outlining his objections to Oates continuing there as a curate."

"And?" It is William's turn to lean forward and prompt Kineally.

"Two weeks later, Oates went to visit the town's Mayor. He gave a sworn deposition that on a certain day, at a certain hour, he had entered the south porch of All Saints' Church and witnessed William Parker, the local schoolmaster and Captain Parker's son, committing an act of sodomy with a young boy."

I feel my face flush with shock. William's face is red, too. Nat's mouth is slack with surprise and Henry's eyes are wide open now. My hand goes to my mouth. Kineally turns his neck a little and raises his eyebrows at Nat, as if to say he had warned us. When none of us speak, he tells us the rest.

"My informant tells me that the Mayor was incredulous, but

that Oates was convincing and his information compellingly detailed."

"The schoolmaster Parker was arrested," Kineally says. "Shortly afterwards, Oates went to the Mayor again. This time he charged the father, Captain Parker, with having made treasonable speeches against the King. The Mayor had no choice but to arrest the Captain and send him to London."

"So, on the word of Titus Oates, father and son were both charged with offences punishable by death?" says Nat.

"Yes. William Parker faced a public trial. Oates was sworn in and made his damning testimony. But Parker defended himself. He was able to prove that on the night in question he had been dining with the parents of some of his pupils. Further, a group of masons had been working on the church that evening and also swore that they had seen no-one there: not Parker, no nameless boy, and no Titus Oates. Parker was freed and immediately began an action against Oates for damages. The Privy Council also released the father, Captain Parker, due to lack of evidence."

"My God!"

"Indeed. Titus Oates was charged with perjury."

"And?"

"He disappeared."

We are quiet no longer. Nat is outraged, but also delighted.

"It's exactly what I've been looking for. My instincts about Oates and his story are justified." He speaks directly to Henry. "There now. Come, Henry. You'll admit I've been right since the very start?"

But he does not. "No. It still won't do."

"Why not? It's a pattern of behaviour. He's done exactly the same here in London, but let his lies encompass a whole religion instead of just one family. Anyone could see that."

"Yes, but they don't want to!" Henry quivers from his shoulders down. "What you don't have, Nat, is any sense of the season, of public opinion, and the politics of the moment! This is not about the truth. God, it is so little about truth I am surprised we still have the word in the language. This is a momentous time. This is about kings and parliaments, about

100

the Tories, about the group calling themselves the Whigs. This is about England: about how it will be in ten years' time and in the century to come. It's about power. Men cannot say what they think without reprisal in times like these. You can't go after the most fêted man in Whitehall without facing consequences."

He slaps his hand to his forehead in despair. "And you were the Licenser, of all things. The man whose job it was to control the extremists, the stirrers up of discontent and sedition. Look at you now. Southwell has tempted you with his offers of money and the good opinion of the King. I should never have let him speak to you."

Henry is full red in the face and on his feet. Nat stands, too. It's awful to watch them, face to face across the table, lost in their disappointment and rage at each other.

"Get out, Henry."

We are all shocked, including Nat, at his harshness. But he does not step back.

"You are wrong," he says, "and I will prove it. Oates should not, must not, be allowed to continue. You did not go to the trial of Godfrey's murderers. I did. There is more than money and my livelihood at stake here, whatever you may choose to think. A man's friends – damn it, a man's *family* – should know him better. I will put a stop to Oates. You will see."

Henry's chest heaves with a ragged breath and I fear for his health for a moment. Then he simply goes and gathers up his coat and hat. The colour has left his cheeks, but he's not finished yet. He comes to me and takes my hands and kisses them. At the door, he pauses.

"I hope you are right, Nathaniel," he says. "I hope we live to see it happen. Yet I am very much afraid that you are creating an enemy who will not hesitate to strike at you in any way he sees fit. Watch your back."

***

Kineally must have slipped away even before Nat threw Henry out. I didn't see him go, but he's no longer in the house.

William leaves soon after, and I clear the plates while Nat stares at the fire. I go and sit with him. I don't hide my tears, but he won't talk.

Only later, warmed by more wine, sealed up in the dark, velvet cocoon of our bed, I run my fingers down the valley of his back and whisper, "Henry worries about you. He should not have said what he said, but it was said in anxiety, not reason."

"You heard what he said about the Licensing Act."

"I already knew about it. From Sarah. You could have told me."

"I should have. I wish I had."

"It doesn't matter. You are doing everything you can."

"I am not just pursuing Oates for financial gain."

"I know that. And so does Henry, really. He is afraid, though. As am I."

"Don't be afraid."

"It is hard not to. Look at how Titus Oates treated William's friend. And now about the poor man in Hastings."

"I won't step back from it."

I can't repress a sigh. "But if you go after him, he will act against you. He'll do something, conjure some lie, buy some witness. You know he will."

"Maybe."

"And then what will happen to me? To us?" I lift his hand and touch his fingers to my lips. "To our family?"

Nat lays a hand on my ripening stomach. "Well, I will have to bring him down first then, won't I? At least I have evidence to use against him now. Kineally is obtaining the court records from Hastings. We will see how long a known perjurer can last as a witness in a court of law. Even in times like these."

Chapter Fourteen

Nat

In the weeks that follow, with Henry and I at odds, I do more and more work in the hot-house that is Sam's Coffee House. The benches are long and I'm able to spread out my papers, useful at moments like this one, when I'm looking over a final drawing I've commissioned called *The Committee*. It is a strikingly vulgar illustration of all the waif and stray religions that abound in London, forming one group under the leadership of the Presbyterians. There are too many pictures of carnal popes and murderous priests flapping on the news-stalls these days. I have heard that they intend to try the head of the Jesuits in London for treason. They say he and his fellow priests conspired to kill the King. All the evidence comes solely from Oates. I hope to do some damage to him before their trial.

In my lighter moments, I like to think I am providing balance. In truth, the pursuit of Oates drives me like nothing in my life has ever before. So many of my thoughts are muddled – hopes and fears for the coming child; guilt over not telling Anne directly about the loss of my post; and frustration that Henry will not come around to my point of view. But in the pursuit of Titus Oates my mind is clear, my purpose sure.

The coffee boy taps me on the shoulder. There is a man here, he says, a Dr. Choquette, who wishes to speak to me about the King's cousin, Prince Rupert. I'm researching him for some small piece of paid work. The bills must be paid, after all. I tell the boy to lead the fellow over.

I quickly find that Choquette is typically French: over-familiar and charmless. He's tall, thin, and sallow. His coat is muddied and worn. I don't like the way he gulps at the wine I offer, too much like a fish sucking in air. Resigned to a wasted hour, I sit back and invite him to give me what information he can.

"To be honest with you," he says in a squeaking accent that sets my teeth on edge, "I have no information about the Prince. But wait!" He's seen me begin to gather up my belongings and leave the table. "Please. I have other information for you. I have been asked to contact you." He stretches across the table, actually laying hands on my coat to prevent me from leaving.

"There is someone who wishes to help you. With Titus Oates."

As soon as he mentions Oates, I have to listen. Good or bad, I want to hear what he has to say.

"There is a man who wants to see you," says Choquette. "A patient of mine. He's a prisoner in Newgate. He is unwell but determined that an interview with you will ease him."

"Who is he?"

"Simpson Tonge."

The name is not new to me. Simpson is the son of Israel Tonge, that half-crazed sponsor of Oates who had first approached the King and, with Oates, lodged the details of the plot with Sir Edmund Godfrey.

I don't like the look of this Frenchman. My instincts tell me to walk away, but the idea of finding more evidence against Oates is seductive. I tell Choquette I'll think about Simpson's request, promising to reply by the end of the day.

I'm sickened by the whole thing in some ways. Tonge, I imagine, will be just another Bedloe, or Miles Prance: some lesser version of Oates, ready to exploit what he knows or pretends to know, without any regard to others or for the truth. I can set little store by anything he'll tell me. But what if he knows something? I can't afford not to find out.

***

Truly this is a hell-hole. A prisoner's life in Newgate is one that no sane person can bear, unless well-equipped with friends and funds to make things even remotely tolerable. First, the stink of unwashed flesh, of piss and shit, of tobacco smoke and misery. Then, the noise. Every time I have the misfortune to come here, I'm appalled by the barrage of noise. It's the clamour of women wailing, of men disputing, of gaolers roaring, and, under all, the rasp and rumble of chains crashing against stone – surely one of the worst sounds in the world. Men like Matthew Medbourne, men with money, can buy themselves private rooms and avoid the miserable sluts and penniless fools, but no-one can escape Newgate's unhappy song.

I'm profoundly thankful that Tonge is not inhabiting the Common side, where lice and cockroaches riot over the huddled and hunched; where typhoid threatens the inmates as much as any sentence passed over their filthy heads. I follow Choquette through the prison, and on all sides, through boards and grills, catch glimpses of squalor and faces written with misery and disease. I breathe steadily through my mouth, trying to preserve my poor nose and keep my stomach even. The Keeper, an ugly giant of a man whose lips fire spittle with every word, takes me to a small windowless cell. Chocquette hands over five shillings and they bring the prisoner up.

Tonge is a slight, inconsequential-looking fellow, with dirty yellow hair and thick lips. He has a nasty boil suppurating on his left cheek. I try not to stare. His eyes are red-rimmed, and the skin below looks bruised. He shuffles into the room like a man of seventy, not twenty-five, and I shift uncomfortably in my seat.

"You asked to see me?"

"Yes," he nods slowly. "I want to tell you about my father and Titus Oates. But I need your help."

I should never have come. I knew he would be after something in exchange for his information, but I'd hoped for rather more finesse in the negotiation, to be a little more engaged before payment was demanded.

"Let me hear something from you that will make me want to help you," I say.

He must hear my impatience because he doesn't argue the

point. He swallows twice, smiles nervously, and then begins to talk.

"My father has known Titus for several years," Tonge says. "When my mother passed away in '75, Father moved for a time into the household of Sir Richard Barker, near the Barbican. I was away studying at the time, so I know little of how he went on there, but he was often in the company of the Reverend Samuel Oates, a Baptist preacher."

I nod. Barker is vehemently anti-Catholic. He would take an ape into his house and give it dinner so long as it could prove it wasn't of Catholic birth.

"My father first met Samuel's son at Barker's house," he continues, "but I did not know him until two years later. I arrived back from university to find Titus living in my home. Father said that Titus was in a bad way: that he was a young Jesuit, but highly disturbed by what he had found in that faith. He had come to my father half starving and in need of shelter some weeks before my arrival. Father was a lonely man and I was suspicious at first, but Titus appeared genuinely interested in his talk.

"To be honest, I couldn't stand Father's ranting, and soon saw that having someone's ear take the strain was very much to my advantage. Although we were the closer in age, it was my father's company that Titus always sought, and while they amused each other I enjoyed the freedom to come and go at will. After a few months, he left. My father and Titus had agreed that something could and should be made of his Catholicism and Jesuit connections. He went to St Omer's College in Flanders, to be, my father said, his eyes and ears in the devil's nest."

All this while, Simpson's been looking down at his hands, but now he glances up and locks eyes with me. I try to look interested.

"In the summer of '78, he came back. Titus had a lodging in Cockpit Alley, off Drury Lane, and he regularly visited my father at the Barbican. They also met at the Flying Horse in King Street and at Titus's father's rooms in York buildings. About this time, Father began to appear excited. He's always been nervous and on edge, but it became more marked. There was an energy about him. I was happy for him." Tonge stops and rubs at his brow, as if trying to order his thoughts and reflections.

"One day, I came across him hunched at his desk as usual, squinting in the candlelight, and poring over some writing with his own pen hovering as though he was making annotations on some text. When I asked him what he was working on, he snapped at me.

"Normally, he's the gentlest of men, but he was frantic. He scooped his papers up into a bundle and told me it was none of my business."

"And you didn't like that?" I ask.

"Would you? I didn't like the way he protected his precious scribbling from me. Whatever it was, I knew he was prepared to share with Oates. Why not me? But I saw them less and less. They had found some house over in Vauxhall. One of the servants said that my father repaired there every morning and often did not return until after dark.

"I didn't even know that Father had been to see the King until weeks after it had happened. I wanted to get closer to him again. I was running up expenses in the city that I could barely afford, and I knew I would need his assistance soon."

For a fraction of a second, Simpson pauses. Perhaps his mind has snagged on his own words, and in this moment he sees himself as I do: worthless, lazy, and undeserving. Or perhaps not. He ploughs on with his tale.

"Despite the coolness between us, I determined to try again. Catching him at home one evening, I began with talk of my mother. That always softens him. After only a few words reminiscing about her sweet temper and staunch love of us both, he opened up to me. He told me that he and Titus Oates had discovered a great plot. He had no doubts. He was adamant that the plot was real. But although all had gone well at first, there were those who doubted them. He fretted that the King was not convinced. He said he was at a crisis point. There was something they could do to take things forward, but he was concerned. He rambled on about the greater good, about means and ends, and much more in the same vein. I said very little; indeed, I'm not sure that he really knew I was there."

Tonge pauses. He looks across the table at me and our eyes meet. That's when I know him for a liar. If a man lies, he speaks words with his mouth, but his eyes hold the thoughts he does not voice. To speak the truth is but one act: thought and word are in harmony. But to lie, a man must hold the truth in his mind, yet voice a different set of thoughts at the same moment. More, he wonders how his lies are being received. The light of speculation is in Tonge's blue eyes. He can barely wait to finish and learn if I believe him or not.

"My father said that he and Titus needed evidence of their plot to make the authorities take action," says Tonge. "They were frustrated and desperate. They wanted their secrets out, for the good of the nation and the safety of the King. So, they were contemplating an act of deception. A forgery. They'd been arguing about it all that day, he said."

"And did they do it?" I ask him.

"I can prove that they did, Mr. Thompson. But I need to know that I count on your help, before I tell you more."

Tonge licks his lips. He has brought me to the sticking place.

"Well, Tonge," I say. "I am a cautious man, but not an unkind one. I'll give you something for what you have told me," I dig in my purse for a few coins – not many, but enough to make a few days in Newgate a little less uncomfortable – "and I will think on things." I stand up and look down at him clutching the silver in his dirty fingers. "If I wish to hear more, I will be in touch through Choquette."

Tonge also rises. "You will not regret it, sir," he says, somewhat sadly. "And I thank you for your goodness. But don't you want to hear of what my father and Titus did?"

I smile. I already know the story he wanted to tell me.

"As I say, I will be in touch."

***

"But I have no intention of going anywhere near the fellow, or that damn prison, ever again," I tell William an hour or two later, over a dish of coffee.

"Whyever not?"

"Because I'm familiar with the story already. Robert Southwell explained it. Simpson's father, Israel, together with Titus Oates, forged a series of letters between those poor priests and Thomas Bedingfield, the Duke of York's confessor. Oates showed them to the Privy Council way back in September when he was first examined. He swore that the priests had disguised their handwriting, but that he knew which was which. Southwell himself was at the meeting, and he personally showed each letter to Oates, folded so that he couldn't see the name signed at the bottom. He correctly identified each one."

"So, they weren't forgeries?"

"Of course they were!"

"But..."

"It will be one man's word against the others. Oates has the support of so many, and Simpson Tonge is simply not reliable. He's already been before the King and changed his evidence at least once."

"I see."

"I wasn't convinced, and I don't trust him. I won't be troubling Simpson any further. In fact, I rather wish I hadn't bothered going to see him in the first place."

Chapter Fifteen

Anne

"Nat. Can you send for Sarah?"

I'm calling from upstairs. He has just walked through the door, but when he catches my tone he drops everything and takes the stairs two at a time. I'm standing in the bedroom doorway, far calmer, now the moment is here, than I anticipated.

"Is it time?"

"Yes. I want my sister."

"What about the midwife? Shall I get her on the way? Shouldn't you sit down?"

"I don't want to. My back aches."

He takes me in his arms. A hot thrust of pain makes me cry out.

"Nat," I whisper. "Go and get Sarah."

Chapter Sixteen

Nat

Her sister comes. They confer upstairs. I'm sent to call the midwife and Anne's mother, who arrives but will not even catch my eye. Women flow in and out, upstairs and down, while I stand in the dining room listening to their footsteps overhead but without any way of knowing how things are progressing either for good or for bad. I hang around the bottom of the stairs, straining my ears, for what? A child's cry? Anne's cry? I hardly know what I want to happen, except for this thing to be over. Eventually, Sarah comes down.

"Go out, Nat."

"What? Why? Shouldn't I stay? Do something?"

She shakes her head and gives me a withering look. "It will be a while. The first always is."

"But what if something happens?"

"Nat. She will be fine. God willing, they will both be fine. Go to Sam's Coffee House. I will send a boy if there is any change. Trust me."

"I…" What do I want to say? That I love my wife. That I might lose her. Or the child. Or both.

Sarah puts her hand to my cheek. "Go. But drink coffee. No ale and no wine. It will be hours Nat. When she needs you, I will have you fetched."

***

Sam's Coffee House has its usual midday mix of tradesmen, the odd lawyer, a few fellow scribblers I know. I avoid meeting anyone's eye and sit down on an empty bench with a copy of the *Gazette*. The coffee-boy brings me a dish and pours my drink, slipping my penny in the pocket of his long apron. At any other time, the familiar mix of roasting berries and tobacco, the loud exchanges, even the touch of the tables and the smooth glaze of the coffee cup, would ease my mind. Not today. I stare at the *Gazette* but read nothing. Instead, I conjure up disasters.

Anne will die. I'm suspicious of the midwife. She's a Quaker, which is, Anne has assured me, a good thing. But is she clean? Does she know her work? I chew on my cheek, thinking I should have been more involved in choosing this woman. After all, horror stories about midwives abound. If a child dies before being born, they often cut off limbs to facilitate removing the poor thing from the mother's body. I imagine blood: Anne's; the baby's. A few years ago, a woman and her child died out in the street, slap in the middle of Threadneedle Street, after one so-called midwife held the woman by the shoulders while another witch ripped the child out of her body, killing them both. Images of Anne fighting for her life have me almost on my feet ready to run back home, but the thought of Sarah's sensible face stops me.

To divert my mind, I brood on Anne's family. That Anne threw herself away by marrying me is an accepted fact. My line of work, even when I was the Licenser, is viewed with derision. My haunting of coffee shops, as I believe her mother terms it, shows a tendency to gossip and idleness that they find particularly disappointing. Perhaps if I was haunting Will's Coffee Shop, rather than Sam's; perhaps if I was a proper writer, like Mr. Dryden, they might think differently. Dryden, famous, popular, and wealthy, keeps his own chair at Will's, surrounded by literary wits. That's Anne's family's idea of what a writer should be. Not the rather grubby news-gatherers, lampoonists, and sharp-tongued opportunists I consort with. Only my loyalty to the Crown brings me any measure of approval. Sarah's husband supposedly reads all my pamphlets, and Anne hopes that one day her younger brother and I might meet and get along. But even when the child is born, I don't expect to be invited to dinner. A thoroughly bad mood settles on me, as thickly persistent as the coffee sticking to my teeth. Time crawls. It's the longest day of my life.

I order more coffee, pick up the *Gazette* again. What is happening to Anne now? Every time the door opens I twist round expecting it to be a messenger for me, yet hours pass and none arrives. Other customers come and go. As space opens up on the long table, I slide further along the bench, away from the fire heating the coffee water and nearer the door so I can keep up my vigil for a messenger. Men, in small groups or alone like me, sit for a while and then leave again. Some nod, some ask me for the news, or to pass a pamphlet their way. Others are as silent and self-contained as I am. Snatches of conversation float my way, but I only really listen when a group of three men sitting on the bench behind me begin talking animatedly of some news they've heard: about, of all things, a midwife. There's a mild buzzing in my head, a coffee-induced fog descending, but I shift back far enough to be able to take in their conversation. Anything to be out of my own head.

"And this woman is a midwife?"

"Apparently. Up to her elbows in Catholic cunny, but with time enough to forge papers describing a Whig plot against the King."

Irresistible gossip. I turn and clap one of the men on the shoulder. He's a broad fellow with the smell of the tanneries on him. My mother-in-law would not like his looks or his language, but to me he's a fellow with a story I want to hear.

"News of another plot?" I ask. The three men shuffle along their bench and make space for me to join them. They know who I am.

"Aye, Mr. Thompson. But is there a tale we know and you do not? Now, there's a turn-up," says one fellow.

"Surprising, but it happens more than you'd think. Tell me about it. You were talking about a midwife? A Catholic midwife?"

"Well," the tanner says, "this woman – her name is Elizabeth Cellier—" He breaks off and glances over, but the name means nothing to me. "She's a right busybody, by all accounts, always doing good works and talking about loving thy neighbour."

"How did you hear this?"

"My sister lives two doors along from her. Says she's forever thrusting her way into other people's houses and telling them how to manage better. Mistress Cellier has busied herself interfering with the neighbours and with visiting fellow papists in Newgate. Made no secret of it, neither."

"And?"

"And so in Newgate, she says, she found out about a plot. A Protestant plot." The large man raises his eyebrows and nods sagely. "Interesting, no? Very handy even. Why, if I was a Protestant plotter would the first person I'd confide in be a fat old chatter of a Catholic? Of course not."

"So, the woman claimed to have uncovered a plot. She made a report?"

"No idea. I was told she claimed that Lord Shaftesbury was plotting to bring down the King and have Parliament run the country again. But her informant changed his song and said instead that she had paid him to make up a plot to disgrace the Whigs, so it was another Catholic plot after all. My sister saw the guards enter the midwife's house. She's been thrown into Newgate, and the whisper is that papers were found in the silly woman's meal tub in her cellar, describing the whole thing. She'll hang for it, I wouldn't wonder."

I thank the men for their time before moving back to the other table. I don't think much of their tale after all. It sounds rather pathetic, but just the sort of foolishness that can easily cost a person their life in current times. And it does nothing to reassure me about the profession of midwives.

Despite the coffee, the warm, smoky airlessness of Sam's begins to prickle at my eyelids. I've no qualms about folding my arms on the table and resting my head for a few moments. I won't be the first man, or the last, to take a little nap in Sam's. When I wake, Henry is sitting opposite me.

"Any news?" I ask, but he's already shaking his head.

"None. I called there less than an hour ago. They told me things were progressing."

"Progressing?"

"Here." He pushes a fresh dish of coffee across the table to me. Just as I remember how long it is since the last civil words we've exchanged, he speaks again. "Drink this and let me occupy your mind. Let's talk. Southwell and I were hypothesising last night. Imagine that King Charles were to die tomorrow—"

"Henry!" Even in Sam's, amongst friends, such words could be misinterpreted.

"Oh, come, Nat. Exercise that brain of yours. No-one is listening. What if he were to die tomorrow? What do you think would happen?"

I take a mouthful of hot coffee. Henry looks expectant. Tangled up with worrying about Anne, I'm relieved that he's with me and recognise the olive branch being offered. "Monmouth."

"No."

I infer that the King's illegitimate son will not inherit the throne, at least not in Henry's opinion. "Why not? He's very popular with the people."

"Ah, but it's not all about the people, is it?"

"True." I shrug. "James then."

"A Catholic?" says Henry with exaggerated horror.

"He is the heir."

"But shouldn't the King defend the Anglican Church?"

"He wouldn't work against it, surely?"

"That remains to be seen. But it may only be a temporary hiatus. James has no sons either. That would be Southwell's view, anyway."

The door bangs and I turn. Still no news.

"So, who's King after James?"

"William of Orange?"

"Dutch. Protestant." He might be married to James's daughter Mary, but could England stomach such a compromise?" I waggle a finger at Henry. "Same argument. Back to Monmouth."

"English. Anglican." Henry is smiling. "Illegitimate."

"Probably."

115

That makes him snort. "Definitely!"

"Well, maybe the King, or perhaps even James, will have another son. A legitimate one." At once, my thoughts swing back to home. "Oh God, Henry, what in heaven's name is happening with Anne? I've been here for hours."

The heavy door creaks open behind me. I keep my eyes on Henry's face. His eyebrows rise in recognition and his chin dips in acknowledgement.

"It's time, Nat," he says. "I will walk you home."

Wild thoughts race around my brain as we stride back through the streets to the house. I grabbed at the messenger's lapels, but the look in his eyes was genuine enough. He knew nothing: just that I was called back. Henry, puffing and gasping, tells me to go ahead, and I take the last couple of corners at a run. I burst through the door. Sarah is at the bottom of the stairs.

"Anne?"

"She will be well, Nat."

But even as relief floods my veins, the hair prickles on the back of my neck. Sarah's face is too still. The house is too quiet.

"The child lives but..." Sarah's face cracks and crumbles like broken pie crust.

I run up the stairs and into our bedroom. Anne's mother is standing by the window, but as I cross to the bed she leaves the room, the swish of her skirts rattling the silence.

"Anne?"

She turns her head on the pillow and looks at me. Her face is bloodless, blanched white even to her lips, although the fragile skin around her eyes looks almost bruised blue. Her beautiful hair is limp, flat against her head like a skull-cap. It strikes me that this is what she will look like when she's dead. Pain slices my chest. Tears slip from the corners of her eyes and her bottom lip quivers. In two steps I'm beside her. I kiss away the tears and we stare into each other's eyes. She slowly turns her head and directs me toward the wooden crib beside the bed.

116

"Listen," she says.

I hear it. There's the faintest rumble, the lightest wheeze or bubble and cracking noise, like a cat is asleep in the cupboard or a whisper of wind is rattling a window in another room.

"A girl. Bring her to me."

I walk round the bed. In the crib, swaddled in white linen, there's the tiniest, most perfect face. She is small, her skin as smooth as her mother's but yellowish, not right. Her tiny head is decorated in inky, black commas; her lash-less eyes are a mole-ish blue; her lips look thin and dry. She's struggling to breathe. With hands like shovels, I pick up the almost weightless form and turn to Anne, my face twisting. I take her into the crook of one arm and trace her perfect, soft skin with one finger, while Anne, sore as an old crone, levers herself up in the bed and holds out her hands for our daughter.

"Can nothing be done?" My voice breaks.

Anne shakes her head. "She won't suckle. She doesn't cry. They think there's something wrong with her lungs. It will not be long."

I take off my boots and climb onto the bed next to Anne and our baby. About an hour later, the little one stops breathing.

***

When the knock at the door comes, we're both startled.

"We can't stay here like this forever, my love," I say softly. I walk back round the bed and open the door to Sarah.

"I'm so sorry." Her voice is almost a whisper.

"It's not your fault, Sarah," I begin, but she shakes her head.

"No! You don't understand. Henry and I... We have tried everything, but we can't stop them!"

"What?" I step back, letting Sarah into the room, and she rushes to take Anne in her arms.

"We can't stop them, Anne."

Heavy footsteps sound on the stairs. Soldiers thrust their way into the room. I stand between them and Anne, to give her some shield, some protection. But they are not remotely interested in Anne. The first of them makes the case very clear.

"Nathaniel Thompson. You are under arrest for treason. If you won't come with us willingly, then I have orders to take you away from here by force!"

Chapter Seventeen

Anne

Our child is dead.

I keep to my bed for three days and nights. Mother, Sarah, Kitty, and the midwife Mistress Gwyd come and go. I drink beer warmed with caraway seeds, coriander, sweet fennel, and sugar to help with the pain. My breasts have been daubed in honey and linseed oil, and tightly bound to dry up the milk I do not need. They tend me like a cripple; washing, dressing, wiping, turning me over and back, but no-one will speak about the baby.

Martha. I dream about a girl with long legs and swinging black hair, skipping with a rope or playing mother with a ragged doll. She has bright blue eyes and dark curling lashes. But when I wake, she is gone, and my smock is drenched in sweat and blood.

***

I am unwell.

Did we bury her yesterday? I open my eyes and I am lying in bed. Perhaps I will always be in this bed. Will Nat come home soon and help me up? The door opens. A woman walks around the bed. She leans in at me. She is my mother, but I won't speak to her. Mother does not approve of Nat. When I have the baby, Mother will be different. I put my hand to my belly. It is soft, like kneaded dough. Pain stabs in my eyes. Martha is already gone.

"I forgot. She is dead."

Mother nods very, very slowly. She is behaving strangely.

Perhaps she is sad, too.

"Are you?" I ask.

"Drink this." She holds out a cup. It looks like water.

I sip it. It has no taste. Perhaps all the taste went out of the world with Martha. Why did God want her? I wish...

"Are you sure about this?"

Someone else is in the room. My hair has been sewn into the pillow, I think, for it tears my scalp to lift my head.

"Henry," I say.

He comes to me and takes my hand. His hands are hot. Or perhaps mine are very cold.

"My feet are cold," I say. "Where is Nathaniel?"

"In prison."

I nod my head. I knew that.

"And Martha?" There's a movement. My mother walks to the door.

Henry pats my hand. "Martha is buried. She is with God."

"I don't remember."

"No. You were ill. Your mother's doctor has sent you medicine to allow you to rest and heal for a few more days."

"Dr. Sydenham?"

"Yes." Henry gives a little smile. "You remember some things then, little one," he says.

"I'm sleepy again, Henry."

"I'll go."

"No. Stay. Stay a moment or two. Your hand feels good." I close my eyes.

***

I open my eyes and I am sitting by the window downstairs. Sarah is sitting opposite me, sewing.

"You should go home, Sarah."

"I have been home and come back many times. But I will leave if you wish to be alone."

"I don't know what I want. I don't know how to be."

"You need to get better. You need rest and time. You need to be thankful that you can heal."

"I can?"

Sarah tilts her head as if weighing me up. "Anne, listen carefully," she says. I blink and try my best.

"Mother is giving you laudanum. It has made you sleepy and confused. I'm not sure it's helping. Do you understand?"

"I don't want to be confused."

"Then you mustn't take the drink again. Can you do that?"

I nod. "I want to talk about Martha."

"Martha is dead."

"I know that."

"Then what is there to talk about?" Suddenly, Sarah is gathering up her sewing, securing her needles, fastening her bags. A new emotion winds its way through the fog. My temper rises.

"She is my baby! My daughter!"

But Sarah is standing and walking away from me.

She opens the door. I stand, but there's a lightness in my head. I have to put my palms on the table, suck up deep breaths. I have to sit down. She is gone.

***

I open my eyes. I am sitting at the window downstairs. William is opposite me, reading a book. He lifts a finger and strokes the side of his nose. Then his eyes come and meet mine, and he smiles.

"How are you?"

I think about this. "I feel nothing."

"And is that an improvement?" he asks.

I think some more. "Possibly. Why are you here?"

"I came to see how you are."

"No-one will talk to me. Even Sarah won't. She has lost children. But she never speaks of it."

"I will."

"About Martha?"

"If you like."

This is good. Now I feel something. "Shall we have some wine?" I say.

121

"Why not?" William goes to the cabinet and fills two glasses.

I take a sip. It tastes hard on my tongue and burns in my throat. I still find no flavours, but I like that burn. "I called her Martha, after my grandmother."

"It's a beautiful name."

"She was so beautiful, William." Tears well at my eyes.

"She had beautiful hands," he says.

"Yes! They were so small, but so perfect. She had tiny nails. Prettier than pearls. And tiny feet."

"I'm so sorry you lost her."

William's face is pale as always. His lips are too red and rich for such a thin, thoughtful-looking face. But his eyes are warm and sincere. He is honestly concerned. It is a hint of comfort in the darkest of times.

"I don't remember the funeral."

"You collapsed. And then you were given physic to help you rest."

"I have stopped taking it. I couldn't think. I need to think."

"You are beginning to heal, perhaps?" He speaks tentatively, there's hope in his voice, but I won't have him misled.

"Oh no, William. There is no healing from this. This cannot get better. This just *is*."

If he tries to tell me I'm wrong, I will be angry. A fist of anger waits in my chest ready to explode if he tells me how to grieve. In my head, I dare him to placate me. Let him try and tell me how to feel, just let him.

But he knows better. Instead, he says, "Would you like to go and visit her?"

"I can?"

"Of course. Are you strong enough to walk a little?"

"I don't know."

"Then you may lean on my arm," he says. "I will call Kitty to get your cloak."

He steps out of the room and I almost call him back. I'm not sure I'm ready. Just to step out of the door seems dangerous. But to see where Martha rests? It will not make it better, but it might help. I let him take me.

***

The noise on the street rains down on my poor head like catapult sling-shots. Carts rumble, a gang of boys run past shoving and shrieking, a man and woman brawl on a corner pulling a loaf of bread between them until it breaks. The woman tumbles back, cracking her head on the stones. She's silent for a moment but then releases a wail that tears through my chest. I shrivel against William's arm. I fix my eyes on my black skirts and wish for a way to shut my ears to the city's harshness. Thankfully, we do not have to go far to find a hackney carriage.

Martha is with my family. The plot has been paid for far in advance, and the fresh-laid earth, without any headstone yet to mark her place, gives me comfort. I will be near her again, one day. She is not far from her name-sake, my grandmother. Or from her cousins, Sarah's children, both of whom died before they reached the age of four. I must remember them and not think so harshly of my sister in the future. I had no idea of her pain, until now.

"Is it harder, William, to lose a person you have been with a long time, or someone you will never have the chance to get to know?"

"Who can say? We all lose. There is no measuring stick for loss that I'm aware of. It's not a case of hard or harder. It is all grief."

He walks away then and leaves me alone with Martha. I'm immensely grateful to him. I don't know how long I stand there, but eventually the heat of the afternoon sends a trickle of sweat running down my back. It wakens me to the sounds from the street, the beauty of the blue sky overhead, and the scent floating from all the roses planted at the churchyard wall. I let him take me home.

"I tried to see Nat," he says when we are only a step from the door.

Nat. Nat, who has not been here when I needed him most.

"Henry and I both applied to visit him, but we were denied. We don't even know what the charge is. Anne?"

"What?"

"Aren't you concerned? Don't you want him home?"

"I…" What to say? We should be bearing this loss together, but I'm alone. I don't have the words.

William keeps talking. "It must be Oates, mustn't it? He must be behind this arrest somehow."

"Oates?" It comes out like a whisper.

I had not thought. I've had no time for thought and no ability either, thanks to my mother and her doctor. But I am thinking now.

Chapter Eighteen

Nat

Our child is dead; our baby, who would have been our little girl. I don't even have a name for her. I don't know who she might have become. Children die every day. I had a sister who died when she was seven years old and I was four. Death is not extraordinary. But the death of our child, of Anne's and my child, this is terrible. It's an open wound in my head, a needle in my eye, a sword in my guts. I would not have imagined it.

They drag me to Newgate. I spend the first night wrapped in a damp blanket in a filthy cage with three other men, one of whom mutters and scratches his arms for hours at a stretch. I don't sleep. When morning comes, the tiny windows send grey shafts of light across the darkness. I make out the forms of tens of other prisoners penned behind similar bars. We huddle in the dark, more shadows than individuals. It is never quiet. Through five nights, not a minute passes when someone is not crying or complaining, singing or shouting. Arguments are frequent, and prisoners fight without mercy. One woman crushes another's face against the bars and shatters her teeth.

It's worse during the day. Guards walk up and down between the cells, swearing, smacking the bars with iron clubs whenever they like, swatting away outstretched hands, and dismissing all appeals. At any moment I expect the door to open. I need to get home to my wife, but no-one comes for me. A man could lose his mind in such a place.

After the fifth day, my circumstances improve a little. I'm told that friends have paid to improve my accommodation. I am led, still in chains, to a different part of the prison and given a small stone cell with a mattress on the floor and a high slit of a window. It is drier, lighter, quieter, and immeasurably safer. I sleep.

I spend two days entirely alone and then I'm taken before the Privy Council in Whitehall. For the sake of the Council rather than myself, I suspect, I'm allowed a change of linen and a wash. I am more than ready.

The number of people in the room catches me off guard. There are six members of the Privy Council and various other politicians, including the Earl of Shaftesbury, who stares straight through me as if I'm a piece of glass. To their left sits Robert Southwell. He nods at me, but nothing in his demeanour gives me grounds for optimism. I'm most affected, though, by the men on the right. Titus Oates glares at me, a sneer curling his fat lip. And next to him, hunched and clearly uncomfortable, sits Simpson Tonge.

They direct me to a stool before the Counsellors, all of whom know me, at least by sight. I'm determined not to be intimidated.

"Nathaniel Thompson," begins Southwell, in his role as clerk to the Council. "You have been brought here to answer the charge that on the 30th of May, you attempted to suborn this young man, Simpson Tonge—"

"Really?" I say.

"You will confine yourself to answering questions, Mr. Thompson. You are charged with attempting to disrupt the work of the Inquiry into the Popish Plot, by generating false evidence against the two men who revealed this late plot to the King and to Parliament, namely Dr. Titus Oates and Dr. Israel Tonge."

As Southwell pauses, Oates leaps to his feet. "The man's a rogue!" he calls out. "He is a papist and a liar." He jabs his finger at me. "He should be pilloried."

The Earl of Shaftesbury raises a lazy hand. "Enough for now, Dr. Oates, enough for now. Your passion is to your credit, but we must follow due process. Southwell?" Shaftesbury is not a young man. He has a hawkish face, thin lips, and pale grey eyes. He speaks slowly, but I don't find his apparent languor in any way reassuring.

Southwell takes up the reins again, reading out a sworn

statement from Tonge, whose eyes never leave his knees. In it, Simpson states that I visited him in Newgate and pressed him to come up with a story about Oates and his father forging letters to add weight to their evidence of the plot. It is said that I offered significant bribes, but that when Tonge hesitated, I paid the gaolers to treat him more harshly, denying him food or any exercise.

It's difficult to sit through. I dare not interrupt again, but with every facial expression I can muster, I show the Counsellors that the story they're hearing is a mare's nest, the most absurd fiction.

Finally, I'm given the opportunity to speak. "This is a clear case of entrapment."

Oates snorts, but I don't dignify him with a glance.

"I was contacted by a man named Choquette," I continue, "a Frenchman and a doctor who told me that his patient, Simpson Tonge, was desperate for me to visit him in Newgate. In no way did I seek out the prisoner or attempt to bribe him into making a false statement. Rather, he was trying to profit by selling out his father and Mr. Oates here."

"Doctor!" Oates is on his feet again, bellowing at me, but I continue to look straight ahead.

"You can prove this?" asks Southwell.

"If Choquette can be found. There will be witnesses to my meeting with him in the Sam's Coffee House. And he should be known at Newgate."

The Privy Counsellors confer for a few moments in whispers. I flick a glance at Oates. He looks satisfyingly frustrated. Then the Earl of Shaftesbury questions me.

"You say that you were invited to Newgate to hear Tonge's evidence?"

"I was."

"And what did he in fact tell you?"

"Very little. He implied that he had knowledge that Oates and his father forged the Bedingfield letters, but I wasn't prepared to pay for something that I doubted could be proved either way. It is very likely that the letters were forged." A rumble from Oates is squashed by a sharp glance from

Shaftesbury. "As I am not in the business of making false accusations, I didn't take him up on his offer."

"Nor did you come forward and inform the proper authorities," says Shaftesbury.

"No."

"Even though this man was either offering you true information—" We all turn slightly as Oates's chair scrapes against the floor, "—or he was seeking to pervert justice through false testimony. At the very least, Mr. Thompson, you should have reported this."

"Arguably." I deem it best to make some form of concession. "But as Simpson Tonge was already being held indefinitely in Newgate prison, I judged his ability to influence events or endanger the country to be strictly limited."

"These are difficult days." For the first time, Lord Williamson, probably the most powerful man in the room, speaks. "I don't believe, however, that arrogance has become grounds for treason. If Mr. Thompson can prove that this Choquette fellow exists, then I don't think we're looking at more than a lapse of judgement in not reporting his meeting with Tonge."

"Begging your pardon," says Oates, rising again. "If I might take a moment of the Council's time?" Williamson nods.

Oates glowers over at me, pressing his chin into his chest. Then he lets rip. "This man is a viper. He is a liar and a papist!" Oates's already shrill voice is strangled with anger. "He is a master of lies and false information. He hides his popish tendencies, but who, having read his cheap rag, cannot see how he has consistently and treasonably attempted to cast doubt upon the veracity of the popish threat? I do not speak of his slanders against myself. I am not so weak as to be hurt by his slings and arrows. But he is a worm, and a danger to us all. He eats away at the truth, seeking to unsettle the people, to confuse truth and lies, to mask the Catholic threat. He is a papist I say!"

"And have you any evidence of this?" asks Williamson.

"Look at his writings! Study his words. Give me a warrant to search his rooms. Then we'll know with whom we are dealing. I say he is a Catholic, and can bring witnesses to prove it."

"If I may?" I keep my voice under strict control. "I would like to state at this point that I believe I am the victim of a deliberate, personal attack from Mr. Oates. I am a member of the Church of England and have been all my days. I have questioned the veracity of this plot, as I have questioned the veracity of this man who accuses me. But I am not a traitor, nor a Catholic."

"So, you admit that you have spoken against the Plot?" Shaftesbury is leaning forward now.

"I have expressed doubts about the level of threat, yes." Again, the Privy Council members put their heads together and murmur for some moments.

"Dr. Oates," says Williamson. "You say you have witnesses to the fact that Mr. Thompson is a secret Catholic. Can you produce one? Now?"

"I can. If I may be given a moment?" Oates bustles from the room.

Within minutes he's back, followed by a thin, delicate-looking fellow who Oates introduces to the council. I've only ever seen him once before, giving testimony in the trial of Green, Berry, and Hill. It's Miles Prance.

"Do you know the prisoner?" he is asked.

"I do."

"Where have you seen him?"

"At Somerset House."

"At the Queen's residence?"

"Yes."

"And what did you see him doing?"

"He was taking mass in the chapel there."

"I was not!" I try to stand, but the guard behind me pushes me down.

"You have been warned about interrupting Council proceedings already, Thompson," barks Williamson. "Mr. Prance, you would be prepared to swear under oath that you have seen Mr. Thompson participate in a Catholic mass?"

Unbelievably, Prance nods. He's thanked and asked to wait

outside.

I turn imploring eyes on Southwell as the Counsellors begin a whispered conference. He sucks in one cheek and shrugs slightly, telling me only what I already know. I'm in serious trouble. Even if they want to, it's hard to imagine the Council will let me walk away from such an accusation.

Nausea grips me and heat rolls under my skin. It's as if I'm on fire from the inside. Oates is grinning at me. The tendons in my neck grow stiff. My legs and arms ache as I hold myself down in the seat when all I want to do is charge across the room and take him by the throat. Real fear, for the first time in my life, turns my insides liquid. I ignore Oates and watch the Counsellors. They are animated. Shaftesbury is talking eagerly, jabbing a finger into the table. I don't need to read lips to know that he wants to make an example of me. But perhaps he's not having it all his own way. Others shake their heads. Southwell is taking notes.

This is the worst moment. I am alone in this. Anne and Henry might be miles away for all that they are probably waiting outside. The only other person in the room who really cares what happens to me is Oates. Finally, I understand how much he hates me.

Henry was right. That thought brings another wave of heat. I might never get back to Anne. I'm on the brink of something terrible. I let myself look at Titus Oates.

He's lolling back in his chair with his arms folded across his chest. His fat, ugly face shines with sweat and his girlish lips thrust forward as he laps up every wave of my discomfort. He is terrifying. The degree of power and influence he has managed to obtain is staggering. It's difficult to comprehend the nerve of the man. He has crawled up from nowhere and carried off his vast charade before the great and the good of the nation. He made sure that I'd be taken from my home at the worst possible moment. He is thrilled now, watching me struggle for my freedom. He is longing, lusting, to see me hang.

Slowly and deliberately, I fold my arms across my chest and force my aching face into an empty smile. His existence is an affront to me. Even if I die for all this, he must never believe he's had the better of me.

Oates shifts in his chair. He doesn't like my smile. Good. His gaze shifts toward the huddled Counsellors. The longer it takes them to decide my fate, the better my prospects begin to look. Only moments later, Williamson turns. Shaftesbury examines his fingernails.

"Nathaniel Thompson. Serious accusations have been made against you, but we have nothing before us that would convict you in a trial by your peers. Let the record show that permission has been granted for a search of your properties, for the seizing of goods as is seen fit, and for a review of all your writings to be conducted by the Commons Committee inquiring into the Popish Plot, led by Lord Shaftesbury. In the interim, the prisoner is to be released."

Relief swoops over me, almost as overwhelming as my earlier fears. My eyes meet Southwell's. He allows himself a small curl of his lips. Shaftesbury glowers at me on his way out. As I turn to my guard, putting forward my hands to be unchained, Oates's breath creeps into my ear.

"It's far from over, Thompson. You can't even begin to imagine what we'll find when we search your little office."

"Secretary Williamson!" Sir Robert Southwell interrupts the general exodus.

"What is it, Southwell?"

"Given that there are issues of credibility on both sides of this case," he gestures towards Oates and I, only inches apart in the centre of the room, "might I suggest that a supervisor be appointed to oversee the search of Mr. Thompson's property?"

It's a stroke of genius. Shaftesbury has already left the chamber.

Williamson wrinkles his nose. "Certainly. A good point. See to it, will you, Southwell?"

"But, My Lord," says Oates. "Sir Robert is a well-known crony of the prisoner."

"Dr. Oates!" interrupts Williamson. "You speak without due consideration. Sir Robert Southwell is a servant of the State and therefore has no *cronies*. You had best consider whom you slander."

For a moment, Oates quivers. Colour rises on his face as if he might do something rash. Instead, he storms from the chamber and is gone.

***

"How is Anne?" I ask Southwell. With freedom, all of the realities of life tumble back into my head.

"She is managing, Henry says. But come. We will go to her now. Are you hungry?"

I blink, and realise that I am.

"Ravenous. But I must thank you. You've saved my neck."

His long face looks grave again. "I may have, but I doubt that Oates is done with you yet. Let's get you home and get you fed. Then we can work out what to do for the best."

***

Dark shadows lie under Anne's eyes. When I take her in my arms, she feels insubstantial and frail. While Henry and Southwell arrange our future for us, Anne sits dully by the fireplace, shuddering at every cart and carriage that rattles past on the cobbles outside our home.

It's made clear to me that Oates has really gone to work on my reputation. Pamphlets litter the coffee shops and taverns, depicting me as that dog, Towser, dancing around the Pope's heels and barking his messages. Henry hands me one, and I turn it over in my hands trying to find some kind of response.

"There have been stones thrown at the door here, Nat," says Henry. "Sarah was abused in the street. They say this is a house of papists, a viper's nest."

"You need to get away," says Southwell.

"While you can," says Henry.

William is here, standing at the window, just behind Anne's chair.

"What do you say?" I ask him.

"Titus is a bully. Always was, always will be. There is a

132

chance that if you disappear for a while, he will find other targets for his vileness."

"But we live here. I work here. We can't just pack up the house and head off into the countryside!"

"And we do not suggest that you do, Nathaniel," says Southwell. "Nothing so rash. But if Oates finds another witness, another Prance, to say you've been seen taking mass…"

"Then you will be arrested again and have to wait who knows how long to have your case considered." Henry looks at Southwell for corroboration and the old man nods.

"What are you suggesting?"

"That we give it time," Henry replies. In a few months, he and Southwell say, the focus of public anger will shift. It always does. I just need to absent myself until they're sure I won't be re-arrested.

"But my life is here!" I insist.

I turn to Anne, but her eyes are fixed on the fire.

***

"It may not be for long." She sounds intensely grave. The others have left, and we've gone upstairs. We lie curled on the bed, too drained to undress, her back pressed to my chest, her hair in my face.

"It has already been too long. I can't bear that I had to leave you that day. I shouldn't be leaving you again. Come with me."

She squeezes my hand. It's all wrong. It should be me comforting her, easing her pain, looking after her, as I promised to do.

"I can't," she says. "I can't leave her here alone."

"She is with God," I say.

"Is she?"

"Isn't she?" It's a poor response, but I am like a blind man, groping my way with my fingertips.

"She is in the ground. I won't leave her. It's only when I visit her that I am at peace. Can you see? Perhaps in a few

133

weeks I could join you. Or perhaps you will be back. I just need time."

I can't see, and I don't understand. But she has asked me to let her stay and grieve for our daughter. How can I refuse? "I love you, Anne Thompson," I say.

"And I, you."

We fall asleep like that. In the morning, I pack a bag and board a coach to Edinburgh.

Chapter Nineteen

Anne

I promise Nat that Sarah will stay with me while he is gone, but after a week I send her home. There is a tyranny open to the bereaved. Henry, Sarah, Nat – all three used to be so sure they knew what was best for me, but not now. Sarah, especially, understands my desire to be left alone.

Two, three, then four months pass. Nat's offices are ransacked but nothing is found. The charges against my husband are not dropped, but with little evidence, Southwell and Henry declare that we will have him back in London soon. Nat's public reputation, however, has never been worse. He is vilified on a daily basis in the Whig presses. They stopped throwing stones at the door when it became known that he had left town, but he is still widely believed to be a secret Catholic. It is Kitty who tells me they are making a straw man of him to burn in the November Pope-burning procession today. No-one else has mentioned it, of course.

I insist on going. It is time I shook the stupor from my bones. There are cross words. Neither Henry nor William are happy, but I make it very clear that I will go, whether they accompany me or not. I am hard as iron about this. I want to see it.

But when I do, this effigy of Nat is the stuff of nightmares.

First, they tie it to a chair. The chair is nailed to a rough platform of wood and juggled up onto the shoulders of six willing men, ready to be paraded through the streets of London. Horses trample past, obscuring my view, filling my ears with snorts and the hard smack of hooves on the cobbles. Men bellow orders as they shuffle and stir the procession into shape. I have never seen such a profusion of purple, such glorious rich deep velvets. All around us, young men shrug on priests' clothes and grab crucifixes and altar books from a cart brimful of goods.

My plan is to stand very still and not panic. I promised Henry and William I would not, and it is not my living, breathing, husband Nat they'll burn. This is only a straw man, thank God. But I cannot drag my eyes from it, all the same. He – it – wears tight black breeches and a many-buttoned waistcoat. It sports a grubby neckerchief and a long dingy coat that has seen better days. They have given it woollen stockings – worn, nubby, and poorly patched. Worst of all are the wig and hat. Its wig hangs limply and is matted with some tacky grime. The hat looks as though it has been kicked across the cobbles before being crammed upon its head. Probably because it has.

They are not his clothes. Nat's clothes, those he left behind, are in our house, cleaned and folded in readiness. Oh, but these are like! That is his cut of coat, his colour of wig, his careless necktie. My husband has been studied most diligently. Where his face should be, there is a painted mask. The body is tightly bound to the chair but the head leans at an impossible angle. They have slung a crude sign around his neck with his name painted on, although no-one in the crowd could have any doubts. Someone has even put a quill pen in one of his hands and piled papers and books on his knee and at his feet.

"Hey!" A whey-faced old man lumbers against me, misting stale ale and tobacco across my cheek. I mis-step and my ankle twists. William grabs my arm while Henry blusters.

"Henry! Enough." I lay my hand on his sleeve and read such concern in his face that my eyes prick. Good, kind friends, they flank me like two sombre guards, ready for me to faint or break down, and who can blame them? I have not been well.

"Where do they get it all from?" William asks Henry.

"One of the Justices of the Peace has been stockpiling since the plot stories first surfaced. On every raid he's seized whatever Catholic paraphernalia he could find. The Whigs have paid for the clothes. They are determined to make a great spectacle."

On this evidence, they will succeed. They have their straw Pope and several straw bishops also tied to platforms, with leather books, altar cloths, crucifixes, and candles heaped about their feet. Where they will place my husband in this macabre pageant?

Immediately in front of us, a live man with his face painted white and his shirt soaked in red dye mounts his horse. He is to play the martyr, Justice Godfrey. Behind him lurks a fat fellow with a merry grin. That one has the honour of being Innocent XI for the day.

After some stopping and starting, the procession begins. There is constant motion. We are jostled and pushed, pushed and jostled. The first few are actors, real people, dressed up and waving, employed to whip up the crowds on every street between here and Smithfield. After them, younger men and boys, dressed as Jesuits and satyrs, line the carts pulling straw effigies of prominent figures in the Popish Plot that will be burned later today. The straw Pope and bishops lead the way. Behind them, men carry five Catholic Lords. Following the Lords is that infamous writer, that suspected traitor – my husband.

From here in Katherine Wheel Alley, they will travel to Whitechapel and on to Temple Bar. They'll rattle up Chancery Lane and along Holborn, before passing beneath the grim walls of Newgate.

We choose a quicker route to Smithfield but are far from the earliest to arrive. People are already forming rings around platforms stacked with firewood.

'Didn't you come here, you and Nat, last year?' asks Henry.

'For the Bartholomew Fair,' I say, remembering. It was another time, another life.

While we wait, the sky darkens and evening comes. Braziers are lit. By the time the procession explodes into Smithfield, all the rich colours visible earlier have grown dark and shadowy. Justice Godfrey's white face is ghastly in the torchlight. The false Pope looks drunk. He sways and spits at the crowd who hurl abuse back at him. Faces twist and sneer in the torchlight.

My feet and hands are numb with cold. I should have eaten. The smell of chestnuts reaches me and my stomach rolls. There are twelve bonfires. The crowd is testy, impatient to witness the promised spectacle. Organised groups of men hasten to hoist the effigies into position. Hate steams up from the crowd's angry fists. It is in their stinking sweat, on their harsh tongues and rotten breath.

"We can go now, Anne," says Henry.

"No. We will see it all."

I glance at William. His eyes roam the crowd.

"He must be here," he mutters.

"Who?" asks Henry.

"Oates." William spits out the name.

"And what if he is?" Henry's heavy eyebrows pinch together. "Have we not learnt enough about what Titus Oates is capable of doing?"

William's eyes flick to mine and then back to Henry. He takes a deep breath. "You are right," he says. "We'll leave whenever you're ready, Anne."

"Not yet," I say.

And so we stand here, we three, silent and still, while all around the crowd rumbles. The pyres are lit and smoke tickles its spice across London's collective nostrils.

Flames lick Nat's boots. They climb his legs, leap towards his painted face. The smoke is soon intense, the smell revolting. Someone has mixed the straw with human hair.

In the end it is the crowd that makes it all too much. It is the cheering and the singing and the swearing. It is the laughter, the throwing of food, the celebration. It is the sound of men screaming for my husband to burn. Their real belief that he is part of some terrible counter-plot overwhelms me. My head pounds. I turn to my friends, eyes wide and imploring. A scream is rising in my chest.

Henry realises. William grabs my arm. We push our way out, following Henry who clears a path. Just as we reach the edge of the mass of people, William's fingers pinch my sleeve.

He says nothing but I follow his gaze.

Titus Oates is only a few feet away. His wide mouth opens and his head tips back as he pours wine down his gullet. He swallows, blinks, and then he sees us. Snatching his hat from his head, he sweeps it down before him, sticking out one leg and bowing.

"Mr. Smith, Mr. Broome, Mistress Thompson. Such a pleasure."

We turn to go in a different direction but the crowd has tightened around us.

"Quite a spectacle, wouldn't you say?" says Oates. "Such dangerous times, but only for dangerous fellows, don't you think?"

"Let us pass," says William. "The lady is unwell—"

"Oh dear, dear, dear. But it is only a straw man burning. No harm in that. The real man in question has run away, has he not? Let us hope that by the time he finds the courage to return, this unruly crowd has settled a little, eh? Although he will perhaps need to live a little more quietly and less in the public eye. Or who knows what could happen? In such dangerous times."

In a flash my hand is across his face, my palm stinging with the pain of it.

Someone, one of his cronies, raises his fists as Oates staggers back. Henry steps in front of me, and at the same second William finds a gap in the crowd. He pulls us away.

***

Henry is outraged. All the way home from the burning, he bothers and blusters about Titus Oates, but beneath it all there is real fear at what I have done. Will Oates set his men on me? Will I be arrested next? I could go to Sarah, to my parents even, but I'm afraid to take this evil to their door. Later, alone, I realise what this is. This is my punishment. This is what I deserve. I wait for trouble to arrive.

Days pass, but the knock at the door never comes. Henry visits frequently. He has written to Nat in Edinburgh, describing the November Pope-burning procession and his continued unpopularity in the city. I also write, but my letters are paltry things. What do I have to write about? Time moves slowly. I spend my hours doing tasks that occupy my hands: folding linen, preparing food, sewing. Reading is impossible. My eyes jump from the page and the words flow without meaning. Sarah visits. I only go out to buy food or visit Martha's grave. I walk with my head down. The city is filled with paper – plastered to bare walls, hanging from stalls, tumbling in the gutters – and I do not wish to see my husband's name or face, except in person.

I long for him to come home.

I'm afraid of what will happen when he does.

Chapter Twenty

Nat

It is abominably cold in Edinburgh; colder than I expected. With such nipping winds whistling about their chops and that boggy dampness mouldering in their boots, it's no wonder the Scots are so miserly. Even the most ebullient character must eventually be brought low by the unkind drizzle, the sleet, and the fog. I've been in Edinburgh for months, and every day this mist they call the haar has hung about the place like a gloomy spectre, blotting out any train of thought that might have lifted my spirits out of the mire.

My room is small, of which I'm glad, as it is the easier to keep warm. The bed is clean and there is a desk and chair. I suffered the landlady's blatant disdain for my thin-blooded Englishman's request for extra blankets, but it was worth it to keep the chill air from seeping into my skin. The threadbare rugs on the floor can't protect my poor feet in the mornings, however. In happier circumstances, Anne would laugh heartily at the sight of me trying to get dressed under my covers, even to my boots, before I emerge from my nest each day.

Anne.

I have some very black days and nights in Edinburgh. I drink whisky till I vomit. I wake in the morning shuddering and sweating, and spend hours lying in my bed, immobile. Guilt and grief sink into my bones.

I spend my time brooding. I keep the little Godfrey dagger that we bought at the magistrate's funeral near to hand, and like to beat a drum with it as I sit and think. My subject is Titus Oates. Every thought I have leads inexorably to him. If I think about Anne, forced to grieve alone, I think of him. I

141

should be with her. That I am not, is Oates's fault. When I consider my career – in tatters since my arrest – I'm crushed by my failure, but that too is Oates's fault. Then there are William, Matthew Medbourne, the Lords and priests in prison cells, and the three fools hanged for Godfrey's murder. I fine-tune my hatred of Oates by running through the list of his victims and re-visiting every loathsome sight I've had of him. I send urgent instructions to Kineally. He must step up his enquiries into Oates's background. He details his discoveries in a series of letters that I fold and unfold so often they begin to fall apart. I become as familiar with Titus's history as any man could.

I learn that Samuel Oates, Titus's father, was a weaver turned Anabaptist preacher, well known for 'dipping'. This form of baptism, where young women are stripped naked and fully submerged in freezing water, usually at night, proved quite profitable for Samuel until one poor girl caught a fever and died. Kineally reported that Samuel Oates was put on trial at the assizes in Colchester but found not guilty of causing the girl's death. He was lucky.

Perhaps because of this incident, Samuel Oates and his wife moved to Oakham, an East Midlands town about a hundred miles north of London. Titus was born there in 1649. During his infancy, Oates's father was repeatedly arrested for holding illegal and blasphemous religious gatherings, although he appeared to have stopped dipping at least. William once told me that Oates's own mother found him a repellent child, but Kineally finds little to add to the picture of Oates as a boy until he joined the Merchant Taylors' School when he was fifteen years old. By this time, the family had spent some years living in London, and Oates's father had found a new vocation as a Church of England parson.

William told me months ago that Oates was expelled from the Merchant Taylors' School for cheating other boys out of their money. Kineally writes that the family next sent him to a village school in Selescombe. He must have muddled along well enough, for in 1667 he was admitted to Caius College, Cambridge. Kineally finds no shortage of men who remembered Oates there, despite him only being permitted to stay in that seat of learning for two short terms. It was a petty matter, but to me it speaks directly to the character of Oates as he became a man. Oates bought a coat from a tailor in Cambridge, but when the tailor asked for payment Oates insisted he had already paid. In fact, he had not only not paid for the coat, he had already sold it to a dealer in second-hand clothes and pocketed the proceeds. When the tailor raised a fuss, Oates was quickly found out. All student monies were handled by their tutors, and the College knew that Oates was lying. He was expelled again.

How Oates managed after leaving Cambridge is unclear, but Kineally finds his trail not long after, in Sandhurst, where he had somehow managed to secure himself the position of curate. From Sandhurst he progressed to a living of his own in Bobbing in Kent, and once more Kineally reports that Oates had been a memorable character. Drunkenness, accusations of theft, and blasphemy characterised his time there. He left before he was forced out. From Bobbing, Oates went to work with his father, who by this time had a parish in Hastings.

I already know the story of the Parkers and Oates's shameful departure from Hastings, but now Kineally has unearthed the record of Parker's trial and Oates's public disgrace. I'm eager to see what Kineally discovers about Oates's time in the Navy, but details are scant. He finds only one written reference to him, which confirms that Oates was thrown out over a charge of sodomy. He might have hanged, had he not been a man of the cloth. Now there is a fact to be bitterly regretted.

After the Navy, Oates settled in London, living again with his father, who had left Hastings and the Church of England, reverting to the Baptist faith. Titus Oates's gift for changing religion is inherited, it seems. This was the time when Oates fell in with Matthew Medbourne. For a short period, he held an appointment in the Duke of Norfolk's household, and began his conversion to Catholicism.

In the few years before he and Israel Tonge suddenly arrived at the house of Sir Edmund Godfrey with eighty-one articles of evidence, each detailing an aspect of the most terrifying Popish Plot, Oates had become a Catholic priest. He was sent to two Catholic colleges: St Omer's in Flanders, and Valladolid in Spain. There, despite being vastly older than many of his fellow students, despite making no friendships or appearing in anyway fit for the priesthood, Titus Oates had managed to access letter upon letter and hear treason upon treason. It was a fantastical account, yet the Privy Council had believed him. Or if they did not quite believe, they dared not repudiate him out of hand. Perhaps it was easier to believe Oates's story was true than to imagine he made the whole thing up.

My instinctive scepticism is confirmed by everything I learn about Oates's past. The seeds of the man he would become are there, in his earlier actions. There's a consistent narrative of anger and deceit. But when he first arrived in London, nothing was known of him. Through his unparalleled audacity, through the sheer scale of his lies, he was believed. Then, once he was in Whitehall and with anti-Catholic hysteria spreading, he was a political gift to the likes of the Earl of Shaftesbury.

As I walk the streets and hills of Edinburgh, or sit in my room, reading and thinking, Oates is my constant companion. I imagine him growing and festering through his strange upbringing into the villain who brought disaster into my life. The look on his face when he had me thrown out of the Fuller's Rent Tavern consumes me. The thought of his hot breath on my ear when he whispered to me in the Privy Council room turns my stomach. Whenever I set down my pen, Titus Oates's face fills the waiting space. A ball of bile gathers in my guts, and it will only disappear when this man is dealt with.

Anne's letters arrive every week or so. They are thin, wretched things. Henry is more forthcoming. Leaving, he assures me, was the best thing I could have done. My office was ransacked. Everything was seized and scrutinised by Shaftesbury's Commons Committee, but they found nothing to complain of, apart from a plea for religious tolerance. In itself, that's not enough to make me a traitor. Miles Prance's evidence remains the most dangerous. As soon as it was widely known that I was suspected of being a secret Catholic convert, I was damned by the public. I'm continually lampooned in the Whig press, and my name has become a by-word for Catholic duplicity and vice. Henry wrote to tell me that my place in the annual Pope-burning procession to Smithfield was secured.

His most recent letter – describing how my fellow citizens thrilled at the sight of a sack full of straw, dressed up in soiled clothes, going up in flames while they shouted my name – gives me nightmares. I hate the thought of Anne witnessing it, and focus instead on Henry's news that three prominent priests are soon to be tried for their part in the Popish Plot. Oates has sworn all three have plotted to kill the King.

Even from here, there must be some way to stop him.

Chapter Twenty-One

Anne

We grow close, William, Henry, and I. Sarah visits, but I am finished with my mother. I write and tell her so in bald terms. She has always believed she has known what was best for me, but she has been wrong twice now: wrong about Nat, and wrong in dosing me up with laudanum. I have a new family, and if it is not the family I longed for, at least we are companionable and kind.

Christmas passes and we slip into a new year. This time last year I was with child. Now I do not even have a husband at home. At least I have seen nothing more of Titus Oates. My fear recedes and I go out more. Henry has employed William in the print shop. Every day I take them food, and when Henry steps out to the coffee shops and taverns, the boys and I help William. They love him as I do, for his gentleness, his thoughtfulness, and his sense of fair play. What a wonderful teacher he must have been, but he is no printer. When William is in charge, the paper dries too quickly and the ink is never evenly spread. He pores over the type, re-thinking phrases, lacking decision and energy. More and more I send him to work with the boys on their letters while I run the presses for Henry. But I don't write of any of this to Nat in Edinburgh. I'm not sure what he would think. My letters to him are a struggle. I have so much to say, but at the same time nothing at all.

That's one of the reasons I decide to accompany Henry to the priests' trial. At least I will have something to describe to Nat. Oh, Henry raises an eyebrow and frowns a little, but he knows better than to argue with me. He confides that Nat has given him detailed instructions. If all goes to plan, Oates will not enjoy this morning's work.

We arrive early at Westminster Hall, because Henry is anxious. He shifts at my side and cannot be still. The great building is mostly in shadowy darkness, but as the sun climbs it fills with light and people: courtiers, lawmen, newsmongers, gossips, civil servants, and businessmen. We sit with Sir Robert Southwell up in one of the balconies erected for such events. It's the perfect vantage point.

At last, the five judges, led by Chief Justice Scroggs, shuffle their way into their seats and the prisoners are brought before the bar. The long indictment of treason is read, and the first witness called.

Titus Oates strides to the witness stand with complete assurance. He has the ease of a gentleman standing before his own warm hearth, or a fond father patting his children's soft curls. He pouts his lips together before he deigns to speak, his brow furrowing with some unspoken distaste, implying a pained reluctance at the necessity of lowering himself to take part in these unsavoury matters. I'm impressed. He is as ugly as ever, yet his presence is remarkable, his arrogance impossible to ignore. I remember the lies he and Miles Prance told about my husband. I don't believe a word Oates says now, but others do, and public opinion remains on his side. In this setting, he is convincing. These poor priests – Father Whitbread, Father Ireland, and Father Fenwick – have no idea what they are up against.

Oates speaks about each of the accused in turn, explaining where he met them and how each man was actively involved in the April 1678 meeting where the King's death was plotted. Oates explains that he was given the task of personally visiting each priest after the meeting and obtaining their written assent to the plot. He also says he spent time in London with each of the accused during the month of August, witnessing their preparations to shoot the King in St James's Park. The Lord Chief Justice Scroggs mutters agreeably throughout, often gesturing to the jury to take note of particular points, and at each interjection Henry shifts in his chair.

"Tell us, Dr. Oates," says Jones, the Attorney General, "what you can, about Father Whitbread."

"My Lord, I endured a great deal while observing these men," says Oates.

His voice is peculiar, but I'm not sure it doesn't make him even more convincing. He is a highly unusual creature. I'm shocked by what he says next.

"Father Whitbread suspected me of betraying his plot," Oates says. "He whipped me, threatened me, and slapped me about the face. I feared for my own life at his hands. He is the main agitator, he is the provincial leader of the Jesuits. With a fanatic's desire, he has paid men to take the King's life and accepted French coin to fund his conspiracies."

Father Whitbread is an old man, his cheeks fanned with lines, his thin lips as pale as his skin. He keeps his face immobile, mask-like. I dislike him. I believe he might use a whip. Fathers Fenwick and Ireland are younger. Both looked cramped with tension and are listening attentively. Fenwick visibly struggles to maintain his composure while Oates weaves his tale.

I'm interested when Oates's evidence reveals more of his own recent history masquerading as a Catholic convert. Nat told me that Oates had been effectively destitute when he arrived in London a year or two ago. Naturally, he glosses over the details but admits he'd struggled to survive in London and was reduced to begging. Father Fenwick gave him alms, he says. But Oates paints this not as an act of charity, but as part of a Catholic snare, a way to attach young innocents to their cause, to recruit and convert them towards extremism.

As the trial continues, all three of the priests' heads droop and their shoulders bend under the weight of the almost inevitable verdict of any treason trial. In the schoolroom with my brother's tutor I remember being taught the words of Cardinal Richelieu, words from another time and another country, but no less apposite here: '*Although in the course of ordinary cases justice requires authenticated proof, it is not the same with those that affect the state.*'

In cases of treason, it is held that circumstantial evidence is enough. Such plots and conspiracies are deemed to be so complex, so secret, and so difficult to prove, that normal laws of evidence do not apply. There are some threats so terrible that they must be stopped at all costs. Suspicion is all that's required.

At last, the priests are given their opportunity to put forward some kind of defence. Whitbread tries to attack Oates. "This man has fabricated evidence as an act of personal vengeance," he declares.

But the crowd hisses and Scroggs is openly sceptical.

"Titus Oates was a student at St Omer's College in Flanders," says Whitbread in a calm voice. "He was the worst, most foul-mouthed, trouble-making, lazy, misbegotten creature we have ever—"

"It is not for the defendant to malign the witness," shouts Scroggs. "Disprove his evidence. Or sit back down."

Whitbread looks rattled. Then he tries again. "In June of 1678, Titus Oates was dismissed from St Omer's College."

Next to me, Southwell and Henry whisper and shake their heads.

"Did you not hear me?" Scroggs's face is purple. "Dr. Oates is not the man on trial today!"

"I apologise, Your Honour," says Father Whitbread, although there is nothing apologetic in his demeanour. "I will speak only of the facts. It has been stated by the prosecution witness that the murder of King Charles was the first order of business at a Jesuit meeting held in London that April. I ask permission to bring evidence that the witness," Whitbread can't keep the dislike from his voice, "was not in fact present at that meeting, because he was abroad, in Flanders, attending St Omer's College."

Henry elbows me. "Interesting," he whispers.

There's a moment's silence. We are suddenly tense, as if an invisible net around us has tightened. All eyes are on Scroggs. Whitbread grips the rail in front of him.

"But what kind of evidence would that be?" says Scroggs. He shrugs and even smiles. "Who could swear before this court that Dr. Oates was in Flanders when we know him to have been in London? Who *would* swear such a thing?" He shifts forward in his seat and the smile is long gone. He jabs a fat finger at Father Whitbread. "More of your kind, that's who! More Catholics." The tension in the crowd loosens. "You will not pull the wool over our eyes so easily. You take us for such fools, but we know what you are." He turns. "Dr. Oates, I presume you can bring witnesses to attest that you were in London in April 1678?"

Oates nods. "I am happy to do so, Lord Chief Justice. My witness is Mr. William Smith, lately schoolmaster at the Merchant Taylors' School."

This is surely a mistake.

I have misheard.

But no. I stare dumbfounded as William, our friend, William Smith, appears in the witness box. Henry can't take his eyes from him, but his hand finds mine and he squeezes my fingers. We both sit transfixed as William swears on the Bible that Oates was in London that April, and that they spent many hours in each other's company.

He doesn't look happy about it. William's usual sombre demeanour is even more pronounced, but I can't get past the first shock of seeing him there, in support of Oates.

Within a minute, it's over. William is despatched back into the crowd.

"You didn't know?" I say to Henry.

He doesn't answer. He's studying Scroggs, who in turn is glaring at Whitbread. Spit is visible on his lips and genuine anger lights his eyes.

"You Catholics," Scroggs hisses. "You are men that eat your God. You are men that kill their kings and make saints of their murderers. And you would have *us* take *you* at your word?"

People all around us gasp.

Whitbread closes his eyes and his lips move quickly, but he has no more words for the court. He's broken. I turn my eyes to Oates. He's standing staring at Whitbread with one arm folded across his chest and his other hand held up before his face. He appears as shocked as anyone, for even the most

150

fervent anti-Catholics in the crowd are silenced for the moment by the urgency of Scroggs's invective. But then I understand that Oates isn't shocked at all; he's trying not to laugh. His shoulders are trembling, his arm is around himself to hold himself in check, his hand hides a smile. As Whitbread sits down, he looks at Oates, who lets his hand drop, giving a glimpse of his true expression to the crushed old man. Whitbread doesn't react. Beside me, Henry sucks in a breath as if scalded. He's seen, as I have, the naked triumph in Oates's eyes.

"It's time," says Henry. He motions to one of the several boys loitering near the back of the Hall ready to run errands or fetch refreshments. Henry presses a folded paper and a coin into the boy's hand, and points out a young woman near the front of the crowd below the witness box. She's wearing a fashionable blue-black bonnet and a grey shawl.

As the boy squeezes his way through to her, the judges ask Fathers Fenwick and Ireland what, if any, defence they might offer. Fenwick, so soft spoken that I must believe he is a total innocent in all this madness, makes little impression, but Father Ireland calls his sister. She's sworn in as a witness and speaks in a clear, educated voice. Miss Ireland is tall, and simply dressed; a good-looking girl with tidy brown hair. Henry's note is in her gloved hands.

She begins by attacking Oates's assertion that Ireland was in London, in August, plotting to kill the King. Her family wishes to offer evidence, she says, that her brother was in St Albans and Wolverhampton for the whole month. There are several witnesses they seek permission to bring to swear to this before the court.

Scroggs raises his hand to quieten her. He scrapes back his chair and confers in whispers with his fellow judges. The crowd, anticipating something unusual, becomes agitated. Feet scuff the floor and whispers pop up like bubbles breaking a watery surface.

"We deny the witnesses." Scroggs glares around the court. 'If it is proved that Father Ireland was out of London for part of August, it is only a mistake in point of time and doesn't

151

invalidate the substance of the accusation. We are concerned with action, in this court, not circumstance of time. Have you anything further?"

Ireland's sister's lips part. She flushes and her eyes fill. I will her to act on the note. Henry has written: *Call upon Sir Denny Ashburnham, MP for Hastings. Request that he be allowed to give testimony. Do not fail.*

She does not.

"Brave girl," Henry mutters.

In a matter of moments, the clerk of the court calls on the MP for Hastings. Oates has gone very, very still. He looks at Scroggs and raises his shoulders slightly, as if to say he knows nothing of Hastings, but his teeth work against his lips. He's nervous.

"Ashburnham?" Scroggs frowns at the MP. "What can you have to say in this matter?"

"I wish to speak, My Lord, of the character of the witness, Titus Oates."

Scroggs slumps in his chair and shakes his great head. "I have to say, sir," he says, "that I am not pleased to hear that, not pleased at all. The court has already expressed its displeasure at the pathetic attempts made to malign Dr. Oates." He pauses, perhaps to weigh up his options.

Sir Denny Ashburnham is a mild, sandy haired man, a respected Protestant Member of Parliament; someone, Nat wrote to Henry, whom Scroggs will know, if not particularly well. Nat's hope is that Scroggs won't be able to shout down such an unimpeachable character. "Well, you may speak up if you must, then," says Scroggs. "But I hope it is to the point. And short."

"I have known Titus Oates for many years," Ashburnham says. "In my experience, he was not a man whose word could be relied upon."

"Not strong enough!" This is Southwell, loud enough for me to hear.

"I have brought with me a copy of an indictment against Mr. Oates for perjury," the MP continues. "I felt it my duty to communicate it to the court, for your consideration."

"You did, did you?" asks Scroggs. He pauses and scratches at his cheek. "Well. You have done so, and we will look at it. But let me ask you, sir, when you speak about Dr. Oates in his youth, when you dishonour a man who stands before us, staunchly protecting the freedom and safety of your fellow Englishmen, what would you have us think of you?"

Ashburnham swallows before he replies. His inner politician has won the day. I can't look at Henry. "Please, My Lord," Ashburnham says, "I would have you think nothing more than that I am a responsible citizen doing my duty. I know nothing of Dr. Oates that would lead me to doubt his testimony now; now that circumstances corroborate his evidence. Were the matter to rely on his word alone, my experience would lead me to harbour some doubts. But that is not the case. I would say nothing against Dr. Oates beyond the matter I have transmitted to the court regarding his record in the Town of Hastings." He bows to the court and Scroggs nods approvingly. Ashburnham is excused. The courtroom is quiet as the judges consider Ashburnham's evidence of the perjury charge.

"Not enough. Not enough." Henry is shaking his head. Southwell is already on his feet, ready to leave.

The five judges confer. There is a degree of liveliness to their debate and I've a late sniff of hope. As Scroggs prepares to speak, I hold my breath, but…

"Gentlemen of the jury, it is of no matter. We have studied the information and find that it is not relevant to the prisoners. There is no need for it to be read. Let us move on."

* * *

Henry is crushed. The moment the evidence of perjury is denied, he follows Southwell out of the Hall. I catch up with him in the street outside and he walks me home in silence. I picture Nat, somewhere far away, imagining events in London in a very different manner than they have played out. How can I write to him of this failure? And what will he think of William's role today?

By the time we reach my door, Henry has rallied a little. "Nat will be disappointed," he says, "but Ashburnham was at fault. Too much the politician. Not enough of a man."

"Those three priests. Do they stand a chance?" I ask.

"No. They will go the same way as Green, Berry, and Hill. The same way as Edward Coleman, although with much less cause."

As he says the man's name, my mind slips back to Coleman's execution, but I don't stop to dwell on his gruesome end. Instead, I remember that I was with child then and that I am not now. The world is a dark, dark place. Thank heavens Henry cannot read my thoughts, and talks on regardless.

"In Coleman's case," he says, "there was some evidence against him, but these priests? You saw it, Anne. They were given no chance. And they will die."

"And what about William?"

"I have no idea what possessed him."

"I suppose if he was subpoenaed and asked the question, then he had no option but to attend the court and tell the truth."

"So it would seem."

"But you will ask him about it?"

"Be sure that I will."

Chapter Twenty-Two

William

They come for me at night. A pair of thugs grab me on the street as I walk home from Henry's print shop. It is nine o'clock and fully dark. Dense cloud obscures the moon and a steady drizzle dulls all sounds so that I don't hear them coming. One moment I'm walking, the next a hand yanks my hair, my head snaps back, and my arms are pinned to my back. With stale breath, they whisper sordid threats in my ear should I make the smallest complaint.

Titus waits in a small private room in The Cooper's Arms Tavern in Rose Street. This time I am not brave or defiant. This time he gives me no choice. Anne will be grabbed off the street just as I have been. Or a fire will start at Henry's print shop. Or Nat will not return to London alive. An accident on the road. Matthew will die in Newgate. He asks for very little in return, he assures me. One small falsehood to avoid such calamities. Indeed, only half a falsehood, because he swears he was where I am instructed to say he was. Not even a falsehood, he says; just the confirmation of something that is true. I agree to the lie. When called upon, I will say that I saw him in London in April 1678. Then they let me go.

I do not immediately realise the enormity of what I've agreed to. A couple of days pass. I visit Matthew in Newgate. Sickness has taken hold of both his body and his mind. His conversation wanders. I'm not sure that he hears or even sees me all the time I am there. One small falsehood, I tell myself. How bad can it be?

I see Anne and Henry and the boys at the print shop and say nothing about my meeting with Titus, even though he is a constant topic among us. Nat has conceived a plan to bring up Titus's perjury in the case of the Parker family in Hastings. He hopes to undercut his evidence during the priests' trial. I am enthusiastic about it, hopeful that this plan will give Titus something more to worry about than this matter that requires me to say he was in London.

How naïve. Weak. Easily manipulated. Educated, yet an absolute fool. This is who I am.

***

After the priests' trial, when I have given evidence that will cause men's deaths…

After the priests' trial, when I have chosen fear and lies over truth…

After the priests' trial, when I have chosen known friends over unknown innocents…

After the priests' trial, when I have been the worst of myself and a coward…

Afterwards, Henry asks me if it is true, what I said under oath in Westminster Hall.

I look him in the eye and say it was.

I lie to his face.

There are no small falsehoods.

Chapter Twenty-Three

Nat

I am propped up in bed with blankets warming my shoulders and cosseting my knees when the idea comes to me. I've picked through Henry's letters for perhaps the fiftieth time. The failure to damage Oates at the priests' trial sent me into a spiral of whisky-filled oblivion, but I don't sink completely. Something in my gut tells me not to give up. Instead, I go back through Henry's letters and find one that brings things into focus. It's the Pope-burning. He's described the procession in typical detail and precision. My reputation, my position, and my prospects all went up in smoke in Smithfield. I let my eyes run over the details again, but this time a name jumps out at me from the page. Justice Godfrey.

A man dressed as Godfrey headed that procession for good reason. The dead magistrate is a symbol for all the turmoil that had gripped the city, his death widely accepted as proof that Jesuit priests were determined to murder the King and turn the country Catholic again. I recall Lord Chief Justice Scroggs, at the trial of Green, Berry and Hill. He said there was monstrous evidence of the whole horrid Plot in that one killing.

But who was the prime witness against Godfrey's murderers? Miles Prance. I thought he was a perjurer at the trial of Green, Berry, and Hill, and then he viciously lied about me before the Privy Council. The more I consider it, the more I'm certain that Prance let three men swing for a crime they did not commit, not to mention letting the real killers run free.

For the first time, I ask myself: if those three men were innocent, then who really killed Godfrey? I drop the letter onto the bedclothes and stare into the fire. Who is to say, even, that his murder had anything to do with the Catholics at all? Something stirs in my ribs. What if the accepted fact that Godfrey was murdered by Jesuit plotters is as false as all the other lies that have brought men to the scaffold and set neighbour against neighbour? People took Godfrey's murder as proof that the Popish Plot is real. What if I prove otherwise? If Godfrey's death has nothing to do with the plot, where does that leave Titus Oates?

I sit up straight and the blanket slips from my shoulders. I reach for paper and a pen and begin to write.

Murder? I write that on the top left of the page and draw two thin black lines under the question mark. Then on the right-hand side, I write *Accident or Suicide?* similarly underscored. Next, in the left column, I quickly make a list: *Inquest, Trial, Miles Prance, Politics.* In the right, I write: *Family, Friends, Character, Physical evidence.* I take another sheet and write *Evidence* at the top. But I stare at that with a frown and then take another. This time I write *Who gained from his death?* The names fly from my pen.

The next morning, I write more letters. I write to Kineally in London. He can begin the work. I write to Southwell, asking him how soon it will be safe for me to return to the city. And then I write to Anne.

There's not much of a view to be had from my room, but as I fumble over what to write to my wife, I take it all in. My window looks out only upon a small passage, which they call a wynd: a narrow run between two tall stone buildings that slopes steeply away from the main High Street. Down below, people scurry about their business, carrying bundles and wrapped up warm. At least this terrible weather keeps down the smell, and the rain is an assiduous gutter-sluicer, something to be thankful for under this iron-grey sky. What does the sky look like over London right now? Where is Anne, this very minute? I long for her frank eyes, her coiling hair, her pale cheek.

My fledgling optimism of the night before dries up with the ink in my pen. I leave the letter half-written, shrug on my coat, and go out to eat. It is a short walk down to a tavern in the

Grassmarket, where I set about some black pudding and a tankard of ale. I'm in no mood for news from the city. Instead, I fish a book from my coat pockets – *Aesop's Fables*, in Latin, my father's copy. As I finger the leather, it occurs to me that after year upon year of frantic rushing and thinking and writing and arguing and reading, I have at last come to a stop. I wake up in the morning and have nowhere to go. At night, I read in bed until the wax on my candle has fully disappeared and I'm embraced by darkness and warm bedclothes. And what am I reading? Not stomach-churning horror stories about Catholics boiling children in vats of oil; not pamphlets about arbitrary government or the expansionist policies of Louis XIV. Just simple fables. A rushing temptation to forget all of it – my so-called career, Oates, Godfrey, all of it – sweeps over me.

There is only person I would not leave behind: Anne. But what damage has been done to us? First, the loss of the child, and now this lengthy separation. I have let her down badly. As always when my thoughts tend this way, I thirst for the scald of whisky on my tongue. Without it, I will struggle to sleep. But I face down temptation and make it through the day.

One day. And then another.

I pass a week in this fashion, awaiting a response from London.

First, a letter from Southwell. He has a suggestion. There might, he says, be a place for a new kind of news sheet in London; a publication that rehearses the arguments between those supporting Parliament and the exclusion of the King's brother from the succession – he calls them Whigs – and the Tories, those who believe in tradition and the monarchy. It is kind of him to think of me. His sympathies are with the King, as mine are, although he can't say so in public. Against all expectation, I'm interested. I scan his words for a hint that it is time I returned to London. There is nothing. But if I am to write this new publication – *The Observator*, I'm calling it in my mind – then I need to go home.

Now that I have turned my back on Edinburgh's many taverns, I have time to walk. One day, I climb to the highest point of Arthur's Seat and let the wind whip at my face. The disappointment of the priests' trial ebbs, although Henry writes that testifying for Oates has cast William into a dark frame of mind. To keep my own demons at bay, I busy myself writing the first several editions of *The Observator*. It's humorous. It's witty. It carries a lightness of tone that I'm nowhere near feeling but strive to conjure up for the sake of the future I pray Anne and I might yet have. I invent two outspoken characters to engage in the kind of coffee-shop debate with which I'm so familiar.

Working helps. I exchange a constant stream of letters with Kineally that have only two topics: Titus Oates and Sir Edmund Godfrey. If at odd moments I still have the urge to throw up the whole venture – to leave London with Anne and start afresh somewhere in the provinces – I've only to look at my work on *The Observator* or reach for Kineally's letters.

Reluctantly, I conclude that my attempts to write the truth about Oates were too late in the telling to change the public's mind. The priests' trial proved that conclusively. I must undermine belief in the Popish Plot itself if Oates is to be brought to account. Godfrey and the truth about his death may be the key. Kineally sends me everything he can about Sir Edmund's life.

Some facts I'm familiar with already. Godfrey was an older man, much older than Oates and myself. He was fifty-nine when he died. I learn he was the son of a Member of Parliament and attended Westminster School before going up to Oxford. Kineally reports that there had been plans for him to follow in his father's footsteps, but Godfrey had suffered from a severe loss of hearing and been forced to change his ambitions. Information about the dead magistrate proves simple to obtain. Kineally has found Godfrey's cousin – a Mistress Gibbon – living in Southampton Buildings, not far from Holborn. She and Godfrey were close all their lives. Her description of him doesn't fit the public picture of the Protestant Martyr. Godfrey was morose, bordering on melancholic. He had been a dabbler in poetry. She describes an honest and kind man who valued his reputation and his privacy.

I also spend a long time dwelling on how it should be that Godfrey was killed by Catholics because he knew the details of Oates's revelations. Why not just kill Oates and have done with it? Or if they – whoever *they* were – felt they must murder Godfrey, why wait until Oates was already installed in Whitehall? By the time Godfrey disappeared, Edward Coleman, several Lords, and the priests, were already in custody. The damage had been done, the uproar was in full sway.

I write to Southwell and outline my thoughts. His response is typically muted, but not discouraging. I point out that there is only so much work I can do on my new paper at such a far remove from the capital. He does not reply.

Time creeps by in Edinburgh. I move forward as much as possible with *The Observator,* and I simmer. Southwell approves the drafts I send him, and Henry reports that he sells out of my new paper within hours. I plan a series of steps to find out what really happened to Sir Edmund Godfrey.

Finally, Southwell writes that it is safe to go home.

Chapter Twenty-Four

Anne

Henry and Nat stop speaking the moment I enter the room. Henry's face is as calm as ever, but Nat looks guilty, like a boy caught stealing cakes in the pantry. He jumps to his feet and offers me his chair, close to the fire. This is what I have become to him: a fragile object to be cosseted and tip-toed around. A few months ago, I longed to have him take care of me. But not like this. Now he pats my cushion, he brings me wine, he asks how I am with irritating regularity, but he has not talked to me about Martha, not really, and he is very quiet about his work. Worse, he has not touched me, at least not in any meaningful way. He has been home for just over a week. I want to scream at him.

"What are you talking about?" I say.

Henry opens his mouth but then defers to Nat.

"Nothing important," he says.

"Then why stop?" I have the satisfaction of watching a blush climb up his handsome face. "If you are speaking of nothing of consequence, you may continue in comfort. And if you are saying something that is important, then you might consider remembering I am an adult, not a child, and treating me as such."

"Anne!" He is at a loss, and flounders for a moment before his desire to defend himself rises up as it always does. "I have never treated you as a child. I simply don't want to worry you."

"Not worry me? Do you think I don't know that you are still the only voice speaking out against Oates and his plot? Do you think I haven't seen or have not read your *Observator*?"

"I…" His voice trails away. Has it not crossed his mind that I would read it? I clench my hands into fists and wait to see if he will duck my challenge or be fair to me. He looks at Henry and Henry, bless him, nods. "All right then," Nat says. "We were discussing the household of Edmund Godfrey. Kineally has tracked down his housekeeper, but she has refused to see me. We were talking about that. Satisfied?"

"Very. And it's very clear what should be done." I give him a little smile to charm him, and am pleased to see it mirrored in his face. "I will go and see her," I say. "No arguments. I will think of some pretext, tell her I need a housekeeper if I must, and then set her gossiping. What is her name?"

"Judith Pamphlin. But, Anne, I'm not sure." His mouth sets in a line. There is argument coming, but before he begins, the door opens. William stumbles into the room.

"What has happened?" Nat asks.

Our friend crumples into a chair and sobs.

Two days later, we attend Matthew Medbourne's funeral.

***

The walls are draped in black cloth. All normal furniture has been removed so that there is only the coffin in the room, set upon two stools and laid open so that the body can be viewed. Nat and I enter slowly, arm in arm. I crush the decorative ticket advising us of the funeral between my fingers. There have been too many funerals of late.

I never met Matthew Medbourne in life. His body has been tidied into a white flannel shift, tied at the feet and hands. He'll be buried with a square of cloth covering his face, but this is put off to one side until his body has been viewed and condolences made to his family. I'm glad there's no mark of the syphilis on his face. No need to picture the fleshy insults hidden by his shroud.

In time, the pall-bearers – one of them William – assume their burden. The coffin is closed, draped in white because Matthew was unmarried, and carried out into the street on six men's shoulders. It's early evening. To the west, pink ribbons

163

of cloud trail up from the horizon, and gradually the greyness of the day shades down towards dark. We are handed wax torches and sprigs of rosemary, and follow the beadle, the coffin, and the family, out into the street.

It's a slow business, this procession from the home of the dead to their burial spot. Often, families take more circuitous routes to better express to their neighbours their sadness and loss, as demonstrated by the expensive accoutrements of a funeral. I don't know the area particularly well, but I've enough of a sense of direction to know we don't take the shortest route to the churchyard. He's to be buried outside, like Martha.

It's fully dark by the time the body is interred. We're on the east side of the churchyard. Torches cast wild shadows across the stone walls and pick out the grass at our feet, a dull mosaic in shades of grey. The air is damp and rain inevitable. More than one mourner's eyes are raised speculatively at the skies overhead. My thoughts turn to Titus Oates.

His actions tell the story of his character. He used Matthew. William and Nat think they are discreet when they talk of it, but I understand fully. Oates took advantage of Medbourne's affection for him. He used him for his money and his contacts, and then abused him for it. Judging from Matthew and William's experiences, Oates is someone who demands sympathy and support but then despises the very people who have helped him. When he no longer needs them, he turns on them. He uses the power he's gained to hurt them – even, in this case, to their death.

As the pallbearers lower the coffin into the ground, I consider all Oates's victims. I count the men who've been executed for treason since Oates made his revelations. There are Green, Berry, and Hill, and others, like Matthew, who were caught up in the panic and did not survive the disease and distress of Newgate. There are five Catholic Lords languishing in the Tower, and several prominent politicians who lost their positions because of the way they dealt with the Plot. There are the three priests I saw tried, all dead now. Then there are countless Catholics forced out of the city, losing friends, livelihoods. Not to mention the pain endured by William, Nat, and myself, through our entanglement with him. I glance at my husband's profile. Nat can't forgive himself that he had to leave me after Martha died, but there's no doubt in my mind about who's truly at fault.

The sound of earth rattling down on the coffin brings me out of my reverie. I want to see how William is faring, but some movement beyond him, near the iron gates, draws my eye instead. Several men are loitering there, peering through the bars at the mourners. There's nothing unusual about that, but the build, the height, and the bulk, something in the way one of them holds himself, makes my nerves scream. I tear my eyes away for a second and then look again. I'm not wrong.

"He's here!"

"What? Where?" Nat doesn't ask who I mean.

"There. William must not see him."

"Stay here. I'll meet you back at the house." Nat releases my hand and slips out of the crowd, half walking, half running, toward the gate. Of course, I follow. Nat moves quickly. He bursts through the gate and is on Oates in seconds.

"You!" He pushes him with both hands so that Oates stumbles back away from the gate and into the road.

"Hey!" One of his cronies tries to take Nat's arm, but he strikes at him with an elbow.

"You!" Nat hisses again, going for Oates, shoving him across the road and towards a narrow alley. My breath catches in my throat. My teeth are clenched. I'm screaming silently – yes, get him away from here, take him by the throat, do more. Hurt him.

One of Oates's friends jumps Nat from behind, but he's ready. He twists away and kicks out, making contact with a fat midriff, sending the man sprawling.

There are three of them, though, and Nat is only one. In the gloom, he launches himself at Oates, but Oates steps aside and Nat staggers forward, off balance. Oates kicks hard at Nat's shins. My hand is at my mouth at the crack of boot on bone. As Nat stumbles, they yank him by the coat and throw him down the dark alley. It's almost pitch black. I grip the railings of the churchyard and hold myself back. I'm desperate to go to him but can only make out dark shapes. Nat pulls himself up, but they kick him as he finds his knees, and he goes down again. They give him a few more kicks as he lies there, and then they begin to laugh. Tears slide down my cheeks.

"Well, Mr. Thompson. What a pleasant surprise." Oates's nasal whine is breathy but thick with satisfaction. 'What a terrier you are. No wonder they call you Towser in the papers. Did you see that picture of Mr. Thompson in the *Weekly Pacquet*?'

His friends snigger. Nat's attacks in *The Observator* have attracted attention, and those rumours that he is a secret Catholic have never quite been dispelled, despite no-one coming forward to support Miles Prance's testimony. Nat continues to be depicted as a snapping little dog, either on a leash held by a priest or sitting in the Pope's lap.

"Might I pick myself out of the gutter?" Nat asks.

"Literally you may. I can't speak for metaphorically." Oates titters at his own wit as Nat struggles to his feet. "Poor Mr. Thompson. I fear you will not look as pretty as usual tomorrow morning." Oates shakes his head, his eyes large with feigned concern. "Shall we go?" he says to his friends.

They turn and begin to walk away, but Nat is not finished.

"I'm fascinated by your recent ventures into publication, Mr. Oates," he calls after them. His voice is strained, every word must be costing him a volley of pain. Oates stops at the top of the alley. "Although the plot narrative remains my favourite. Yes, something in the nature of a Homeric effort, I thought. I even had some time for your style and turn of phrase. A better grasp on the truth might befit a man of the cloth, however."

"The truth?" Oates doesn't move. He doesn't sound worried – why would he, with those two thugs flanking him? – but he is listening.

"I'm very fond of the truth," Nat says. "Passionate about it, even. And about history. Personal history. I like to know where a man comes from. What his record says of him. After all, any man can call himself many things: an apothecary, a lawyer, a man of property, a Doctor of Divinity even, but for all these there must be evidence. Evidence of truth."

Oates stares. His eyes bulge angrily, and the words that would send his thugs back onto Nat are surely twitching at his fat lips. At that moment a coach clatters down the street towards them. All three turn their heads at the sound, and Nat manages to stagger a few more steps up the alley. A group of men walk down the street towards them. With witnesses coming, they surely won't attack him again. Nat takes the opportunity to goad Oates further.

"I know all about Hastings, Oates. I know what you did to Parker there. An interesting tale you told. I wonder what you took as inspiration?" Oates flinches and Nat plunges on. "I know what kind of man you were in the Navy, and what kind of man you were in the Fuller's Rent Tavern. You, Titus Oates, have climbed up into this city's heart on the bodies of innocent men. Every day you walk the street in the robes of my religion you are an affront to me and the rest of London. And one day, Oates, they will see you as I do."

I long to clap my hands and cheer my dear, brave, foolish husband, but dare not make a sound. For a moment, Oates's face squirms with anger and hate but then, as if a fragrant smell had wafted under his nose, he breaks into a smile. "Fine words, Mr. Thompson. But then you are all words, aren't you? When you speak against me, what happens? Nothing." With that, he claps the shoulders of his friends and they move off without a backward glance.

I'm across the street and in Nat's arms the second they are out of sight.

***

He has to lean on me and clutches his ribs as we stagger home, but his grin is as wide as the Thames. I kiss away the blood on his lip.

"You were wonderful," I say.

"I took a beating!"

"I wanted to hit him myself."

"Anne!" He is smiling down at me. We are nearly home.

"In fact, I did slap him in the face once. At the Pope-burning procession." His jaw falls open and I begin to laugh, but then stop. "I want you," I say.

Nat's eyes widen in shock.

We hasten home and rush to couple together. It is hot and tender; such a release that when it's over I bury my face in the pillow to hide the tears. When I turn my head, I find that he has done the same.

Chapter Twenty-Five

Nat

Two days after Medbourne's funeral, William and I set out for Primrose Hill. It is raining again but easing away to a thin drizzle, so we save ourselves the cost of a coach and walk. William urged me to let him help find out more about Godfrey's death, and I am glad of a companion, even a miserable one, after all those quiet months in the north. It's no weather for chit-chat, but at one point I mention Anne and this nonsensical idea that she should visit Judith Pamphlin. William, like Henry, finds nothing wrong with the idea.

"It's too much for her," I say. "After all she has been through."

"Your wife is stronger than you think."

"She really struck Oates in the face at the procession?"

"Full in the face. She did not hesitate." For the first time in days, William smiles.

The walk takes nearly an hour, so when we arrive I'm more than ready to sample the wares at The Horseshoe Tavern. My ankle and ribs ache as a result of that run-in with Oates, but the bruises spur me on. This pursuit of Oates began in my desire to find favour with the King and line my coffers, but there is much more at stake now. His affronts to justice cannot be allowed to continue. *He* cannot be allowed to continue. This morning, we are making enquiries about the night Godfrey's body was found. Why was Godfrey strangled in Somerset House, but then found with a sword in him, all the way out here? There must be a reason, but as we walk up the rough path to the tavern door my optimism falters.

It's not the most enticing establishment: a squat, square, two storey building, more weathered grey than white, and with a series of stables and outbuildings unsteadily shambled up next to it. There are cracks in the glass of several windows, and inside is not much better. Light from the windows crosses the worn wooden floor like the bare struts of a broken fan. Otherwise, it's generally dark, and the damp mix of wet wood and spilt liquor puts me in mind of mildewed sheets and wet stockings. As we make our way to the bar, the soles of my shoes stick. I dread to think when the floor was last washed. Nobody appears to have heard the door open and close. William tries a polite cough.

"What is it?" calls a gruff voice from below. Moments later, a bald head and broad shoulders rise out of a square hole on the other side of the bar, and our host ascends into view. "Sorry, sirs," he says, breathing deeply, "just down checking on barrels while all was quiet. What can I get you?"

"Ale, please." We watch him pour our drinks. "Are you Rawson?" I ask. He looks up at me and nods. His face resembles a worn leather football, shiny and badly-shaped through overuse. "Often this quiet?"

"Sometimes. Never very busy this time of year. But mostly busier than this."

"Wasn't this where they held the inquest over that magistrate who was murdered a while back?"

"It was." Rawson turns his back and begins wiping down bottles.

I sigh and clear my throat. "Perhaps you could join us. We've an interest in what happened to Godfrey. I'd be happy to buy you an ale or two. If you could spare us the time?"

That catches his interest. I ignore William whispering that if we have to bribe every witness, we'll be in serious trouble in short order. And besides, it works. A gulp or two of beer and John Rawson becomes refreshingly loquacious.

"First I knew of the whole affair," he says, "was when two of my regulars came in on the Thursday afternoon. They were talking about how they'd seen someone's sword scabbard, stick, belt, and gloves left lying in one of the fields at the foot of the hill. They thought some fellow might have been sleeping it off down in the ditch, but I'd seen soldiers hunting

170

hedgehogs around there a few days before and suspected the young fools might have left something of value. I gave them a drink on the house to show me where this ditch was, and so when the rain let up – about five o'clock it was – out we went. Right enough, the scabbard was still there. Then we saw it. The light was bad but there was definitely a long dark shape down in the ditch. Something was there that shouldn't have been.

"We scrambled down, none too willingly, mind, but we did it. He was face-down, thank God, and his head was covered. I wasn't ready to see his face. I left the two of them there while I went for the local Constable, John Brown." Rawson picks up his tankard and drinks deeply.

"Where does he live, this John Brown?" asks William.

"Not far. Near St Giles Pound. He'll be here any minute. Always calls in on his way home."

'Would you take us to the ditch?"

"You are mighty interested, aren't you?" A light of speculation crosses his eyes, but then he blinks, and it's gone. Rawson doesn't care why we want to see the ditch or hear his story, and that suits me very well. He shrugs. "Not I," he says, "but Brown will." He nods at the door. "Here he is now."

Constable Brown has the air of a man who has told this tale many times over but does not tire of it. Godfrey's murder made him well-known in these parts, he tells us. After knocking back a pint of dark ale, he is more than happy to show us where the body was found.

I have one last question for the landlord. "Have you seen much of Miles Prance lately?"

Rawson's eyebrows lift, creating waves that ripple the skin over his wide bald head. "Who is he?"

"A silversmith. A small man. Sandy hair. I was told he was a regular here."

"Never heard of him."

Outside, Brown leads us down a couple of deep rutted lanes running between the patchwork of fields, and then points across to a drainage ditch just at the south edge of Primrose Hill. In a sense it is remarkable for being so unremarkable. It's not particularly large, or deep, but it runs at least ten feet along and is a mess of brambles and briars. The ground falls away steeply from where we stand.

"Where was Godfrey's scabbard and so on?" I ask.

"Right here."

This is significant. Why bring a dead man to a place like this and then stab him? That must have been what occurred. Otherwise, why would the scabbard be here? "And where was the body?"

Brown looks at me and then at the ditch.

"In you go," he says. "I'll tell you when you're in the right spot."

I take a moment to add a good pair of shoes and stockings to my list of Oates's victims, and clamber down. Freezing water floods my toes. I slosh along – thoroughly ridiculous – but to my relief, Brown doesn't keep me down here longer than necessary.

"Stop!" he calls. "There, where you stand now, that's where the head was."

"And the feet running that way?" I gesture along the ditch away from where Brown stands.

"Yes."

What a drab end. The sky is a band of grey, and the green of the grass has been sucked away in the gloom.

"Tell us about the body being moved," I say, once I've struggled out.

"It was early evening, the light was gone, and I was keen to move quickly,' he says. "I went down, same as you did. I found a tall man lying face-down, with a sword run through him so that the tip stuck out of his back some seven or eight inches. I called a couple of the lads to help roll the body to its side, so I could look at his face. As soon as they did, I knew what we were dealing with."

"You recognised him?" I ask, glancing at William. For all his willingness to join me, now he barely seems to be following the conversation.

"At once. He was well known, particularly to those of us working in the law. A fine man. I am sorry to think of him dying in that way and at the hands of those damned papists. It was a travesty."

We walk back to the tavern in silence and bitter disappointment. Brown is no help. He is as convinced as everyone else that Godfrey was murdered by Catholics. I'm tempted to let it drop and go home, but that means admitting failure.

"What did you do next?" I ask.

"I made sure I was clear in my mind about how the body lay and pulled out the sword. I carried his hat and wig in my own hands as the men brought the body here."

Pushing through the tavern doors, he points at a long trestle table under the windows. "We laid him out on that table. Rawson brought candles. The place was busy for once – wouldn't you know it – and I had some trouble keeping back all the nosy bastards, pressing forward, trying to get a look at the corpse. Everyone knew the man was missing, I suppose. It took some stern words before I could get the space I needed to do the necessary. I searched the body first."

"What did you find?"

"Enough to show it was no robbery. There were several guineas in one pocket, as well as some pieces of gold and half a crown. In the other, he had some silver and a couple of rings. He wore another ring on one finger, and of course there were also the sword and the scabbard, his gloves, and his stick. I had them all laid out next to the body and left three fellows on guard."

"While you…?"

"Went to notify the family."

Brown says it was around ten o'clock when he arrived at Hartshorn Lane. "That old manservant – Moor was he called? – answered the door and took me into the parlour where Godfrey's two brothers, Michael and Benjamin, were in conference with Sergeant Ramsay. He's an officer of the court. Sir Edmund's disappearance was a matter of grave concern, as you know. It was my unpleasant duty to confirm the family's worst fears."

"How did they take it?"

173

"Much as you would expect, I'd say. One of the brothers swore a little. Damned and blasted, said he had known his brother was dead, that kind of thing. The sergeant from the court slid off to take the news to Whitehall."

"Who identified the body?"

"Benjamin Godfrey. The other, Michael, was keen to remain in town in case they were wanted at Whitehall. He's a very fine fellow, and very full of his own consequence. I remember he was full of talk of repercussions and implications."

"What did you take him to mean?" I ask. William has stopped paying any attention. He's been no help at all.

"That's clear enough," says Brown. "He thought his brother had been killed for political reasons. He hadn't been robbed. It was political or personal. Had to be one of the two."

"I see. And you brought Benjamin Godfrey back here?"

"Yes. He was very shaken up at the sight of the body. Upset by the dark bruises round his brother's neck. He wanted to know where Godfrey's cravat was, but it wasn't found with the body. He made us take him out by torchlight to look at the ditch. After that, he agreed to go back into town and give the news to the rest of the family. I reported to Sergeant Ramsay, who assured me that the Middlesex Coroner, Mr. Cooper, had been notified. It was a long day, but all done right and proper the way I like it."

Rawson brings us another round of drinks without being asked. It pains me to pay for them, or to stay there a minute longer listening to Brown who is shaking his head and opining over it all.

"He was left lying like a dog, face-down in a ditch, Godfrey was." Brown says. "Murdered for what he knew and because he was a good, upstanding, honest Protestant."

I down my drink, hope souring with every swallow.

***

On the long walk back to the city, my irritation at William can't be contained.

"What the hell was that about?"

"What?"

"You barely said a word in there. Were you even listening? I'm not sure why you bothered to come."

He is silent for a moment or two while I simmer. When he does speak, he surprises me.

"Why Miles Prance?"

"What? What do you mean, why Miles Prance?"

"Why did you ask about him?"

"Because he said at the trial of Green, Berry, and Hill that he was a member of a club here and that leaving the body here was his suggestion. Another lie, clearly."

"Another lie?"

I tell William about Prance's appearance before the Privy Council where he claimed to have seen me taking Mass.

"I did not know that was Miles Prance."

I have plenty of choice remarks I could make about Prance at this point, but I hold my tongue. And besides, William is not finished.

"That tavern," he says. "It's not the sort of place Miles would ever go to. It's far from his home. It's falling down. I doubt he has even heard of the place."

"Miles? You know a lot about Miles Prance, suddenly."

"Not suddenly. I have known him for several years."

I swallow. "You did not say so."

"You did not ask."

I don't like his tone, but remind myself that William is grieving. He has not been the same man since his arrest and the loss of his job, truth be told.

"Well, I am asking now," I say. "Prance lied at the murder trial. He said he was a frequent visitor to this tavern. The rest was surely lies, too. Maybe the key to this mess is getting him to tell the truth now. But why would he do that? Lord knows what kind of hold Oates has on him."

"Can't you guess?" says William. "Miles Prance is a member of the Fuller's Rent Tavern. Just like I am. Just as Matthew was."

"But he's a married man! His wife was at the murder trial,

175

shaking her head, denying he was tortured."

William laughs softly. "You are more naïve than I imagined, Nat," he says. "Let me put some pressure on Miles Prance. The fact that he has a wife might work in our favour. He is a weak man. I should know."

Chapter Twenty-Six

Anne

Nat does not embrace my proposed visit to the housekeeper, Mistress Pamphlin, but neither does he forbid it. He is unhappy after his visit to Primrose Hill, for the first time faltering in his certainty that there is more to Sir Edmund Godfrey's death than is currently known. I need to help. Nat is not the only one who Titus Oates hurt last summer. And so, I walk past the rising mass of St Paul's Cathedral, flinching at the sound of metal on stone, and thinking furiously about what I will say to Mistress Pamphlin. For the past couple of days, I have thought of little else, working up convoluted stories to explain my arrival at her door uninvited, but this morning the way to do it came to me clearly. Since then, I have been rehearsing what I will say. I have only one chance to impress her.

She lives in a small back street, just far enough away from the Cathedral to escape the dust of these years of rebuilding. It is a tidy property. Her windows are clean and there are drying marks at the doorstep. Mistress Pamphlin has been at work already this morning. With my heart in mouth, I raise my knuckles and knock.

"Yes?" An old woman with a long nose and a small frowning mouth opens the door barely wide enough for her own head and shoulders. She regards me less than favourably.

"Mistress Pamphlin?"

"Who is asking? I hope you are not selling anything." She cranes her neck to see if anyone else is here.

"I am alone," I say with a smile. "My name is Anne Thompson. I was hoping, if you were not too busy, that I

177

might introduce myself and ask you a few questions."

"Questions? What kind of questions? What sort of funny business is this?"

"Nothing untoward, Mistress Pamphlin, please, let me assure you. Here." I have a basket over my arm and I lift it toward her, pulling back the cloth to show her some warm scones I have baked. "My name will mean nothing to you, I am sure, but my husband has written to you. Nathaniel Thompson?"

Her eyebrows rise in recognition, and she releases her grip on the door a little. "So, when I refuse to see him he sends his wife to bother me? What kind of a man does that?"

"Oh, no. He has no idea I am here. And please, if I am wrong, please take these scones as an apology. It was simply that he mentioned you frequently and remarked that you must know so much more about Sir Edmund than anyone would realise. I thought how true that must be. And then I thought that perhaps you would rather be visited and spoken to in a friendly way over a cup of tea and something to eat than be sent letters and be quizzed and questioned. And so here I am."

"I have nothing bad to say about my employer."

"Of course not!"

For a moment or two we stand on the threshold. I have pinned my hopes on the idea that her loneliness mixed with my very nearly truthful appeal will be enough for her to invite me in. She looks me over. I have dressed simply and neatly. The scones smell good. I am no threat to anyone.

At last, she shrugs. "I will heat the water then, come inside."

Mistress Pamplin's room is simple but comfortable. She has a starched white tablecloth and an ordered basket of threads and wool next to her chair. A faded green and red hanging screens off a section where I presume she sleeps.

As soon as I am seated, she proceeds to question me. "So, Mistress Thompson, your husband is a writer. Not the most stable profession, but common enough in this day and age. No children yet?"

"No," I say. "There was a child. But she died." I brace

178

myself for words of sympathy, but she offers none.

"You are young. I imagine there will be others. Your husband has made quite a name for himself."

"He has."

"But he is on a wild goose chase now, you realise that?"

"I have thought him wrong before, but found that his instincts were correct."

"And his instinct now is what? That what they say happened to Sir Edmund is false? That was what he implied in his letter. But no-one hangs themselves, stabs themselves, and then finds their way into a ditch now, do they?"

"No, they do not."

She has not yet sat down, although I am seated by the fire with my hands folded in my lap. "So, you agree that you are wasting your time, yet here you are all the same?"

I give her the most disingenuous smile I can muster. "Who doesn't like a scone, a cup of tea, and a gossip?" I say. "At least you will not be troubled with any more unwanted letters."

Behind her, the kettle begins to bubble and the iron set of her jaw relaxes.

***

"Sir Edmund was a very sombre and serious gentleman," she tells me. "Not one for laughter, or if he was, I didn't know it. He had some kind of illness in his youth which affected his studies. Although he was a fine gentleman, he was not one to flaunt his accomplishments. He ran a plain house and lived a simple, good life. I would like to tell you more, but am not sure what there is to tell."

"Anything you tell me is helpful," I say. "And your tea is excellent." I grope for something to add. "Your work day began early, I imagine."

She settles her narrow hips in her chair.

"Of course," she said. "Young Elizabeth was up first – she was the maid."

"Worth her hire?"

"I would say so," says Mistress Pamphlin, although her

179

expression suggests that she has not always thought so kindly. "She was responsible for making up the kitchen stove and lighting a fire in the master's study. I would be up not long after Elizabeth. The master had a taste for fresh bread, and he always praised my rolls and my pastry." She smiles down into her teacup. "First, though, I made breakfast for myself, Elizabeth, and Henry."

"Henry?"

"Henry Moor. Sir Edmund's valet. Amongst other things."

"You did not approve of Henry Moor?"

"He was a tricky one, that's all I'm saying. Nothing more than that."

I take a sip of tea and regard Mistress Pamphlin over the rim. "And after breakfast?"

"Then the master would either work in his study or go out on business. That could be him gone until ten in the evening, or only for a few hours. No day was the same. He would call me to him before he went out, and give his instructions for dinner." She puts her head on one side. "He was not one for parties, but what a man for meetings," she says. "He was forever out here and there, discussing parish business, or lawyering, or visiting property, or seeing to the coal and the wood business. He kept his hands busy, that one."

"And when he was at home? How did he amuse himself?"

"Like any other gentlemen, I suppose. Reading and writing letters."

She breaks off, and we are silent for a few moments thinking about the dead man. It is a melancholy picture. What kind of man spends all hours at work and then closets himself up alone? Where were his friends, his pastimes, his diversions?

"No friendships?' I ask.

"Not many. He saw his family. His brothers. His cousin." Her voice trails away.

"And?"

She shakes her head. "You will likely not have heard of him, but he did have a friendship with an Irishman; a faith healer, would you believe? With an outlandish name. Valentine

180

something."

"Valentine Greatrakes? My mother is much taken with him." I roll my eyeballs, and am pleased to see Mistress Pamphlin nod in agreement.

"I don't hold with that sort of nonsense," she says. We sip our tea and she takes a second scone. With renewed confidence, I press on.

"Were you there when Titus Oates visited Sir Edmund?"

"Yes. He came twice, Dr. Oates did, both times with another man, Israel Tonge. Sir Edmund had many visitors and kept many papers secured on his clients' behalf. But those two did stand out. Even before we knew what they were involved in."

"In what way did they stand out?"

"Voices were raised. An argument of some kind. Sir Godfrey showed them the door himself when it was his normal custom to call on Moor for that. And after that second visit, he stayed in his workroom for hours. He refused his supper and would not even let me bring him wine. Whatever they said to him, he was most unhappy."

"What can you tell me about his disappearance?"

Mistress Pamphlin takes a deep breath and blows out her cheeks. Suddenly there are tears in her eyes. "To live in a house where a person has been murdered, and a good person at that, is not a happy experience. You know he went missing on the Saturday? At first, it was a normal day, just ordinary. But then..." She bends toward the fire and gives it a few firm thrusts with the poker.

"I was in the kitchen around dinner time, making a sauce, when Henry Moor appeared in the doorway. He was all of a fidget, full of questions. Had I seen the master that morning? What orders had he given? When did I expect him home? I'd no time for such chatter and told him so directly, but still he hung about the doorway. I asked him what need he had of the master anyway at that time of day. He gave me some cheek about pestering him with questions. Before I could point out that he was the one with all the questions, he was off again. I went on with my work, but Moor's jitters set me thinking." She stops and appears lost in thought.

181

"What were you thinking?"

"Well, I don't know why I'm even telling you," she says, shaking herself slightly. "It has nothing to do with the matter. Yet, it is all in my mind now, so you shall hear it. Moor's tetchiness reminded me that Sir Edmund had been rattled the night before. I had knocked at his study at nine o'clock to see if he needed anything further before I retired. I found him out of his seat and stuffing papers in the fire. He was in shirtsleeves, with the arms rolled up and his collar band discarded on the floor beside his chair. His hands were full of folded documents, which he was thrusting furiously into the flames."

"My goodness! What was it? What could he have been burning?"

She looks up at me tight-lipped and slightly pink in the cheeks. "I thought it might have been something of mine. I had a cottage mortgaged to him. I feared he might be burning my deeds in with Lord knew what else. But no. He said my deeds were safe and that I had nothing to fear. He said that for me, all was safe."

"And what did you take to be his meaning?"

"I took nothing from it at the time, except disliking his manner of speaking to me. Later, I wondered if he was hiding something. If he was, it did him no good. They killed him anyway."

A hundred ideas about what Godfrey might have been burning wheel around my mind. "How did he say the words? With what emphasis? He said that you had nothing to fear. Was there any implication that although you were safe, *he* was not?'

"Oh certainly," says Mistress Pamphlin, folding her arms across her chest. "And that was how the brothers, Mr. Michael and Mr. Benjamin, took his meaning. They said it meant their brother knew his life was at risk. And he was right."

"When did you realise he was missing?"

She tells me that the uneasiness felt by Godfrey's household grew throughout that Saturday. When the master failed to arrive home in the early evening as expected, the three servants held conference in the kitchen. It was agreed between them that Henry Moor should go to the brother, Michael Godfrey. He returned with the instruction that they wait until morning before taking things further, so they each took a small brandy and then retired for the night.

The following morning, she confirmed with her own eyes that Godfrey's bed had not been slept in. Moor then fetched the two brothers, Michael and Benjamin, and between them they tried to contact Godfrey's close acquaintances and business colleagues – anyone who might have seen him the day before. Mistress Pamphlin had tried to be optimistic, but the brothers and Moor were shaking their heads. As early as the Sunday, she overheard them talking about papists following Sir Edmund around the city.

"Is it true that the brothers were very clear and vocal in declaring that Sir Edmund was murdered by papists? Did they ever indicate what led them to that conclusion?"

She shakes her head. "Not really. But we were all at sixes and sevens. Moor was absent all hours of the day and night. Mr. Michael spoke to me and Elizabeth and made it clear it was the papists they feared. Then the body was found. And there's no doubting the fact that the master was much put about by being involved with Titus Oates."

"Can you remember anything else about Oates's visits? Do you know what they argued about?"

"No. I only know that after their second visit he was particularly distressed. He wouldn't eat or drink. He only called for more candles and then sent Moor out delivering letters."

"Where is Henry Moor these days, do you know?"

"Not the least idea. He disappeared into thin air, not days after the funeral. But he's no loss to anyone, that one."

Chapter Twenty-Seven

Nat

Our investigation into Godfrey's death isn't moving forward fast enough. I want – I *need* – to see Oates brought to heel. In order to undermine public belief in him and his plots, I take regular aim at him in *The Observator*. In every edition, I make sure to launch a personal attack on the good doctor. I dwell on the lack of evidence for his doctorate and his bizarre career, particularly in Hastings and in the Navy. I send Kineally back to every place where Titus has lived and worked, and have him gather criticism upon criticism of Oates's lifestyle, his language, his religious attitudes, his drunkenness. Anything that is said against Oates, Henry and I print. I invent a series of dialogues featuring Titus and one of his fawning little cronies. My trick is that the friend is terribly dim and keeps asking questions that Titus does not wish to answer. When Kineally finally obtains evidence that Oates's doctorate from Salamanca is a complete fiction, we devote a whole page of *The Observator* to Titus being probed by this "friend" for details of his time studying divinity.

"He is still dangerous," cautions William, sitting back in his chair at our dining table.

"What can he do that he has not done already?" I say.

William opens his mouth as if to speak, but then closes it again. Anne, bless her kind heart, asks him a question about one of Henry's print boys who has been unwell. The awkward moment dissolves. William continues to be morose but Anne brings out the best in him. We are all assembled – Henry, William, Anne, Kineally and I – to review what we have learned so far about Sir Edmund Godfrey's death. Anne describes her visit to Mistress Pamphlin.

"What I want to know," she says in summary, "well, there are several things I want to know. First, where is Henry Moor?"

I nod at Kineally. He will take that on.

"Then, what did Godfrey burn the night before he disappeared?"

"That may be relevant," said Henry. "A man does not usually know that he is going to be murdered. Murder victims are not known for putting their papers in order before they die. A suicide, on the other hand..."

"True," I say. "Yes. I would very much like to know what it was."

"Then there is the question of Oates and this other man, Tonge," says Anne. "Why was their business so upsetting to Sir Edmund?"

"I will go and visit Israel Tonge," I say. "Although after what his son did to us, I may struggle to keep a civil tongue in my head."

"Use it to your advantage," says Henry. "He is a lonely, crazed old man. Tell him he is lucky that you have not sought revenge against Simpson for his attempt to entrap you. Tell him he owes you some answers."

"I shall. Anything else?"

"Only Valentine Greatrakes," says Anne. "Such a strange choice of friend for the magistrate."

I agree with her. "Does anyone know anything about him?" The men around the table shake their heads, but Anne bites her lip.

"I do," she says. "My mother is one of his clients."

***

The next day, as I head off to see what I can shake out of old Israel Tonge, I mull over the matter of the Irishman, Greatrakes. I told Anne that it is probably not worth pursuing. She has her reasons for not seeing her mother and I have agreed with her, at least in part because it suits me to forget their disapproval. When I returned from Edinburgh, she told me that she was finished with her family, excepting only Sarah, and I did not shed a tear for her decision. But now? How much have I thought about what is best for Anne? And am I even thinking of her now, or do I just want an easy route to talking to Valentine Greatrakes about Godfrey? Perhaps a little of both? The man I was before those months alone in Edinburgh was never so introspective or questioning.

Israel Tonge is perfectly horrified to see me. I lean against the door frame with my arms folded, and smile broadly at him as he peers out. Behind wire frames, his large eyes blink in alarm. Brown liver spots dance across his bald head and grey hair sprouts from his fleshy ears. They stretch south like melted wax.

"What?" He is all bluster and spittle as I push open the door and stroll past him. "I shall… I shall call a constable!"

I find my way into his little parlour room. He has no choice but to follow.

"Mr. Thompson," he begins, his hands fluttering. "My son —"

"I'm not interested in your son," I say. "I want to sit down and talk to you, not about Simpson, but about you. Where shall I sit?"

He is flummoxed, but gestures to one of the chairs and then sits down opposite me.

"I want to talk about Titus Oates. And about Sir Edmund Godfrey. I take it you can spare me half an hour." The room is full of open books and disordered papers. Under the window, a large oak table is piled with manuscripts, and towers of papers are stacked up against the walls. Israel's reputation is well known. If the disorder in the room is reflected in his mind, then rumours of his weak hold on reality may be well-founded.

"Why should I speak to you?" he snaps.

"Mmm." I pretend to consider this for a moment and then bend forward, glaring directly into his mossy eyes. "I said I wasn't interested in Simpson – and I'm not, at least not right now. But that could change. I would argue your family owes me some assistance, after what he did last year."

"But you are not after him?" Tonge seems genuinely worried for his son.

"No. I won't touch him. But you must answer my questions honestly. Can you do that?"

Tonge nods.

"Excellent."

They say Israel Tonge's mind was shattered when he lost his living to the same Great Fire that had brought Godfrey a knighthood. He's a fanatic, one of many who have laid the blame for every disaster in London at the door of the Catholics. He has been finding out plots and foul conspiracies every year since 1666. Once he knows I am not after revenge against his fool of a son, he becomes quite talkative, as lonely old men often will.

"Did Titus ever stay here?" I ask.

"Yes, yes, of course he did." Tonge's forehead erupts with wormy wrinkles. "He had nowhere else to stay, poor man. He was so harshly treated by those Jesuits." Tonge's fingers dig into the arm of his chair.

"Was he a good companion?"

"Yes. He was always busy, mind you. In and out. In and out. And then working on his evidence." Tonge gestures towards the table by the window and I try to picture Titus there, pen in hand. It is a struggle. In my mind, Oates is always swaggering around, with his flock of followers in tow.

"This was the evidence that you took before Sir Edmund Godfrey?"

Tonge nods.

"Why Godfrey?"

He looks up at me sharply. "Why Godfrey?"

"Yes. How did you come to take your evidence to him? There are so many magistrates in London. Why choose him?" Tonge looks unsure. I wait.

"We were advised to," he says.

"By?" It's like walking through mud.

"The Lord Chief Justice."

"The Lord Chief Justice? Scroggs?"

Tonge sneers at my surprise. "Yes, of course Scroggs. He

was tasked by His Majesty to investigate our findings, and did so thoroughly. Then he asked us to lodge Titus's statements with Sir Edmund Godfrey, and tell him to show them to no-one. And so we did."

"And when was that?"

"The first time was in the beginning of September."

"And you both went? You and Oates?"

"Yes."

"What was your impression of Godfrey?"

He stares off into the fireplace for a few moments. "Well, he was very stiff." I send a silent invocation to the heavens to help me find some patience.

"He was formal – which I suppose you would expect – but he was cold to the point of rudeness, very distant. Titus detested him, but then he is quick to take dislikes, isn't he?" Tonge may have forgotten who I am, speaking about Oates so familiarly, but I have no intention of interrupting his flow of thought.

"He was reluctant to take our evidence," Tonge continues. "Godfrey asked numerous questions before he'd even look at Titus's statement. Perhaps that was what Titus didn't like? What do you think?"

I manage to shrug my shoulders. No doubt Tonge is a little wandered in his understanding, but his grasp of the past is firm so I keep probing. "Can you remember any of the questions?"

"I suppose so." Tonge works his fingers backwards and forwards across his brow. "He asked what it was about. And Titus said it was about fires. About criminals planning fires in London. Then he asked who these criminals were and Titus mentioned the priest, Fenwick. Godfrey said he knew him a little. He was even stiffer with us after that."

"Is that the Fenwick who was hanged with the other priests?"

"Yes. He was tried with Whitbread and Ireland."

"And do you remember anything else about that visit with Godfrey?"

"No. Should I?"

I suppress my dislike of him. "Why did you visit him

again?"

"Because Titus had more evidence."

"Of the plot?"

"Yes, of the plot." Tonge looks at me wide-eyed. "Titus was in the hands of those murderous priests right up until the morning that we saw the Privy Council. I barely saw him through the month of September. We knew that his secret could be discovered at any time, but he had promised to find as much evidence as he could, and was risking his life for his country."

I rather think that he was spending his hours in the Fuller's Rent Tavern sponging off Matthew Medbourne, but there is nothing to be gained by sharing that. "And how did Godfrey receive you that second time?"

"Very rudely. He was most irritable." Tonge knocks his teeth together, once, twice, three times, while he considers. "He didn't ask any questions. Or offer refreshments. I was anxious myself. We had been called before the Council. Our revelations were to be shared with the King and his closest advisors. It was a momentous day." Tonge's voice trails away, and I suspect he is no longer seeing Godfrey's face. Instead, he is remembering appearing before the King and his council, being given lodgings in Whitehall, finally being taken seriously. I doubt there is any point in asking anything further, but I do it anyway.

"So, the visit was without incident?"

"Not entirely," says Tonge brightly. "Titus and Godfrey argued about how Godfrey tied up the papers. Titus was afraid the pages would become disordered. Godfrey lost his temper. He was blustering at Titus all the way to the door. When we saw who was walking down the street towards the house, though, we were all astonished. I remember it precisely."

"Someone on Godfrey's street? Who was it?"

"Edward Coleman."

I'm completely taken aback, and Tonge relishes the fact. "Yes! Can you imagine? What a trick of fate. Titus had just lodged his evidence against Edward Coleman, and there he was, large as life. I don't think he saw us. He crossed the road and disappeared."

"And Titus? Or Godfrey? What did they have to say about Coleman?"

"Godfrey disappeared back into the house without another word, but Titus? Titus was most disturbed. He believed that the Catholics were following him. He feared that they knew he was informing on them and would set their assassins on him. But by that evening, we were lodging in Whitehall and he was quite, quite safe."

The thought of Oates safe and snug in Whitehall is never one that has pleased me greatly.

"So, do you see him much nowadays then? Titus?" I ask, as I prepare to leave.

Tonge shakes his head. "Oh no,' he says. 'Never at all." For a moment he looks off into the distance, as if to some brighter space beyond this room. "He is an important man, you know," says Israel Tonge. "Titus is very busy. I'm very proud of him. Very proud."

Chapter Twenty-Eight

William

In the weeks after Matthew's death, Nat's point of view finds a growing audience. A year or so ago, the air was so full of panic that no-one would listen. But the hysteria of the early months of Titus's revelations has dissipated. *The Observator* sells well. Anne's father writes to her, suggesting that the family may be coming round to her choice of husband. Titus still dines out on his stories and draws crowds when he preaches about the Catholic threat, but there is no doubt his influence diminishes.

That only makes me more afraid. Any cornered animal will lash out, and I fear for my friend who every day attacks Oates. Nat will not drop this until Titus is disgraced, and the creature will fight that at every step. I want to kill him. I dream of lying in wait outside a tavern door and stabbing him in the neck and chest. But God knows, I am no hero.

Three priests were hanged on the basis of my false evidence and a tide of prejudice that is only now abating. Matthew is dead. The damage is irreparable.

Some things, once done, cannot be undone. This is the kind of talk I used to give the boys at school. Second chances are few and far between. Mistakes are made, but we must not let our mistakes define us. We move on. We repair what we can. These are maxims that I have rattled out for years. Now it is my turn to put my own homilies into practice.

I visit Miles Prance. I know him; I know that he lied for Titus Oates and I understand why. I threaten him. I threaten, as I am sure Titus did, that I will tell his wife about his friends at the Fuller's Rent Tavern. It is a side of Miles's life that no wife could ever understand. He is not a bad man. He is only a weak man, like me. I promise that if he tells Nat the truth, we will make sure Titus is too far down the road to Newgate to retaliate. He can take his wife and leave London if he wants to, but he must come clean first. Thank God, the man has a conscience. In many ways, Miles is another of Titus's victims. He will come to Sam's Coffee Shop and tell his story to Nat.

***

Miles arrives later than expected, and Nat is agitated. He has high hopes of this interview, but he's also still angry about the lies Miles told the Privy Council. He has agreed to let me take the lead, but when Miles finally appears, Nat struggles to be civil. There are a few awkward moments. While the coffee boy fills three dishes, we sit in grim silence.

"Mr. Thompson." Miles's voice comes strangled from his throat, and Nat sits back in his chair with his arms folded. "I would like to begin by making you an apology." He wipes a pale hand across his forehead. "Last year, I was persuaded to take part in… to make a statement… to—"

"To give false testimony that I was secretly a practising Roman Catholic. Yes, I do remember it."

Prance nods weakly. "And it was a false statement, for which—"

"I hope you didn't come here just to tell me that, Prance," says Nat. "I was aware at the time that you were spitting out a stream of lies. I imagine you had a reason, but as William says, what is done is done. I'm still here, after all."

"I just wish to offer an apology." Prance's lower lip presses forward in the manner of a sulky child, although I told him to expect something like this.

"What Miles has agreed to come here for," I say, "is to tell us the truth about the Godfrey trial."

"You're going to tell me that you perjured yourself?" says Nat.

Prance bites down on his lip, "Yes."

"And you will sign a statement to that effect?" I say.

Prance nods miserably, but Nat brightens like a sky cleared of clouds. "Then you are very welcome here, Mr. Prance," he says. "And you may consider your apology to me accepted."

Prance almost buckles in relief. He has pale, sandy lashes, and when he swallows, thin freckled flesh quivers over his Adam's apple like plucked chicken skin.

"Take your time, Miles. Have some coffee." I say. "Just tell Nat here what you told me. I'll take notes. Nat, Miles has promised me he will answer any question you have."

He needs no encouragement. "When did it begin?" Nat says. "How did you become involved?"

"I was arrested. One minute, I was arriving at work, the keys to my shop in my hand, the next I was being bundled along by three constables and thrown in a cell in Newgate."

Nat and I nod. We know what that feels like.

"Did they tell you why?"

"Eventually. They left me alone for three days. There was no window, no bed, just straw and shit to sleep on. You know about the noise there? And the smell?" He shakes himself a little and pushes the candle on the table to one side so that half of his face is in shadow. "At last I was taken to a different room. I was interrogated by Captain Richardson." Prance's throat trembles. "A girl, a neighbour's daughter, had informed on me. She told the authorities that I was away from home in the week that Godfrey was missing. I am a Roman Catholic. That was enough to make me a suspect."

"Were you away from home?"

"Yes. I was miles away from London. Visiting my mother."

"Why would this girl inform on you?"

"I had caught her stealing."

"Stealing what? And where?"

Prance sits up straighter. "I'm a silversmith. A good one. I've made pieces for the Queen. When I made something, I liked to take it home to show it to my wife. The neighbour's girl was forever in the house, gossiping about nothing. She would ask Hannah what I was working on and ask to try things on." Prance's nose wrinkles. "Hannah had a liking for her company. I let her try a bracelet one day. She tried to go home still wearing it. Oh, she played it all for a joke; Hannah took the whole thing as forgetfulness. But I knew. I had seen her look at the silver. I caught up with her the next day and told her I knew what she was. She informed on me for revenge."

It is a commonplace tale. In the madness wrought across the city by Titus Oates, it was not unusual for neighbour to turn on neighbour, if one was Catholic and the other not.

"And Richardson? What did he ask?"

"Very little. He asked me where I was, and I answered him as I've answered you. Then he talked. He told me that no-one would believe me. He told me that no-one would support my story. That I'd better start coming up with the truth about what had happened to Justice Godfrey or it would be worse for me than I could imagine. I didn't even know who Godfrey was, but all the prisoners were talking of it. Anyone who was a Catholic was accused of the murder."

"But still," says Nat, "you gave up Green, Berry, and Hill, to save yourself."

"No!" Prance looks horrified, but then a self-disgust that I recognise all to easily washes over his face. "At least, not then."

"Explain yourself."

Prance looks down at the table. "I was taken from my cell to be charged with secretly attending mass and cultivating Catholic clients. I was a silversmith to the Queen! And they used that against me. The courtroom was busy, even busier outside. I had spent days in the dark in Newgate, and then I was dragged out into sunlight, crowds. We were kept waiting for hours. I saw Titus Oates there, with another man I knew – not from London, but from my home. I thought it was a sign that I still had friends in the world. I begged them to help me and they promised to do all that they could.

"But when I returned to Newgate, I was taken in front of Richardson again. He said a reliable witness had seen me with the body in Somerset House. I was not even in London! They said the body had been found at the Horseshoe Tavern by Primrose Hill, and that they had witnesses who would say I was a regular there." Miles breaks off and drains his coffee cup.

Nat lowers his voice. "Did they torture you?"

"Little Ease," Miles says. "Have you heard of it?"

"No," says Nat.

"It's a hole. Somewhere in Newgate. Somewhere underneath, down one of those stairways. It's maybe ten feet high. Not wide enough to stretch your arms across. I could sit in it, but only with my knees buckled up to my chest like a snivelling schoolboy. The walls weep. They lowered me in and left me there, in the dark, for days."

"Did they feed you? Speak to you?"

"Oh no." Miles seems to find Nat's questions amusing. He sounds slightly unhinged. "After a few days in there, I told Richardson everything he suggested was correct."

"Everything?" says Nat.

"Yes. He explained what was required of me. Implicate Somerset House. Catholics. Make sure Godfrey was strangled, beaten, and stabbed, but make the stabbing later, some kind of afterthought. They would not bring me out of Little Ease until I was ready to tell them everything. That's how I came to name Green, Berry, and Hill. I knew them. They were Catholics. They knew Somerset House, as I did."

"Why three of them, though?" Nat has his hands pressed against his temples.

Miles laughs then, an ugly bitter squawk. "I thought if I named three of them then they might have more of a chance. Green wasn't even Catholic. That should have helped him. I thought between the three of them, one would be able to prove they were somewhere else. I thought that between the three of them, my story had to fall down somewhere. But I don't expect you to believe me." Miles waves a limp hand across his face and fishes in his pocket for a handkerchief.

"I don't know if I believe you or not. Either way, those men are dead," says Nat.

There is an edge in my friend's tone and disgust in his face. I will never be able to tell him the truth about my lie at the priests' trial. Bile rises in my throat.

"You have no idea," says Prance, shaking his head. "No

idea what it is like to be a Catholic these days. We are hated. Spat upon. Glared at. Ignored. People whisper behind our backs. Neighbours who once smiled and wave now turn their backs. My business has suffered. My wife is miserable. And we have done nothing."

Nat raises an eyebrow but doesn't respond to this directly. "And was it true that you went to the King and retracted the whole story?" he asks.

"It was," says Miles. "But that just bought me another trip to Little Ease. It was so cold down there that I would have cut off my own fingers and toes to stop the pain."

I'm unable to look at either of them. None of us, not Nat, myself, or even my poor Matthew, suffered such privations in Newgate. Prance's perjury can be understood. I cannot say the same of my own.

I'm so lost in my own dismay and guilt that I almost miss Nat's next question, yet it proves to be a masterstroke.

"And why, how even, did they choose you to be their witness?" he asks.

"It was Oates. He knew I could be manipulated. He promised to help me, and then did the opposite. Moor, too."

"Moor?"

"Yes. Henry Moor. He was Godfrey's manservant. He's the man I knew that was talking to Titus at the courtroom that day. They were looking for someone to frame the story the way they wanted it, and there I was. A gift."

Nat smacks his hand on the table.

"Moor," he declares. "I have Kineally looking for him already, but he has found no trace. Come on, man!" He reaches across the table and shakes Miles's shoulder. "You say you know him from your home? Well, where is that, damn it? He may be the answer to the whole riddle!"

"Ely," says Miles. "That is where you will find him."

Chapter Twenty-Nine

Nat

The evening before I leave London to track down Moor, Henry and I spend a quiet hour in Sam's Coffee House.

"Like old times," I say.

Henry shakes his head. "We cannot live in the past, Nathaniel. You are a better, stronger man since you met Anne. She has been good for you."

"You did not always think so."

He shrugs and throws me a half-smile. "What do I know of marriage?"

"You will make sure she is safe while I am away?"

"Of course. Our man will continue to follow her and watch the house. I will see her in the print shop, and if William does not walk her home, then you know I will."

I try for a little levity. "One could argue, you know, that she has also made a better man out of you. Every day, a woman in and out of your shop. I would not have imagined it. Wasn't there a Henry Broome I once knew who thought a woman in the workplace would be far too distracting? But I suppose she is helpful with feeding the boys."

He shoots me a wry look, but then he changes the subject. "What about this link between Godfrey and Edward Coleman? Have you thought any more on that?"

***

Later, at home with Anne, I tell her she has turned Henry from a confirmed misogynist into an ardent admirer.

"He is like family to me," she says.

Family.

We do not talk of Martha every day, but the loss is always with us. I kiss her hair on the pillow next to me. Hopefully, we will have another chance to be a family, although the thought of going through such pain a second time is dreadful. I let my hand run down her body and rest on her stomach.

"Soon," she whispers. "Soon, God willing."

Again, I kiss her hair and the smell of her diverts my thoughts.

"Amen to that," I say.

***

In the morning, she kisses me farewell on our doorstep, and I am pleased to see Henry's man stationed at the corner, covertly watching the house. William has come to walk me to the coach house, and later he will return and accompany Anne to Henry's shop.

He is tense this morning. It's in the way he walks, in the way he keeps cracking his fingers, in those long, tired sighs of his.

"Travel safely," William says, gripping my shoulder so tightly that I wince.

It saddens me to see how he is changed. Bringing Miles Prance to me, getting him to sign a confession to perjury in the trial of Green, Berry, and Hill, giving me this path to finding Henry Moor and perhaps the truth finally about the death of Sir Edmund Godfrey; none of this progress has helped William. The death of Matthew Medbourne has affected him far more deeply than I imagined. Instead of working his way through his grief, my friend is becoming lost in it.

"I'll be fine," I say, climbing into the stagecoach. "I'll find Moor and see what he has to say for himself. I'll be back before you know it."

But William surprises me by mounting the coach rail and hissing at me. "You must do more than see what he's up to!"

"Rest assured, William, that I will do what I—"

"You must do what it whatever it takes, Nat. Whatever it

takes. Choke the truth from him, if you must!"

What is this? Choke the truth? William is a far more bitter man than he was before Oates took his job and his friend from him. I have not asked him how he persuaded Miles Prance to tell me the truth. But I imagine much unpleasantness.

"I will do what needs to be done, I swear," I say. "We nearly have him. It is nearly over."

"Nearly is not enough, Nat. For you, for me, for Anne, all of us. We must be rid of Titus Oates."

***

I associate Ely with Cromwell and his New Model Army, with the Civil War that raged at the time of my birth and left me fatherless. I expect an austere, unfriendly place. Yet, a few hours away from London, when the horses slow and the coachman directs me to look out of the window to the left, I'm pleasantly surprised. It's a cloudless day. Flat fields of golden rye spread away into the distance. It's as if there is nothing in the world except this bold expanse of nodding crops and the bright, blue sky. Then I shuffle forward and look at the road ahead. The skyline is broken by a looming, grey building erupting out of the earth, still some five miles off. Ely Cathedral.

At the close of the journey, golden fields give way to fruit crops. Young cherry trees and strawberry hedges remind me that I've not always lived in the city. One step out of the coach, however, and I'm quickly brought back to sober reality. We've pulled into the yard of an inn, but the whole area is inches deep in water. Drainage is clearly a pressing issue in Ely. Wrinkling my nose, I resolve once more to go about my business and return to London as quickly as possible. It doesn't take long to discover Henry Moor.

While Ely might lack the polish of London – its menfolk more concerned with the price of wool than with the immortal soul of the next King of Great Britain – certain aspects of society are little different. I find Moor at lunch-time, in a thick-walled, bustling tavern, eating mutton pie, washed down with a strong ale. My recollection of him from my one sighting at the viewing of Godfrey's body is hazy, but once I clap eyes on the small, stiff back, the grey curling hair, and his sharp beak of a nose, I'm sure it is him.

After Moor leaves, a modest outlay to the landlord buys me information about the former servant's life since his return to Ely. To my reckoning, Moor must have left London very soon after his meeting with Prance. But in the miles between city and town, he underwent a transformation. Moor arrived in Ely with his pockets well-lined. He bought up the row of houses where he had lived as a boy, and leased them out. He brought his wife with him and purchased a substantial house near the river on the south side of the Cathedral. Then he set about elbowing his way into parish affairs. There is no gossip about Moor himself, except that the old man has picked himself a much younger wife and mayhap wishes he hadn't. He is rarely found at home, the landlord says, and it is widely believed that the little woman has a sharper tongue than the old boy bargained for.

I take myself out into the streets then, and spend an hour taking in the sights of Ely. The Cathedral is wonderful to behold, especially its octagonal tower panelled with stained glass, through which the sun spills a rainbow of colour. I pace the marble floors thinking about Moor and how best to approach him. My thoughts centre on his money and his new young wife, and I decide to take a look at their home.

The house is not far from the Cathedral and it's a pretty property, built of sturdy split beams, set well back from the street with a neat box hedge. White wisteria has insinuated itself up and around a dozen little windows. There's no doubt that Moor has come into money, and I'm flushed with certainty that his success and my mystery are connected.

I stop some ten yards or so from the house and have a hand above my brow to keep the bright sun from my eyes, so that I don't see her until she is almost past me. Only the lightest clicking of wooden heels alerts me that someone is approaching. A slim young woman, dressed in a deep blue gown with a muslin shawl across her shoulders, swiftly crosses to the house, slips up the path, and is inside in a matter of moments. I catch only a fleeting glimpse of her, but it's enough for me to recognise Elizabeth Curtis – Godfrey's former maid, the one who gave evidence at the trial of Green, Berry, and Hill. She is dressed very much as the lady now, though, and must be, for there is no other explanation to be had, married to Henry Moor.

I can use this.

***

By eleven the following morning, I've given myself a new name and inveigled my way into Moor's house. I confront Godfrey's maid in her own well-appointed parlour.

"Well, sir," she says. "Your note said you had important family news for me from London?"

"Yes, it did." I make her a small bow, and a vain little smirk replaces her haughtiness. "But sadly, I lied."

Unhappy thoughts ripple across her face like wind wrinkling cloth. She is pretty but has a weak chin and small eyes. I take a seat, uninvited, and her mouth falls open.

Perhaps it's unkind to threaten such a young girl. She is twenty years old, at most, but she has that look about her that makes me think she has seen a thing or two. I don't waste any time. I tell her I know who she is, and that I'm prepared to advise anyone in Ely who will listen that the fine lady they are treating so well is no better than a kitchen maid.

She doesn't like the idea. "What do you want?" She takes the chair opposite me and folds her hands in her lap.

"Information."

"About?"

"About the death of Sir Edmund Godfrey."

She doesn't like this, but neither does she look particularly surprised. "And who are you? Why do you want to know about the old man?"

I say nothing.

"Perhaps," she says, "you might be satisfied with something other than information?" Her words are heavy with suggestion.

201

"I'm not interested in your money."

"And do you think I've nothing else to offer?"

The kind of offer she has in mind is all too clear.

"Understand me, Mistress Moor, I'm here solely for information. I've come here for the truth about what happened in London. I want to know why you lied in court, and I want to know who has paid you and Moor so handsomely. I want to know what you and he did, to earn all this." I stand and spread my arms wide to indicate the fine furniture, the maps, the ornate little clock, all the trappings of her new life. She turns, flushed and open-mouthed, about to say more, but I raise a warning finger. "Believe me, I will know what happened and I will hear your tale today. I will wait in this room. When your husband returns, you'll convince him to tell me the truth. If not, I will ruin you both. I have heard that you manage your husband very well, Mistress Moor. Manage this, and you will not hear from me again."

With that, I pick up a slim volume from the bookcase near my chair and sit back. I begin to read and don't so much as glance her way. After a few seconds, she leaves the room and closes the door behind her.

About an hour later, Moor enters. His face is fixed like a mask and his hands are tight-clenched at his sides. He orders me out of the house, of course, and has some choice comments on my appearance, including – in his assessment – my obvious lack of physical strength. We bandy a few insults back and forth. William might be right. I may have to choke the truth from this man.

But Mistress Moor is not finished. She bustles into the room with teacups rattling, and although she tries to cut off my view, I see her grip her husband's ear between one finger and thumb and twist it. She leaves us but doesn't close the door. I'm sure she's right outside, hanging on every word.

Grudgingly, Moor begins to talk. He says Sir Edmund Godfrey was out of sorts for some days, possibly weeks, before he vanished. He was curt, off-hand, preoccupied. By the Saturday afternoon, the first day of his disappearance, Moor claims he knew something was seriously wrong.

202

Godfrey had failed to meet a business acquaintance at five o'clock, and such a thing was unheard of. Moor's first action had been to inform his master's brother, Michael. From that moment, all had been in the Godfrey brothers' hands.

"In the early days, they asked me to keep the disappearance quiet," he says. "But when the Tuesday came and there was still no word – when rumours began to spread that their brother had been murdered by papists – then they went to the authorities. Up until the Tuesday, there had only been me, working alone, searching all Sir Edmund's haunts, tracking down anyone he might have spoken to, looking for witnesses, and trying to keep the other servants back in Hartshorn Lane from falling into a panic."

There's a note of pride in his voice that makes him believable.

"How did it come to be rumoured that he had been murdered by Catholics?" I ask.

"I have no idea. But I wasn't surprised. I spoke to anyone that might have seen Sir Edmund and anyone that knew him. That was a lot of people. And I'm sure that they spoke to their friends, who discussed it with their friends. You know what London is. The coffee shops thrive on gossip and speculation. And the master was most upset after the visits of Dr. Oates. Didn't he tell some of his friends he was afraid? No, I wasn't surprised by the rumours. And of course, they were proved right."

"But what did you – what did the brothers think – when the body was found in such strange circumstances?"

"Honestly?"

I nod.

"I gave it barely a thought. I'm not ashamed of it. When a master dies, a servant has his own future to look to. I'll admit I was surprised when they found him near Primrose Hill. I had been there myself, earlier in the week. Passed the very place, and there was no sign of him. His body must still have been in Somerset House." Moor shakes his head. "But you see, Elizabeth was very upset. None of us servants knew what would happen to us. I did what I could for the family in the hope that the master's brothers might offer me another position, but they did not. I saw nothing of them after the funeral, and was given notice to leave the house before the end of November."

"Yet you are remarkably comfortable here."

"Aye. I've been a lucky man. An aunt of mine died and her son with her. Quite sudden, but timely for me. I've no other family living. But now I hope for a son. Do you have any children?"

"I... no. No, none." The question throws me. Moor is more suited to be a grandfather than a new father, and I'm suddenly furious. Imagining that this venal, old liar might soon have a child on his knee while Anne and I just wait and hope, burns me inside. I turn on him. "Yet your wife perjured herself at the trial of your master's murderers."

"Did she? Who says so?" Moor's tone has changed, as mine has. He raises his eyebrows and looks belligerent.

"Miles Prance."

It's a direct hit. Moor unbends his knees and stands up. "We should walk a little."

He leads me out of the house and into the garden in silence. His mind is surely busy, wondering what I know and what he might have to tell me. I have a boiling need to finish this and get back home to Anne. When Moor steers me into a tunnel of dog-rose, the hairs on my arms stand up.

We're side by side when Moor twists away, as if his coat's snagged on a thorn. In the next moment, he has a blade at my throat. He pins me back against the foliage, one hand gripping my neck-band and the other pressing his steel into my skin. He's shorter than me, but there is strength in the wiry arm against my chest.

"Who are you?" he demands.

"No-one."

"Who sent you?" His spittle lands on the side of my face.

"Does it matter?"

"Answer the question."

I take a step into the unknown. "Michael Godfrey," I say.

"What?" Moor blinks rapidly, and the pressure of the knife

at my throat eases a fraction. It's enough for me to shove him back and punch him in the jaw. He drops the knife, and I grab it while he clutches his face. I push the blade against his skin just below his right ear. A line of red appears.

"You set up Miles Prance. You and Titus Oates came across Prance and saw an opportunity. But that kind of service doesn't bring this level of reward. There must have been more." William's desperation to have this finished spurs me on. "Tell me the rest or I'll kill you."

My free hand is on his throat. My fingers press so hard that his eyeballs roll and he's gasping for breath. Anger rolls through me. "Tell me what you did and who you know, or I'll kill you, and when I'm done I'll go and visit your pretty wife." My breath is on his face.

Then I smell it. Warm liquid spreads across Moor's breeches and his mouth gapes open. I grit my teeth and push the knife a fraction harder.

"I'll tell you, you bastard," he says, tears of shame rising his eyes. "They found the body. I don't know where. The brothers found him and sent for me. They paid me to make arrangements. They told me nothing of how he had died but said I must hide the body. A few days later, they told me to leave it somewhere – a place with no connection to anyone in the family. I was to stick a sword in him, so everyone would know he'd been murdered. The money was beyond anything I could have hoped for. It's not as if he left me anything. I was jobless and desperate, and he was already dead. I just made the best of it."

"So, you put the body in the ditch at Primrose Hill?"

"Yes."

"It was never at Somerset House?"

"No."

"And why did you choose Primrose Hill?"

"I had to choose somewhere. I knew that the Horseshoe Tavern was friendly to Catholics. By the time they told me the body should be dumped, half the city was certain Godfrey had been murdered by Catholics. It was as good a place as any. The rest I've told you already."

He is less afraid now and, thank God, I am myself again. I let the blade off his skin.

"What happens now?" he says.

"You go home and change, and I go back to London."

"And the Godfreys? Will they find out I've told you?" His eyes narrow. I need to let him go and then get out of Ely, before he decides to come after me.

"I don't know, Moor," I say. "You will just have to wait and see."

Chapter Thirty

Anne

Nat is different after his trip to Ely. He tells me what he has learned about Moor's part in the Godfrey mystery, but where I expect him to be jubilant, he is sombre: no less passionate to destroy Oates, yet more subdued than I anticipate. He tells me little about Henry Moor, beyond the astonishing fact that Moor and the housemaid are married. I must call on Mistress Pamphlin and let her know. Her mouth will form a perfect 'o' in surprise.

When I ask how he got the truth from Moor, he shrugs off my questions. I'm hurt, although I won't show it, and old fears re-surface. I dread him retreating from me and returning to the way he was in the early days of our marriage when he kept his thoughts and plans so close to his chest. But a couple of days later, Nat gives me the draft of his new edition of *The Observator* to read – even before he takes it to Henry. It's casually done, and I don't remark upon it. I simply take the paper and sit down to read by the window. But my heart pounds and I am close to tears. This is the first time he has asked my opinion of his work.

The piece declares that Nat has found the truth about the death of the magistrate, Sir Edmund Godfrey. He writes that Godfrey killed himself on Saturday, October the 12th, 1678. He hanged himself, and the fact that he was not robbed supports this theory. The only thing missing was his pocketbook. Who, Nat asks, might not want Godfrey's personal notes left in public hands? Next, Nat announces that he has new evidence about what happened to the corpse. The accepted tale of his body being moved from room to room at Somerset House is utter flim-flam. The reason no soldier saw Godfrey's body being removed in a sedan chair, as Miles Prance testified it was, is obvious. The body was never there in the first place. Nat takes a side-swipe at Prance, too, and declares that the little silversmith is shortly to be arrested for perjury.

"Is this true? About Prance?"

"Being arrested?" says Nat with a smile. "No. It ought to be. But he is long gone."

I smile back and read on.

He quickly demolishes the physical evidence of murder. The doctor, Skillard, is a drunk. With witness testimonies from patients, Nat easily discredits Skillard and his confusing evidence at the trial of Green, Berry, and Hill. More witness evidence comes from people present at the hasty inquest held in the Horseshoe Tavern. Several jurymen complain vigorously about the length of time the inquest had taken, the muddle of the evidence between the broken neck, the stab wounds made by his own sword, and the bruising to Godfrey's chest and neck.

"I like this bit," I say. Nat puts a hand on my shoulder as I point to a passage where he anticipates the counter-arguments. He acknowledges the possibility that Godfrey was beaten first and then hanged. It is undeniable that the body was somehow transported to a ditch and impaled upon his own sword. Rawson and Brown's evidence is incontrovertible. But what kind of murderer acts in this way? His fingers squeeze my shoulder, and a burst of happiness fills my stomach.

"What about this section with Lazenby?" he asks, and I read about this other physician Nat has found. Lazenby has read up every description of the marks about Godfrey's neck, and spent hours mulling over the bruises on his chest. He will swear that the neck damage is as consistent with self-strangulation as with strangulation by another. As no blood had been found in the ditch or on Godfrey's clothing, he suggests that the bruising might be due to a pooling of blood.

"It isn't watertight," he says.

"You don't mention Henry Moor," I say, still greedily reading.

"I won't until I need to. That will come in time."

"I love this section on motive." This time, his hand grazes my cheek and I raise my free hand and stroke his fingers. What kind of murderer, he has rightly asked, strangles a man and then ferries him halfway into the countryside to leave him with his sword in him, in a ditch? To what purpose, to what end, could such proceedings relate? It makes no sense. And it made no sense because the story told at the trial of Green, Berry, and Hill, was not founded in sense, but in nonsense. Nat has employed all the tricks he has honed in *The Observator*, setting up the argument he opposes, and then grinding it into the dust point by point. Why would the Catholics murder Godfrey? Obviously, because he had knowledge of their Plot. But by mid-October, Oates's deposition had been accepted by the Privy Council and the Commons was in uproar. That bird had flown.

I put down the paper and turn to embrace him. "We will win this," I say.

His mouth is in my hair. I tug at his shirt to run my fingers across his back. I want my husband. I take his hand and lead him up the stairs.

***

Afterwards, we're in the mood to celebrate. We hurry to Henry's print shop, deposit Nat's work, and propose a trip to the theatre. Henry demurs – he has meetings with an illustrator and, he says, waving Nat's papers, some fireworks to light. Our optimism, in Henry's case, is infectious. He embraces us both and sends us on our way with good cheer. William is another story, but we drag him out. He is more in need of a diversion than anyone.

Our friend is quiet all the way down Drury Lane, but Nat maintains a steady stream of observations and is in high humour. At the theatre door, we join a press of people waiting for the ticket booth to open at midday.

"No, no. Let me." William reaches for his purse, but Nat insists this is his treat. Nine shillings procures us three tickets for the pit.

"You wouldn't have preferred a box?" he asks, as we push our way down a narrow hall and into the amphitheatre.

"Not at all. There's so much more to see here. From above, we are a sea of wigs and shoulder padding. Whereas here," I gesture across the rows of green cushioned benches that are filling quickly, "there is much more to meet the eye."

"Look!" Nat nods at an enormous old lady, dressed in reams of purple silk. "Very fine! And there, see?" He points to a narrow stalk of a man in a tight coat and curling wig. He's perched at the end of a bench, taking snuff while attempting to keep his chin up, stiff as an artist's mannequin. "What does he look like?" Nat whispers. William, to my relief, joins in with the game.

"Look at that gold lace," he says. "And over there. The buttons, the ribbon."

"I'm not sure that young lady's intentions are entirely honourable," Nat says, and I clamp a hand over my mouth as the woman in question bends over a timid-looking fellow whose face grows red and hot at the glorious vista she's placed before him.

"Don't even look, William," Nat says. "It's all very shocking!"

Smiling, William offers to buy some oranges. We have heard that the theatres have suffered while the city has been so disturbed by rumours of plots and fires, but there's no evidence to support this. Londoners of all qualities, plumed, perfumed and powdered, squeeze their way onto benches.

The play begins at last. It's a comedy, and slightly bawdy, as one might expect. The audience is even noisier once the performance starts. With thick candles on the stage and more swinging high overhead, there's plenty of light for Nat to continue observing the audience as much as the players themselves.

"Did Matthew ever play here?" I ask William.

He shakes his head. "He would not have thought much of this."

I have to agree. I glance to my left to see if Nat is enjoying it, but his eyes have strayed up towards the boxes to my right. He is staring, lips slightly open and nose pinched tight.

At the front of the box are three figures in a row. They're all men – the two at each end quite young, good-looking fellows, with lace generously crowding their throats and wrists. The man in the middle, however, wears a plain surplice, and in front of his chest holds his familiar wide-brimmed black hat, trimmed with silk ribbon. Above the hat, there is the chin. And atop the chin, the nasty little eyes and mean forehead of Titus Oates.

Nat's face is white. His jaw is tense, his hand lifeless when I take it in mine.

Everything: the buffoonery on stage, the people shuffling and shifting on the row behind, the woman in front, primping at her hair, all these distractions disappear. There is only Nat's face, his naked anger and pain. For a moment, I hesitate, not knowing how to respond. Then William is out of his seat. He's also staring up at Oates, and now Oates is glaring down at us.

Nat stands, too. He moves as if to take William by the shoulder and pull him back down, but his fingers slip off the wool of his coat as William lurches away. He pushes and shoves along our row, his eyes still fixed on the box, not caring whose dress or feet he tramples. Nat dives off after him and I follow, my head in a spin.

"William!" Nat calls, running after him through the stalls, but I doubt William can hear him in that well of chatter, even if he's disposed to listen. What is William thinking? He's making for the stairs. Nat looks back at me for a second and then takes off after William.

"I've come to pay my compliments to Dr. Oates," William says loudly, as I come up the stairs behind them.

The hallway is narrow and dark, its red walls lit by a series of flickering candles in brass sconces. I hang back, hoping to stay out of sight. The door to the box is open, and William tries to push his way in past two of Oates's friends. Nat stands a foot or two behind.

"Dr. Oates!" William raises his voice. "Titus! No time for an old friend?"

211

But there's nothing friendly in William's expression or stance, and when Nat calls to him he just lifts one hand as if to warn him off. Then comes the familiar voice.

"William Smith. What a surprise. I didn't think you were much inclined towards the theatre these days."

"Or I you, Titus." William steps back as Oates comes out into the narrow hall. "Developing a belated taste for culture?"

"Oh, not at all. I've always had an affinity for the stage." On the word 'affinity' William takes a step forward, his fists clenched. Oates's friends don't like that.

"Not enough of an *affinity,* as it turned out," says William. "I don't know how you can live with yourself!"

But that only makes Oates giggle. "Oh, believe me, my darling, I live very well, very well indeed. As you see, I have some charming new friends. They're very protective of me; that's more than can be said for you. Still missing Matthew? I did hope you'd move on with your life. But I gather I hoped in vain. Choice of friends says a great deal about a man, you know."

Oates looks over William's shoulder now, glaring at Nat. Nat steps forward, but again William waves him off. He looks pale, but very calm.

"You really are quite poisonous, aren't you, Titus? I'll never understand how Matthew tolerated you. Perhaps there's a sickness in you. Indeed, your mother implied as much to me when she—"

There's an angry cry and Oates bursts forward. He shoves William up against the opposite wall with one hand around his throat.

"Never mention my mother!" he shouts. "Never bring your long, ugly face near mine again. Or do you want to end up like your beloved Matthew? Do you?"

Nat clears his throat and taps Titus Oates on the shoulder. "I'd be grateful if you released my friend."

Oates slowly turns his head, his face marbled purple and his eyes bulging. "Don't speak to me!"

"I hadn't the least intention of it. I have been far too busy imprinting the scene in my mind. A fine picture of a man of the cloth at play, don't you think? And I have a meeting with my illustrator later this afternoon. I'm sure he will do the situation justice. But I'll need to work on a title."

How I love my husband! Oates's hold on William weakens as the door of every other box opens and the hallway fills with of spectators. This drama quite trumps the one they've paid to see.

"Doctor Oates on a matter of doctrine?" Nat muses. "Or *The grateful pupil* perhaps?'

Oates lets go of William. He turns and shoves his friends back towards their box, but Nat is not done with him. He grasps Oates's shoulder. "Oh, come now, Titus! Don't hurry away," he says. "We meet so rarely, and yet I know so much about you."

"If you don't release me at once, you will know more of me than you want to."

"Promises, promises, Titus. But the game has changed." Nat lets go of him, turns and smiles at the crowd of onlookers.

"I'm afraid the good doctor is a little out of sorts today and cannot entertain us further. But do not worry, my friends. There will be much sport to be had with him soon. Look out for the next edition of *The Observator*. Indeed, the next several editions. There is much to be learned there about the true history of Mr. Oates, of his so-called plot, and the so-called murder of Sir Edmund Godfrey. He has sent many men to Newgate. Perhaps it's time someone sent him there."

Oates's eyes narrow and his chin juts forward, but instead of attacking, he whirls around and disappears into his box. Nat bows to the onlookers and they too return to the play. Within a moment, there are only the three of us left in the hallway.

"By God, I enjoyed that!" Nat says wrapping one arm around my shoulder and his other around William's.

Fools that we are, we laugh all the way home.

Chapter Thirty-One

William

I can't sleep.

Have I lost my mind? What possessed me to attack Oates in the theatre in that way? So many things. It was his face. It was his intrusion on one of the few happy days I have had in months. It was the never-ending presence of Titus Oates, and the fact that he is there, always there, when others do not live and breathe any more because of him. I wanted to kill him. Instead, he intimidated me, and only Nat's friendship and sharp tongue rescued the situation. Afterwards, Nat and Anne were elated. They truly believe that Titus will soon be disgraced. I hope they are right, but remain very much afraid of what he will do in the meantime.

At night, I lie awake and stare at the ceiling. During the day, I suspect people are following me. I almost ask Henry about it, but I am afraid that he will think I've lost my mind. Earlier today, I had that sense, that prickling of the hair on the back of my neck, on the way back from church. Titus has men watching me, I am almost sure of it. I call at Nat and Anne's house to see if Anne will come and help me in the printshop, but she is already out. Even Kitty is absent. It is early. I decide to go and see if Anne is at Martha's graveside, and then wander back again. It is a fine morning and the sky is a calm, pale blue. The streets are busy with people with places to go, but my senses are smothered. Nothing seems real. Nothing is clear.

She is there. I don't disturb her, just sit and wait while she talks to her daughter in peace and privacy. When she straightens and turns, her kind smile warms my skin. I

214

swallow the worm of guilt that is my perjury in Titus's favour, and smile back. We stroll slowly back to her house and the world comes back into focus.

But as we turn the corner to Nat and Anne's home, she drops my arm. There's a knot of people in front of their door. There are men with buckets. We rush forward and hear the worst word for any Londoner. Fire.

Anne is pushed away before she can reach the door.

"I don't understand it," she cries. "We have not so much as lit the fire this morning. Nat left early and Kitty was at her mother's house last night. How can there be a fire?"

I point at the window. It has been smashed inwards, there is no glass on the street. I have no doubt that Titus is behind this. This is our punishment for laughing at him. Anne stares dumbfounded as the flames take hold of the second floor. Smoke billows out and fills our nostrils. Heat forces us back. This is a full scale attack.

"What chance you can save it?" I ask one man who has been trying to fight the fire.

"None. Nor the poor bastard who pushed his way in there and ran up the stairs."

Anne has not heard. Neighbours envelope her and steer her away.

I can hardly bear to say the words.

"The husband? Nathaniel?"

"Not him."

All the blood that has drained from my veins rushes back through my body like a tidal wave.

"Then who?"

"A fat, old fellow. Shoved his way past us and up the stairs calling for the wife, but I'm told that no-one was home."

"You need to let me in." I shove him and run for the door, but another man stops me and the first one grips my arms behind my back.

"No! No-one else is going in there. If I have to tie you down, I will, do you hear me?"

He pulls me from the door and throws me across the street. Sprawled on the cobbles, I stare up at the house engulfed in flames.

With my eyes closed, I see smoke climb up to meet him. It spikes up his nostrils and oozes down, to settle like treacle in his lungs. His flesh is on fire, his hair, his hands, his mouth, his eyes. I imagine him screaming.

Henry.

Chapter Thirty-Two

Anne

The fire has been out for several hours before Nat and I learn that Henry has died. When Nat arrives at our neighbour's busy house there is much lamenting and talking and discussion before anyone tells us that someone has been killed. In that moment the nightmare of the day expands like a fissure in ice. When we realise that it is Henry, everything collapses. Now we are truly drowning. I have been thinking of clothes and furniture and letters – of nothings – and all the while, Henry is dead.

We stagger out to look. Only the shell of our house remains, black and smoking, gaping open like death's dark jaws. Nat hurries me to Sarah's house, where my sister, bless her, takes control.

***

In the days that follow, we have another funeral. Hundreds of people attend. Henry had a rich life. It's hard to believe there is a soul in London that does not want to shake Nat's hand. Our private loss becomes public. Nat finds it all so hard to bear, especially when William fails to appear.

"What would you have me do?" asks Nat. Sarah and James have left us in their little sitting room for the evening while they attend some party or other. It is dark, and we have not lit all the candles. It is hard to be in brightness at such a time.

"Do?"

"I could shut up the print shop. We could leave London."

"Nat!" I am shocked. This is not the way my thoughts have

been tending.

"It's my fault."

"No!"

"It is. This pursuit of Oates. Henry warned against it. I brought this violence to our door."

"Henry warned against it in the beginning, yes, but that was long ago. He printed your words. He read them. He was proud of you. He had faith in you. I saw it in him every day."

"Yet how can we continue? Henry is dead. William has abandoned us. What danger are we placing your sister in while we stay here?"

That gives me pause. "We must move."

"You shouldn't be living like this. You need a home. We ought to be living like a family, not like vagabonds."

"Enough! Enough of what you believe I need, or think you are duty bound to provide." Surprise lights up his eyes but I barrel onwards. "Here is what we will do. Tomorrow you will take lodgings for us – somewhere small, somewhere out of the way, and in false names. We won't tell anyone where, not even Sarah. You will write. We will bombard the city with the truth about this man until he cannot show his face in public. You will see Robert Southwell and demand he find a way to arrest Titus Oates. Some way – any way – must be found to put him in prison, and we must not rest until we find it."

"Are you serious, Anne?" He bends and peers across the candlelight at me.

"Never more so."

"But how can we publish? The boys cannot run the print shop. Where the hell is William?" Nat slams his hands against the arms of his chair and slumps back. "We can't just hire someone. I trust no-one."

I take a deep breath. "But you do trust me."

"You know I do, but Anne—"

"No buts, Nat. I will run Henry's presses. Indeed, I have been doing so this many months."

"What?"

"While William has taught the boys to read and count, I have worked with Henry." I stumble here, not quite sure in this moment why I haven't told him before now, not quite sure how to say this right. "I wasn't certain you would be happy to have me do it. You have always been so set on providing for me. But I wanted something, I *needed* something to do after Martha. Henry let me try the work. I can do it, Nat. If you will let me."

"Let you?" His voice is a whisper, and I am afraid for a moment that this will not end well. "My God, that we should talk of me letting you do anything! You can run the print shop, Anne? You can move to some secret place and work with me to pull this monster down? You do not need my permission, not for this or anything."

He opens his arms and I walk into them, happier – despite all this unhappiness – than I ever thought to be. His kisses are on my neck and his hands find my skin. I have one last thought before we seek a quiet oblivion in each other's arms. But I will not raise hope in Nat when it may all come to naught.

The next morning, he sets out to find us new lodgings and I seek out Sarah. I tell her we are going to visit Mother. I need to talk to her about Valentine Greatrakes.

Chapter Thirty-Three

Nat

Strengthened by Anne's resilience, I set out to secure us a room south of the Thames where we can hide from Titus Oates. It's a grey morning. Low cloud settles only inches above the rooftops, threatening rain. Cold air bites at my fingers and feet as I brave the river crossing, but I welcome the sensation. Pain is good. Pain is being alive, when Henry is not. The reality of his death is hard to grasp. I have to keep reminding myself that he's gone. I close my eyes to fool myself that none of it has happened. It is easy to conjure him in my mind. He is at work, as usual. He shouts at the boys and mutters as he reads. There is a war going on in my head between what I long to be true yet know to be false.

It does not take me long to find a room, and a woman working at a nearby tavern promises to clean it for me by the end of the day. In short order I'm back waiting for a boat, listening to the rhythmic slap of water on timber. By the time one arrives, I've made a decision. And at this hour I stand a good chance of finding Sir Robert Southwell at home.

***

Within minutes of knocking at his door I am in his study and launching into my story of Henry Moor and Godfrey's brothers. I tell him about Moor interfering with the evidence by abandoning the body in a ditch and thrusting him through with his own sword.

"Michael and Benjamin Godfrey would have lost all their brother's wealth if it was known he had taken his own life."

"*If* he took his own life." Southwell knocks the wind from my sails with one sally from the other side of his grand oak desk. "Sit down and take a breath. Why do you suggest suicide?"

"Why else have Moor go to all that trouble? The anti-Catholic hysteria created by Oates was a gift to them. It was in many people's interest to make the Popish Plot credible. I'm sure the brothers could hardly believe their good fortune. But without this cornerstone fact of Godfrey's murder, Oates is vulnerable."

"Perhaps," Southwell says. He holds up a hand when I start to speak. "I have read *The Observator* and applaud your efforts. Do I take it that Henry's accident does not deter you?"

I swallow and think of Anne. "I am only more set on seeing Titus Oates in gaol."

"As am I. Henry was my friend for more than forty years." He reaches down and strokes the head of a spaniel that I had not even noticed sitting next to him. "You need to lie low," he says, and nods in approbation when I explain my morning's work. "Good. Because when you print these accusations, you will be highly unpopular with Oates. Your lives will be at risk, if they are not already. The Godfrey brothers may well want to speak to you, too. At least Shaftesbury is unwell and not in a position to make trouble. That makes the brothers less influential, too, at least for the moment. It may be worth hinting that they were politically, as well as financially, motivated to obscure the facts around Godfrey's death. And I'd certainly advise you to disappear for a week or so."

"They won't be charged over this?"

"You have no proof that it was suicide. And only Moor's word against theirs."

"It doesn't seem right."

"Ah, but never forget that this is a means to an end," he says. 'History is full of innocent men who've hanged, and guilty men who've died in their sleep in their own warm beds. You are no lawyer, and you can only fight with the tools you have to hand. Thus far, you're doing an excellent job."

"So, what do we aim for, for Oates? A treason trial?"

"Hardly that!"

Hearing the derision in Southwell's voice, my temper catches fire. "Why not? The man has lied and made fools of everyone. Not to mention the deaths he has caused!"

"Yes, but think of the implications, Nat. Think beyond Titus Oates." Southwell leans forward and jabs a finger at me. "Did Henry Broome teach you nothing? Such arrogance you have. That's been your problem all along, young man."

"What implications?"

"Who has thrown their weight behind Oates? Who has publicly praised him? How many fine dinners has the man eaten? In whose houses has he run tame? You said it yourself. He has made fools of everyone. But not every fool wants to be known as one."

"So, truth and honesty, these things mean nothing any more?" I'm out of my chair, pacing the room. 'It's all about politics and reputation and keeping steady, regardless of the cost. Damn it, where's your *soul*, Southwell? You cast up Henry to me, but he was not as cold as this, by God. He would have seen this as I do. I'm sure of it."

"Really?" Southwell is as calm as I am outraged. "Henry was, as I am, a pragmatist. We've been through things in our lifetimes that young men like you don't even dream of. Did you see a King's head taken from his shoulders on the steps of Whitehall? No. But we did. Have you seen Englishmen killing Englishmen, heard Cromwell thunder? Did you see the city fill with colour at the Restoration, or then turn black with plague and fire? No. There is a difference, Nat, between knowing the truth and knowing what to do with it. Actions have consequences. A lesson I thought you might have learned."

"But where's your passion? How can you tolerate what Oates has brought on us?"

"Don't underestimate the situation, Nat. Look at the King. He has no legitimate children. James *will* inherit, and there *will* be a Catholic King in England again. What will that mean for us all? Perhaps if we waited for a few years. Perhaps if James was King, Oates could be tried for treason."

"Perhaps. What good is perhaps?"

"What good is any of it?" Southwell gets to his feet and starts poking at the fireplace. "I mean for what, or for whom, are you doing this, Nathaniel? Even if Oates is tried for treason and hanged, what will have changed? Henry will still be dead."

His words silence me. While I ponder, he pours us some wine.

"I am not without passion," he continues. "I am a courtier, though. And I do know, whether I like it or not, what is possible and what is not. You are right that Titus Oates is an affront to honest men. You are right that something should be done about it. But it will not be a treason trial. That puts too many reputations at risk."

The wine tastes burnt on my tongue. The disappointment is crushing, but I have promised Anne that we will pursue this to the end. I force myself to focus, and piece by piece I walk Southwell through my attack on Titus Oates. I show him a new pamphlet, re-visiting the trial of Godfrey's supposed murderers.

"However the man died, it was certainly not at the hands of Robert Green, Lawrence Hill, and Henry Berry. As you know, Oates's plot revelations were known to the Privy Council days prior to Godfrey's disappearance. I'm ready to wager that the Queen's residence and the Savoy next door were already under observation. Inside Somerset House, it's a warren of rooms and apartments. You know that every bit as well as I. On the night of Godfrey's murder, I will prove that the King and his whole court were there."

Southwell nods.

"Is that the place that any sane person would choose to stage a murder?"

"No."

"I've interviewed all the witnesses, the Catholic witnesses whose testimony was outrageously disregarded during the trial. Even the greatest dunderhead alive could not argue with it. There is simply no way those men could have hidden Godfrey's body in Somerset House. On the day Henry was killed I was out visiting the apartments Prance alleged were used." From my bag I pull an illustration of the rooms in question and we pore over it together. "The body was supposed to have lain in a small chamber off the main living apartments of a Dr. Godden. Godden, his niece Mary, and their servant Mistress Broadstreet, all gave me clear, straightforward statements. Every night they ate supper beside the door where the body was supposed to have been concealed. Every night Hill helped Mistress Broadstreet serve them, and then their doors were locked for the night while they read or played cards together. The little room was barely more than a cupboard. It had only one entrance. If Hill's witnesses had not been Catholic, it was certain that he would never have been found guilty. The story makes me sick to my stomach."

"You must impart that sentiment to your readers."

"I will."

He hands me my papers and his eyes flit toward the clock in the corner.

"I had some other ideas about Godfrey," I say.

"Go on."

"As you said, I have only Moor's word for it that Godfrey killed himself. I don't know if I will ever be able to prove it. I have been thinking, though, about why he might have done so. What motive did he have to take his own life? If I find that, I destroy any vestige of support for Oates's claims about Godfrey's so-called murder."

"I like your reasoning."

"Good. It occurred to me that Godfrey might have given someone access to Oates's deposition."

"What makes you think so?"

"Henry."

"Explain."

"When Henry and I viewed Godfrey's body, he talked about him a little. You know what Henry was like. He collected titbits of information like cat hair on a blanket. He told me Godfrey was friends with Edward Coleman."

"He did?" Southwell's voice betrays his interest. Good.

"And then there is old Tonge. Israel Tonge told me he saw Coleman outside Godfrey's house on the morning that they went to Whitehall. I put myself in Godfrey's shoes. I have this incendiary deposition in my hands. I've been given it by two clear rascals, neither of whom I'd trust an inch. I'm a shrewd man, a fair judge of character, and I know my politics. If this story grows wings, then my friends, all of us, are in danger."

"Why wouldn't Godfrey have believed them? Instinct? Experience?"

"Probably both. Tonge has never impressed anyone and Oates was poor back then, with no-one but Israel Tonge standing between him and vagrancy. He'd been begging alms from priests outside Somerset House only weeks before. Imagine how he must have appeared to Godfrey. Godfrey probably knew from instinct and from fact that Oates was a liar. Tonge said Oates spoke against one of the priests, Fenwick, and that Godfrey knew him as well as Coleman. Perhaps that's how he knew it was a pack of falsehoods. He decided to tell Edward Coleman what was happening."

Southwell says nothing.

"It makes perfect sense," I say. "Godfrey let Coleman read his copy of the deposition, and Coleman took it straight to his employer, the King's brother, James, Duke of York."

For a full minute we stare at each other.

"You would have confided in Henry," I say.

Southwell gets slowly to his feet and goes to the fireplace. "It's ironic really," he says, his back facing me as he stares into the fire. "Henry would have enjoyed this aspect, I am sure. You see, Godfrey did have everything to do with the Popish Plot being taken seriously, but not in the way the public imagines.

"The truth, Nathaniel, is that the King was trying to hush it all up. His advisors were toying with Tonge and Oates while working out the easiest way to get rid of them and their outlandish claims. But Godfrey told Coleman, and Coleman told James. The King's brother is not known for his politicking, is he? In front of the Privy Council, he insisted that Charles investigate these slanders against Catholics most fully. It was Godfrey's actions that caused the plot to reach the public. Not his death, however that came to be construed."

225

It's so enormous and yet so simple at the same time. Godfrey had told Coleman. Coleman had told James. Godfrey, arguably, had committed treason.

"Sir Edmund Godfrey was an upright, uptight, moralist," I say. "Yet he suddenly found himself embroiled in something totally abhorrent to his whole code of living. We have witness testimonies that Godfrey had been in fear for his own life in his last days. His housekeeper told Anne he was burning papers the night before he disappeared. The explanation of his suicide is there, crystal clear."

"But there is still no evidence. And I will never confirm this conversation. You know that."

I do know that, but him saying so dashes me to despair yet again. If there is a way forward, I am struggling to see it.

"What about a charge of perjury?" I say, finally. "Surely we must be able to disprove some of Oates's statements. He has lied many times under oath. I'll look at the court records. Find discrepancies."

Southwell, back behind his desk, takes a long sip of wine and slowly inclines his head. "That is much more likely. And now that your friend William Smith has come forward—"

"He has *what*?"

"You didn't know?" Southwell is smiling, back to his smooth, cold self again. "Your friend came to visit me the day after Henry's funeral. He was much distressed, but in the end, he told me something highly significant. He is to sign a statement to be taken to the Privy Council."

"A statement? To what effect?"

"That he perjured himself in the priests' trial. Oates forced him to do it, he says."

"My God."

"Quite."

"I haven't laid eyes on him since Henry died."

"He is greatly ashamed, and avoiding both you and your wife."

"I need to see him!"

"I am not sure you would find him. He has refused to furnish me with an address. But if you choose to wait and promise to be gentle with the poor fellow, I am expecting him here later this afternoon. He will need his friends around him if he is to stand up in court and condemn Titus Oates to his face. Perhaps you will return later and hear his story for yourself?"

"You know I will."

***

William looks haggard and unwell. At the sight of me, he staggers, as if his legs will go from under him. I grab his elbow and manoeuvre him into the chair in front of Southwell's desk. With a tact I had not suspected him of possessing, Sir Robert removes himself from the room for a few minutes.

"You could have told me. Why didn't you tell me?" I ask.

"I wanted to. I should have done. I sincerely wish I had. If only I had told you earlier. If we had acted against Titus sooner… I have nothing but ifs and regrets." William smacks his fists against his temples. It's an alarming sight. "I should not have been so rash at the theatre. I should never have lied for him. I haven't been able to face you and Anne. You have lost your dearest friend. And all my fault!"

"No."

"Yes."

"No, William. Listen to me. Heaven knows, what you say is an echo of what I have been saying to myself every moment since that damned fire. I should never have spoken out against Oates. I should not have written as I did, or fought with him in the street, or attacked him at the theatre, or insulted him every day. I've pursued this relentlessly, desperate to destroy him for any number of reasons, not all of them noble. Even after being forced to abandon my grieving wife, I could not give it up. Now I have lost a man who was a second father to me, and to what end?"

"You are a good man, Nat. Anne believes in you and so did Henry. Oates did this to him, no-one else."

"If that's true, then the same holds true for you, William.

Titus Oates's men set that fire. We must not forget it. Whatever the provocation, the act and its consequences are his responsibility, not yours."

A half smile. "Or yours."

The storm in his eyes eases a little. We are both bruised. Both guilty. But not totally responsible.

"I want to put this right, Nat," says William. "In as much as I can."

"The evidence at the priests' trial was a lie? He threatened you? While I was in Edinburgh?"

William nods. "I had to swear that Oates was in London on a certain date or he would make sure that Matthew would die in Newgate." He presses his lips together, keeping his obvious emotions in check. "Amongst other things."

I want to say that I understand, but we have always stepped carefully around this friendship of William and Matthew's, and I don't want to make a mistake now.

"So, you will give evidence to your own perjury? You could go to gaol yourself."

"I will do so gladly, so long as the same is true for Titus Oates."

From the door, Southwell interrupts us. "It may not come to that, but it is well to consider the possibility and be prepared. Mr. Smith, you might also think about staying south of the river, near your friend here, for a period. I will prepare the grounds for Titus's arrest with the Privy Council but you, Nat, are in charge of the court of public opinion. This time we will need our Catholic witnesses to be heard. Hide out and stay safe, both of you. When the warrant for Oates's arrest is ready, I will send word."

Chapter Thirty-Four

Anne

Not long after Nat leaves to seek out new lodgings, I knock on Sarah's dressing room door.

"Can I talk to you for a moment, Sarah?" I ask.

"Of course, dearest." She pulls me in to sit by her on a narrow couch. "What is it?"

"I have decided to go and see our mother."

***

Two hours later, we are admitted to our parents' house. I have planned what to say and how to act, but I dread this meeting. The splendour of my old home surprises me. I was once so accustomed to all this finery – the high ceilings, the liveried footmen, the army of candles like a small forest – but now I see with new eyes. No wonder Nat has been afraid of disappointing me and nagged with doubt about what I had left behind. I must let him know how little it means to me.

Sarah whispers her hopes that we will heal the rifts in the family, but I've no serious intention of reconciliation. This visit is purely a means to an end.

My mother sweeps into the room and greets us both as if we were acquaintances arriving for tea, not her own children. She and Sarah have similar colouring and features, but where my sister's expression is always warm and welcoming, my mother has a perpetual look of suspicion on her face. She is on the watch for disappointments or slights, and she broods on what she finds. I'm thankful that we have been able to keep news of the fire at our home from her. This would be an impossible task otherwise.

"I have come to apologise, Mama," I say, squeezing my fingers together in my lap. "I hope you will forgive me for being distant for all these months."

"Distant? Is that what you call it?" Her shoulders are tight and her lip quivers. There is anger there, but also anxiety, and I'm surprised by a tugging desire to comfort her. The next words I have planned to say are far from easy to deliver.

"I'm sorry. My letter was unkind. I was ungrateful."

Beside me, Sarah's lips part. "Are you actually apologising, Anne?" she says.

"Yes! I told you that's why I wanted to come. Is it so shocking?"

"Frankly yes!" says Sarah. "When have you ever apologised for anything in all of your days? I can't wait to tell Roger."

"Our brother has nothing to do with this!" My sister has broken into laughter now. "Sarah!"

"You were ever the hothead, Anne," says Mother, with an eyebrow raised.

"Are you both serious?" My task and purpose are quite forgotten. "A hothead? Who never apologised?"

"Never. Oh, you were always the sweetest of girls, Anne," Mother continues, "but once you were set on a course, I never saw you dissuaded. Your father and I should have thought more upon that and behaved a little better when you were first married."

I blink. This is an olive branch I had not anticipated.

"I have also thought," she says with one hand on her chest, "that I have been a little slow to consider you an adult, capable of making your own choices and decisions. And I am sorry for it."

"Thank you, Mother," is all I manage to say. We eat tea and discuss a hundred things, from my mother's friends and Sarah's in-laws, to Nat's growing reputation among her friends' husbands – a factor, I am sure, in her change of heart toward me. She even says that my father will have been sorry to miss my visit. Truly, the times have changed.

230

In a lull in the conversation, I take a deep breath and ask my mother about Valentine Greatrakes. I tell her that I wish to consult him, and when her lips form around the words demanding to know my reasons, I simply lay a hand on my stomach. Her face reflects her thoughts so clearly – I would laugh if it were not so important. She believes I wish to meet the Irish healer to ask him why I am not yet with child again. If I am completely honest, I may also want to ask about that, but only after I have quizzed him about Sir Edmund Godfrey. Of course, Mother knows exactly where to find Greatrakes. She dispatches a letter to her friend Lady Verner and tells us we may present ourselves at a gathering at the Verner house later this afternoon.

***

As we walk past the footman and up Lady Verner's grand marble staircase, I am quite composed. The sitting room, as always, is full of flowers. I catch their scent: tall vases of dusky pink roses, very charming. Card tables are set out the length of the room, and many ladies are already busy playing Ombre. Sarah leads me on to meet our hostess. Now my nerves begin. I have not been in such circles for a long time and several girls I used to know are present, including Miss Alice Peters, whom I have never liked. Her eyes meet mine and relief heats my cheeks, until her gaze moves seamlessly past as though I am invisible. Lady Verner, however, is perfectly kind and directs us into another, smaller sitting room, where a lady – if she is prepared to wait – may have a private consultation with Valentine Greatrakes.

Here, I spot a small child who has been allowed into the party for a few moments and escaped his tutor's clutches. He peeks out from a table near where Sarah and I stand. He has such naughty blue eyes. I lift my hand a little and wave. My heart aches to see him wave back and grin. There is a crowd in this small room, and I only catch glimpses of Greatrakes through the crush. He has wild red hair – no wig for him.

Finally, the melee around Greatrakes thins and I'm

permitted to take a seat next to the man of the moment. He is older than I had imagined, and his leathered face makes me think of a rocky path on a sunny day.

"What is your name?"

"Anne Thompson."

"And what ails you, Mistress Thompson, or would you like me to hazard a guess?"

"Do you guess people's ailments? Is that what you do?"

"Not always. Some people tell me at once what is wrong. Others don't know or can't say what ails them. But often enough I guess right."

"Often enough?"

"Enough to persuade people that my fabled powers are real," he says.

"And are they?"

"I believe so. And soon you can tell me yourself if you concur. Now, let me try to guess."

Greatrakes takes up both my hands and turns them over and back. His eyes are light green. He's like a force of nature. I force myself to breathe.

"You fear you are infertile," he says, and I flinch. "You have suffered a loss." He frowns as if weighing some thought up. "A baby died, shortly after birth."

"Yes." Sarah's hand reaches down from where she stands behind my chair. She squeezes on my shoulder.

"Lady Verner?" Greatrakes waves our hostess over, treating her more like a serving girl than the wife of a peer of the realm. He speaks quietly to her for a moment and then Lady Verner smoothly ushers all the other ladies from the room, even Sarah.

"Do not be alarmed," says Greatrakes, settling himself back beside me. "If a matter is urgent, it is quite agreed between myself and Lady Verner, that she and her other friends will withdraw for a time."

"Urgent?"

"Isn't your reason for seeing me urgent?"

His voice is soft and persuasive, his lilting Irish accent almost hypnotic. I have sudden empathy for my mother's interest in the man. This day is far more emotionally charged than I had anticipated.

"I do wish to talk to you in confidence."

"On your own behalf or on your husband's?"

My eyes widen, and my mouth goes dry. "How did you know?"

"Tell me your story, honestly," he says. "If I can help you, I will tell you."

I'm here to ask questions about Edmund Godfrey. But he has asked for honesty. I take a deep breath and begin with Martha.

I talk about the hopes and fears I had when carrying her. I talk about Martha's birth. This is difficult. When I hesitate, he waits, and in the silence I find the words I need to describe it. The memory of her few hours of life almost overwhelms me. He brings me a cup of hot honey and lavender from a dish on a table in the corner. It's sweet and instantly calming.

"Nat was there when she died. His face and his pain, it felt almost worse than mine. And then he was arrested."

For the first time, Valentine Greatrakes interrupts my story. "Why was your husband arrested?" His voice is as honeyed as the drink warming my hands. Never in my life have I unburdened myself in this manner. But I answer easily, as though he is someone I have known for the longest time.

"My husband was – *is* – entangled with Titus Oates. Nat is a writer. He was the Licenser, but when the Popish Plot was all anyone could think of, he lost his position. It wasn't his fault. He didn't like Oates, he didn't believe him from the first, and so he went after him – with words, you understand. He attacked him, and Oates could not tolerate that. He trapped Nat and had him arrested only hours after Martha died."

'But you say he is still entangled?' Greatrakes bends down to a large satchel at the side of his chair. He begins sorting through bottles, placing them on a small table.

"Yes. At this minute he is out finding us rooms where we can hide from Oates. Our home was burned to the ground. Our closest friend died in the fire."

Even as I talk, I'm questioning myself. Here is this man, of whom I know next to nothing, yet I have confided in him about the worst day of my life. He is like a pool of calm water, immense yet graceful, busy yet restful, focussed and relaxed all at the same time. I have no idea how I'm going to get him to speak about Godfrey. He is only a breath away from me, but his thoughts could be in another continent. He has so easily won my confidence, but I've not the first idea of how to gain his.

"I am afraid that Martha's birth may have damaged me. We wait for another child, but I have not conceived again."

"There may be many reasons for that. These other recent losses – of your friend, of your home."

This is my chance. "Nat believes you were a friend to Sir Edmund Godfrey. He has evidence that Godfrey wasn't murdered at all."

"I don't see how that helps you now."

"It helps because your friend's death was taken by all of London as proof that Oates's stories were true. Everyone accepted that Godfrey was murdered by Catholics as part of the Popish Plot. But if he was not murdered – if there is some other explanation for the poor man's death – then doubting Titus Oates is no longer strange. Questions can be asked. Evidence re-examined. Three poor men were hanged for your friend's murder. It breaks my heart. They were innocent. All of them."

Greatrakes stops sorting through his supplies.

"I met him through treating his sister,' he says. He rests his head against the back of the chair and lets his shoulders curl and relax. His eyes are closed. "We became friends. We liked each other, although he was very sceptical about my business – rather like you."

His eyes are still closed. He's not testing me, just stating the facts.

"Edmund suffered from melancholia. His father had suffered similarly, so he had no illusions. There was not much I could do for him. There is no cure. But I like to think I helped him live with it a little better. I gave him some herbal medicine to take when the black mists came on him. I was

234

someone he could talk to. You are much more eloquent than your husband, you know."

"I am? What makes you say so?"

"He has written to me several times, asking to meet with me to discuss Edmund, but I did not reply."

"Why not?"

"Because he never told me why. He was not open or honest. Not like you have been."

I grow a little hot. I've an impulse to defend Nat; he is much more open than he was, I want to say, but I keep to the task before me. "You are easy to talk to. And you knew about my fears for a new baby. You knew at once."

"That is a small matter. You are too thin. Look at the wedding band on your finger." I touch it and it slips round easily. "Your sister looks at you with a mother's eyes. You are pale. You look as though you do not sleep well. You stared at Lady Verner's grandchild with longing."

"I did?"

"You did."

"Here." He picks up a bottle from the table and hands it to me. "Bergamot. Make tea with it each morning. It may help you, or it may not. More likely an end to this matter of Titus Oates is what you truly need."

I take the bergamot gladly and he waves me away when I offer payment. I stand then and thank him for his time, but he is not finished with me yet.

"Is there not one more thing that you would ask me? About my friend?"

Perhaps it is something in the tilt of his head. Or the tone of his voice. Or the light in his so green eyes. I tingle with anticipation and unexpected hopefulness. "Do you have any idea of what truly happened to him?" I ask.

"Yes, I do. My dear friend killed himself. His last letter to me proves it."

Chapter Thirty-Five

William

Anne's recovery of Godfrey's suicide note from Valentine Greatrakes is the tipping point. Nat publishes the true story of the magistrate's death, and suddenly we are not the only voices questioning Titus Oates and the whole of his calamitous Popish Plot. Southwell insists that Nat amend Godfrey's letter to remove Edward Coleman's name, but Anne prints the rest:

My dear friend Valentine,

The darkness is coming on me again. I write to you and hope that you will send me some more of that cordial you so kindly prepared for me last year, and also, to be direct, in the hope that you will visit. Things go ill for me in London. A year ago, I almost left it all behind and came to you in Ireland. Would that I had done so.

There is much nonsense talked of in the city. Or nonsense I thought it when I warned my friend Edward Coleman that he was the subject of some wild claims I had the misfortune to come across in my role as a magistrate. I fear I have caused displeasure. At best, I have been a fool; at worst, precipitated a crisis that should never have been. The nonsense becomes more serious every day.

If I am found to have betrayed this confidence, I fear the consequences. But no-one can be harder on me than I am myself. Did I ever imagine myself fit for a higher office? I know now that my deafness only prevented me from failing in a more spectacular fashion. My judgement is not what I thought it, Valentine. Do you see? I have lost faith in myself again.

Come soon, Valentine, if you can. But please, if you do not

hear from me again, please know that it is by my choice and my hand. Know also, that although I leave you, I loved you well. Your lightness always lifted my darkness, and for that I am truly thankful.
Your friend,
E.B.G.

***

They work well together, Anne and Nat. It heartens me. They climb their way out of the pit of despair that the fire threw us in, but I remain in the dark until Titus is dealt with. I must have my chance to unsay the words I spoke at the trial of Fathers Whitbread, Fenwick, and Ireland. That is my every waking thought, and nothing – not my friends, not the boys, not the lifting attitude in London – can shake me from it. My guilt over their deaths keeps me firmly in the pit. At last, Southwell sends the message we have been waiting for.

***

It's late, nearly midnight when Nat and I cross the Thames. As the waterman works his oars, Nat's fingers rap against the side of the boat. I study the sway and glint of the lanterns on other boats criss-crossing the river. I've a dream-like sensation; a disbelief that such a longed-for moment is finally upon us. The high walls of Whitehall gradually grow larger as we eddy onwards. In a few more minutes we are berthed beneath it. Nat pays the boatman and we clamber up steep stone steps. Henry would likely not have come with us to see this done, but he is in our thoughts tonight.

A sharp wind hits us as we reach street level. We cut through an alley at the side of Whitehall and then slow our pace as we enter the courtyard. The palace is brightly lit still, although most of the street torches in the city are out for the night. A burly guard approaches, and Nat shows him a paper bearing Robert Southwell's seal. He's satisfied to let us linger. The courtyard is out of the wind, built several storeys high on all sides. We stand just inside the south gate, and I take in at least five different entrances through which Titus might be brought.

"You're sure they will take him out through this gate?"

Nat nods. He has his arms folded across his chest and stands very upright, although he sways forward and back on his feet a little. Which way will they bring Titus? On the east and west wings there are large iron studded doors that stand open in the daytime but for now are closed and guarded by eight men. The guards appear relaxed. Murmurs of conversations and the occasional crack of laugher echo up into the night. On the north wing there are three possible routes for the soldiers to bring Titus. The central doors are also closed, and a sturdy oak beam is posted across them. But on either side near the corners are two smaller open doorways, and in the torchlight I make out the beginnings of a stairway. One guard is posted at each of these, but most likely at the top of each stair there will be a guard station.

"I'm freezing." Nat turns and flashes me a grin. "Listen," he says, and he makes his teeth rattle against each other like a dice in a box.

"Surely it will not be long now? Southwell was certain?"

"Look!"

The guards step away from the east doors as they grind open. A soldier emerges and takes a moment to confer with the men. He crosses over to the south gate for a whispered conference with the officer who spoke to us. That's when we hear the first shriek.

"Bastards!" The familiar voice shoots through the east door. His screeches explode over the trample of the feet of four or five soldiers, dragging him out by brute force.

"Whore-sons!"

I clamp my hand over my mouth. With every inch of his strength, Titus Oates squirms and struggles against the guards who've been sent to arrest him. Nat and I glance at each other, our eyes on stalks as Titus, spitting and kicking, is manhandled into the courtyard.

"I am a man of position! I'm a man of the cloth, by God!

You shit-breech windfuckers will be sorry you ever touched me. I will have your guts for my supper! I will eat—" The first guard moves swiftly up behind Titus and stuffs a cloth in his mouth. His eyeballs swell out in shock and anger. In another moment his arms are tightly bound, but he still struggles violently, twisting and bucking, refusing to walk. He is half kicked, half dragged towards us.

Nat and I step forward into the light. The group halts while the guards exchange papers and cast a derisive looks at their struggling prisoner. Titus's chest heaves, his face is choked with bile, and his large head still resists, swaying and turning like a cornered beast. When his wild eyes fall on us, all colour drains from his face. His nostrils flare and he strains forward as if to charge, but the soldiers have him held fast. I remove my hat and nudge Nat, who does the same. We grin at each other. And then, both putting our best legs forward, we give Titus our compliments, bowing with as much ceremony as we can muster.

As we straighten up, the guards pull him away. Veins rage in his neck as he twists back to glare at us. The guards drag Titus off to gaol. Our laughter surely echoes in his ears as he goes.

***

After several hours of sweet celebration, Nat and I stagger back over London Bridge. We have no money left to pay for a boat and are only just able to recall the route to our temporary lodgings. The wind howls over the bridge, and although drink warms my body, my fingers and face are chilled.

"Bastards!" From behind me, Nat calls out in imitation of Titus and dissolves into a fit of hysteria. "I am a man of the cloth," he says, sounding more like a strangled cat than anything else. A window above us opens and a basin of water is thrown out. It misses, but not by much.

"Come on, come on. No more shouting. You'll get us arrested, and then where would we be?" I stop up short and consider two narrow roads leading off to the right. I push my fingers up under my wig and scratch my head. "This way," I decide. "Come on."

Somehow or other we make it back to Nat and Anne's lodgings. My new, tiny room is only a few streets away. We pause to say our goodbyes.

"Will there ever be a finer moment?" I ask for the umpteenth time.

Nat grins. "Could he have taken it with less dignity? What a performance. I could not have written it half so well."

"You are right." I jab a finger up towards Nat. "He is a disgrace of a man. And you knew it, right from the start. Why, I am sure you were not such a banshee when you were arrested."

"I was not!"

"And I am sure I was not either," I say.

"Nor Matthew," he says.

I can't speak then. I wander away and leave Nat to fumble his way indoors and up to Anne. Our losses – of Matthew, of Martha, and of Henry – crash down on my head as I walk the rest of the way alone. The taste of beer sours on my tongue. This is but one small victory. And while Nat and Anne may nearly be finished with Titus, I'm afraid I will end up back in Newgate.

Even so, our day in court cannot come soon enough.

Chapter Thirty-Six

Nat

With Titus Oates under arrest, Anne and I are able to return across the river and settle into a new home not far from the print shop. We go to work together every day – I to my office upstairs, and Anne below, marshalling her boys. William appears only sporadically, and on Southwell's advice still keeps a low profile. It is clear to me that he needs this trial to happen as much, if not more, than we do, but to a degree I envy him. William can act, where I only watch. In giving evidence against Oates, he can make reparation for Henry's death, even though he must admit his own perjury to do so. I have done all I can with my writing, but still it tears at me that it was my crusade against Oates that brought this misery to our door. Now I'm left to wonder what I might have done differently. Such thoughts bear fruit in grey hair and furrowed brows; the scars of living, I suppose.

At last the day of Titus Oates's perjury trial arrives, ushered in under a pink and orange London sky. I am thankful for Anne's arm in mine as we walk to the Old Bailey together.

"Poor William," she says. "He was restless yesterday. He is so intent on this. Desperate, even. He will be happier when his evidence is given, I hope. Oates will be found guilty, won't he?"

"I believe so. I pray so." We pause outside the courthouse walls. Witnesses and spectators are gathering in the yard. We find a path through them all and enter. It is a fine new building, another one rising from the ashes of the fire of '66 – in this case, a stately three storey building, in the Italian style. They have kept the building open on the courtyard side to promote the circulation of air and reduce the risk of infection carried in by prisoners from Newgate next door. "Come." I squeeze her hand in mine. "The sooner it begins, the sooner it ends."

Falling in with Sir Robert Southwell, we take our seats in the balcony. There's a sea of noisy humanity beneath us: lawyers; clerks; scribblers like myself; witnesses, of course; and a jumble of curious spectators, pushing and shoving to establish a vantage point. Anne is restless, rubbing her hands to keep warm and craning her neck, trying to catch sight of William. Southwell, on the other hand, looks as disinterested as ever. I don't know how he does it.

"This trial will be a memorable one," I whisper to Anne, "if his exit from Whitehall was any indication."

Titus Oates does not disappoint.

He's led in with his wrists shackled but his head held high. Oates makes much of looking about himself, twisting his fat chin from shoulder to shoulder. At the first opportunity, he speaks up in that loud, braying tone. As we know too well, this man is nothing if not versed in the ways of our courts of law.

"My Lords, it must be recognised that I am to speak here in my own defence. I have papers, records, testimonies." He waves his hand over the small space allotted to the defendant. "I cannot manage my affairs like this. Pray, let me have space to manage my own trial."

With a disgruntled look, the Lord Chief Justice Jeffreys, an old fellow with watery blue eyes and skin like crackled glaze, inclines his head and orders that an area at the bar is cleared for Oates, who makes much of setting out of his precious papers. The crowd stirs a little, but soon the business of selecting the jury begins.

"Not Scroggs this time," whispers Anne.

"No. He has fallen from favour. Some of his views on Catholicism have cost him," says Southwell. He follows this comment up with a groan. "This will take forever and a day. Watch. Oates will object to every one of these jurors."

He is right, near as damn it. Oates interrupts proceedings whenever he can, asking the jurors questions or objecting to their selection without any grounds whatsoever. He has maintained much of his swagger in gaol, although he is thinner and his skin colour is not good. Eventually, the jury is sworn in and the formal charge against Oates is read out: perjury in the matter of the trial of the priests Whitbread, Ireland, and Fenwick.

"It shall be shown that the defendant, Titus Oates, of the parish of St Sepulchre, was a witness in the aforementioned trial," the clerk reads. "At that trial the defendant did state under oath that there was a meeting held on the 24th of April of the year of our Lord, 1678. The defendant told the court under oath that at this meeting Jesuit priests did consult together in the White Horse Tavern in the Strand, and that they did there plan to form a revolution against our Government and murder our King. Titus Oates claimed to have later witnessed these Jesuits sign a document committing themselves to this treacherous plan.

"The truth, however, is that the defendant, Titus Oates, was in no manner present at such a meeting. There was no truth in his claim to have heard any man plotting a revolution and the death of the King, yet on the 5th of February, in the year 1680, Titus Oates did, under oath, declare that he had seen and heard the aforementioned priests, Whitbread, Ireland, and Fenwick, in such an act of treason. The court will prove that this man has wilfully and voluntarily committed an act of perjury in this matter and you, gentlemen of the jury, will be asked to say if he is guilty or not guilty in this regard."

Oates is set on interruption. He makes various complaints about the indictment, including some nonsense about wording and Latin that inspires harsh words from Lord Jeffreys. Next to me, Southwell "tuts" and Anne looks disgusted at Oates's behaviour. I had expected to revel in this. I have longed to watch Oates squirm. Now I'm not sure how I feel.

The prosecution outlines their case. They will prove that Oates was out of the country from December 1677 until the end of June 1678. For all that period, Oates was at St Omer's, excepting one night only, in January 1678, when he turned truant and spent a night in a place called Watton, about two miles away from the college. Many witnesses will prove this, but first the jury will hear evidence of what Oates said in the trial of the priests.

A witness is called, a Mr. Foley, who served on the original jury. Foley testifies that in the priests' trial, Oates swore he had attended the consult on the 24th of April and then had carried the document from lodging to lodging where he saw the various priests sign their commitment to a Catholic uprising.

Oates is granted the opportunity to examine the witness, but his questions do little to help his cause. Can Mr. Foley recall whether he had said that he'd seen the priests sign the document, or only that he knew it had been signed? Does Mr. Foley remember whether he had said where it was signed: at the tavern, or in their lodging? Had the meeting at the tavern taken place in one room, or several? I imagine Oates's intention is to make the witness appear unreliable. Jeffreys certainly thinks so and steps in, warning him that attempts to insult witnesses will not be accepted.

"That's a little rich," I mutter to Anne. "Consider the way Catholics were treated when trying to give evidence in the trials in '78 and '79. No-one had any problem insulting those witnesses."

Some of those very same discredited witnesses soon take the stand. The first is a Mr. Maxwell, a student at St Omer's in the same class as Oates. He's well dressed and a little nervous initially, but articulate and clear in his answers. He says he left St Omer's the day before the supposed Jesuit meeting in April, and Oates had been at the college at that time. Maxwell had not travelled with, or seen, Titus Oates on his journey to London, and his testimony very plainly shows that Oates is a liar. We turn our eyes on the defendant who bridles in his chair and jumps to his feet.

"If I may ask a question," he begins, "I would ask the witness of what religion he may be and where he lives."

At a nod from Jeffreys, Maxwell answers, "I am a Roman Catholic, and I live in the Inner Temple in London."

"And when did you first go to St Omer's, and how long were you there?"

"I arrived there in 1672. So, for six years."

"And what was your business there?"

Maxwell hesitates. He looks at Jeffreys.

"That is not a pertinent question, My Lord," says the Attorney General.

"It is my question, however," insists Oates. "And I will prove it to be pertinent."

Jeffreys clears his throat. "You will not, Mr. Oates. You will not ask questions that may ensnare a witness. Not in my court."

"Mr. Oates, you notice," says Southwell. "Not Doctor. You did your work well, Nathaniel."

Below us, Oates holds his arms out in supplication. "I merely ask the questions that will support my own defence, My Lord. It is a relevant question and I have good reason for asking it."

"But I will not have it asked, Mr. Oates. There is an end to it. Have you anything further?"

"Yes." Oates looks disgruntled, but he is nothing if not persistent. "Mr. Maxwell," he says, "when did I first come to St Omer's?"

"In November. November 1677."

"And what manner of place was this that we met in? Was it not run by priests and Jesuits?"

"Mr. Oates!" Jeffreys is red in the face and the Attorney General is on his feet. "Mr. Maxwell, you are not obliged to answer that question."

"But what is to say that he has not been put upon by his superiors to say these things about me?" whines Oates.

"Nor is that a suitable question either, Mr. Oates!"

"Then I am hardly used, My Lord, most hardly used. How can I conduct my defence without questioning the witness?" Oates wheedles, but his eyes are on fire with anger and frustration. For a moment he and Jeffreys glare at each other. Anne leans forward, her lips open, absorbed by this exchange. It ought to feel beyond good to have Oates come under the thumb of the law. Jeffreys draws in a breath and grows larger in his chair, looming over the courtroom.

"I do not care, Mr. Oates, to hear your opinions on how you are treated. You will ask only questions that are within the bounds of the court's discretion. When you ask questions that are impertinent, extravagant, or ensnaring, you will be corrected and kept within the proper limits."

Oates's shoulders drop. He rubs at his chin. He looks downcast, but still he is not done. "Then, My Lord," he says, "I would like to ask Mr. Maxwell if he was a witness at the trial of the Jesuits Whitbread, Ireland, and Fenwick."

"A fair question," says Jeffreys. "Mr. Maxwell?"

"I was."

"And then I would ask him how his evidence was received at that trial?" Oates folds his hands across his chest, a very priestly gesture, and gazes wide-eyed and expectantly at Jeffreys.

"What? What kind of question is that?" barks the judge.

"A fair one." His chin juts forward.

"No indeed, it is not a fair one at all."

"Yet he came to London in the matter of that trial, and his testimony was not believed or credited at all." The whine creeps back into Oates's voice. "I wish to ask why he thinks his tales of my whereabouts will be better received now."

"Because of you, Nat," whispers Anne.

"He comes because he was subpoenaed," snaps Jeffreys.

"Well, I wish to know if he will receive any reward for coming here."

"Will you?" Jeffreys turns to Maxwell, who shakes his head. "There. He was not paid. Are you done, sir?"

Oates's frustration is evident. His chest rises and falls. His brow comes so low down over his eyes that they are all but lost between his wig and chin. He can do little more at this point. Maxwell confirms that he had heard there was a Jesuit meeting that April, but that it was of no special significance. Oates suggests that Maxwell could not be certain that he'd seen Oates every day of their time together at St Omer's, but his argument is weak, and shortly afterwards the witness is dismissed.

"What do you think?" Anne says to me. "You don't look

happy."

"It is pretty much as expected," Southwell says, wrinkling his nose.

"There has been rather a *volte-face* though, hasn't there?" I say. "It is a rough form of justice, I suppose. It pains me greatly to say it, but Oates has a point and is not being given a fair hearing. Maxwell's evidence is the same. But now it is believed, whereas only a short time ago it was not."

Anne's face registers her surprise and Southwell rounds on me.

"Come now, Nat! It is a little late to be pitying the man, isn't it?' he says. 'Was Oates in London in April 1678, as he said? No, he was not. Did his false evidence lead to the deaths of innocent men? Yes, it did. That he will be punished is largely thanks to your efforts to turn the tide of public opinion. Sit back, man. Watch. Jeffreys is in a fine temper. Enjoy it."

Enjoy it? No, I don't enjoy it. But I do try to put the question of fairness out of my mind. Southwell is right. This may not be fair, but at least it is true. I squeeze Anne's fingers. I just want it to be over – for all our sakes, but most particularly for William's.

Chapter Thirty-Seven

Anne

After Maxwell, and a brief break for refreshments, the prosecution continues producing witnesses placing Oates firmly in St Omer's, not London. The crowd perks up during these testimonies. There is no love for Oates amongst his old classmates, and they speak against him damningly. Man after man describes Oates as foul-mouthed, boisterous, short-tempered, slow-witted, unpopular and, therefore, highly memorable. Next to me, Nat makes a few notes. Some of their stories will be reproduced in the next issue of *The Observator*, no doubt. After a time, the stream of witnesses from St Omer's begins to pall. Their evidence is more of the same, driving home the inescapable truth of Oates's whereabouts that April. I turn my eyes on the wider courtroom and my thoughts to William.

He is down there somewhere. Nat, Southwell, and I have been given excellent seats in a balcony. We look directly down on Oates and miss no moment of his discomfort. Only the heads of the jury men and the back of the Attorney General are visible from here, but I've a clear sight of Jeffreys at all times and the milling crowd of onlookers who fill the standing space below. There's almost constant movement in that section as people come and go: some just stopping in to catch a glimpse of the Saviour of the Nation in the toils; others, friends to a particular witness, who shuffle out after their companion's testimony is complete. There are men and women there, a fine mix of wigs and bonnets from this vantage point. It's so very typical of London that a trial, in many ways, is just another opportunity to show off one's finery.

I search but can't see William. Perhaps he has been told to wait outside. I have no idea how long it will be before he is called. He has been like a taut string these last weeks, even more subdued than usual, only saying, when pressed, that he will be fine when this is over. I am worried for him. To have to stand and declare himself a liar, to have to admit that he has committed perjury and acknowledge that he allowed himself to be blackmailed, these are hard truths for a quiet and honourable schoolmaster. What will they ask him, and how will he answer? Most importantly, will he be sent to gaol?

Down below, the parade of witnesses from St Omer's is over, and Oates wrangles again with Lord Jeffreys over the Latin wording of the indictment brought against him. He is a fool. Jeffreys quickly silences him on the point but Oates moves on boldly, bringing up the matter of Ireland's conviction for treason.

"I desire that a point of law be considered, My Lord," he declares.

"Ah-ha!" Beside Nat, Southwell mutters and nods his head, as might a man arriving in good time at an expected destination.

"My point," says Oates, "is whether or not the conviction of Ireland and his fellows – that they did treasonably conspire to murder the King at a consult meeting on April 24th, 1678 – ought not be taken as sufficient legal proof of the fact. For how can that meeting be false, while their conviction remains in place?"

"You see," Nat hisses at Southwell. "He should be tried for treason, not perjury!"

"No. Listen."

And indeed, Lord Jeffreys is not in the least perturbed. "There is no question to argue," he says. "God forbid that if a verdict is obtained by perjury, that the existence of the verdict should prevent the perjurer being prosecuted for his false oath. Where would the justice be in that? We are not concerned with the conclusions of that trial here, but with the testimony that was made. And if the testimony is false then the perjurer must be prosecuted."

"But is the conviction not incontrovertible evidence of fact, until – and if – it is reversed?"

"Yes, against the party convicted. But if the verdict was founded on perjured evidence, then I say again, the perjurer must be prosecuted."

Oates bows his large head and spreads his palms on the papers. When he straightens he speaks with great deliberation. "With permission, there are some observations I would like to make to the court and to the jury." Jeffreys rolls his eyes but allows it. "First is the matter of these witnesses. The jury may wonder, as I do, about all these witnesses offering new evidence: where were they in 1678? And then, what of the others? Some of these men did give testimony at the priests' trial and they merely repeat their statements today. Last time, the jury didn't believe them. Why? Because these men's religion and education betray them as men of artifice whose word is never to be trusted."

Nat grips his knees in reaction to Oates's bigotry. Jeffreys appears resigned to letting Oates have his say.

"And I would further observe," says Oates, "to you, My Lord, and to the gentleman of the jury, that I have been most harshly dealt with in this case." The emotion is back in Oates's voice. All eyes are on him as he lifts up some papers and reads: "In the case of the trial of Fathers Fenwick, Ireland, and Whitbread, it was said by Lord Chief Justice Scroggs that an 'unexceptional verdict had been found'. Why, he said that 'all objections against the evidence had been fully answered', that 'the prisoners had nothing to argue over', because 'the thing was as clear as the sun'.

"And yet, now," says Oates, "this plot, which was firmly believed in by both Houses, by judges in the highest ranks of the judiciary; this plot is now a subject of scrutiny. So, I must ask you to consider what is more likely. Is it, as I would suggest, that this is another part of one of several attempts to baffle us and disguise the truth? Have we not recently seen—" and here, the creature turns his eyes and stares directly up at Nat, "—some vile and bold attempts to overturn the murder of Sir Edmund Godfrey? Is this not another assault in the same vein? Or have our judges no sense? Have our juries no intelligence or honesty, conscience, or understanding? Have our judges and juries accepted and believed in a false plot, and therefore drawn the blood of innocent men upon their heads and the head of our Nation? Which shall it be?"

"He is bold," whispers Southwell. Oates runs his eyes around the court, letting the implication of his words settle, but Jeffreys is quick to respond.

"No, no. You go a deal too far, Mr. Oates. Judges and juries shall not take a share in that blood which was spilt on your testimony and oath!"

"But I declare it was as true then as it is now," says Oates. "The evidence from these St Omer's men was once recognised as to be part of a malicious, devious plan to over-set my revelations of the Popish Plot. They must be seen as such again, and I must be acquitted. There is no question. Thousands of Protestants in this land believe in the Popish Plot and know it to be true."

This is dangerous ground. Oates is nothing if not brave. Where I've previously held sheer meanness of spirit to be his defining feature, it comes to me that perhaps his greatest weapon is his audacity. We all look to Jeffreys. It's for him to steer Oates away from all this talk of religion and the truth, or otherwise, of the earlier verdicts.

He doesn't do so directly. Outwardly patient at least, Jeffreys asks Oates to confine himself to the question of whether there was a Jesuit consul held in April 1678, and to prove that he was in London on the 24th of that month.

Oates won't comply with Jeffreys's directions at once, but that's not unexpected. Instead, at his insistence, we must sit and listen while the full judgements against the three priests are read aloud to the court. Another break in the trial is called for but we remain in our seats. When the court reassembles, Oates is asked to summon his witnesses to prove that he was in London as he claimed.

Nat whispers in my ear. He wants to give William a few words of support before he's called. He slips past me and disappears. I lose sight of Nat, but down below I finally spot

William. He looks, from his fingertips to the ends of his hair, as stiff as a dog on point.

Chapter Thirty-Eight

William

Titus calls a Mistress Mayo, and a man named Butler. I remember them from the priests' trial – a shambling pair. Jeffreys easily finds and exploits the discrepancies in their evidence. Both were servants in the household of Sir Richard Barker but he's apparently too unwell to appear himself. Both say Titus visited Barker's house, in disguise, towards the end of April 1678. Jeffreys pushes them to describe Titus's hat and style of wig. They're asked to detail every time they saw Titus and explain over and over again how they were able to date each occasion. Better men and women would falter under Jeffreys's close questioning. In the end, they differ on the details of his wig, of all things, and grow less and less certain about when they saw him. After the St Omer's men, their testimonies come as something of a light relief to the crowd, but anxiety balloons in my guts.

Jeffreys clearly enjoys the cut and thrust. "And this is all you can offer?" he says to Titus. "What about your lodgings? You say you were in London for several months. Did no-one else see you here? Only an old woman who barely knew you, and a rambling coachman? Where did you stay all that time? Where did you eat?"

"I can tell you where I lodged," says Titus.

"Do so then. Let us hear it. It will benefit your defence."

"But is that the point in question?"

"Upon my word, yes! It is the main point in this case. Where did you lodge?"

"Well, My Lord, I stayed mainly with Father Whitbread."

Jeffreys smiles and leans back in his chair. "With Father

Whitbread, the priest, hanged by virtue of your own testimony and therefore not able to give testimony?" He curls his upper lip and sniffs once or twice. "A shame for you. It sticks with me, this lack of evidence that you were here. I have to say, it does not satisfy. Have you more witnesses?"

"My Lord, I take this very hard," Titus whines. "Many months have passed. Witnesses have moved away, become ill or infirm. I take it hard that I am asked to prove something now, something already proved to the satisfaction, to the enthusiastic satisfaction, of the courts, the judiciary, and even Parliament, at the time. I would move to another part of my defence." He bends and rakes through his papers. I imagine that he's busier controlling his temper than finding anything in his bundles, for he comes up empty-handed yet plunges forth in strident tones. "I would contend, in my defence, that I am not the guilty party here, but a victim. It is clear to me – and to many here, I am sure – that this whole event is part of a wider conspiracy to cover up and deny the history of the plot."

"Really?" Jeffreys throws his hands up in distaste, but Titus won't be deterred.

"We have seen the recent attempts to baffle the public over the death of Justice Godfrey; we have all been subject to a torrent of misinformation and—"

"Mr. Oates!" Jeffreys bellows down. Impassioned though he is, Titus freezes, his mouth hanging open.

"Mr. Oates, I must and will keep you to evidence that is proper. Evidence of fact, not opinion or hearsay. The jury will not attend to that which is not proper evidence. Confine yourself to the question of this meeting in April 1678, or the jury will be asked to quit the chamber until you can behave appropriately!"

It's stormy, even by the usual standards of our judiciary. My stomach heaves. Sweat forms on my brow. My voice must not fail me. I must be steady.

It seems Titus had planned to distract the jury from the question of his being or not being in London, by parading a gallery of public figures from the House of Commons and the Lords to testify that he should be believed now, as he once had been. Unfortunately for him, the majority of the great and the good whom he's subpoenaed, quite simply fail to appear. Some are ill; others have been present, but left; some are too busy, or their whereabouts are unknown. Finally, Titus spots one peer in the crowd, the Earl of Huntingdon, and asks if he might be called. Huntingdon takes the stand and is sworn in as a witness, but he does no good to Titus's defence. When asked to give account of what credit Oates had been given by the House of Lords, he doesn't mince his words.

"Mr. Oates's discovery, it is true," says Huntingdon, "found a good reception in the House of Lords, but this was grounded on the opinion that he was an honest man and that what he said was true. Indeed, had the matter been true, it was of the highest importance that it be examined. But since that time, it has become apparent that his evidence was so full of contradictions, falsehoods, and perjuries on which innocent blood has been shed, that I believe a great many men are heartily sorry for what happened in those earlier trials and regretful of their part in what took place. I do believe, My Lord, that the majority of peers have quite altered their opinion of this man and of his evidence, and think – as I do – that his evidence was completely false."

"Do you have anything to say, Mr. Oates?" asks Jeffreys.

"Only that the Earl was asked to give evidence of opinion in the past, not the present."

Titus has grown sulky. He knows things are not going his way.

The Crown begins to call its witnesses against Titus's character. The temperature in the courtroom rises as more spectators arrive. We are pressed too close together for comfort. The man beside me smells of onions. I force a mouthful of bile back down my throat and shuffle though the press of bodies to find a different vantage point. The Queen's physician, George Wakeman, who was tried but acquitted of involvement in the Popish Plot is called and appears to enjoy himself on the stand. Wakeman testifies that the claims Titus made about Jesuits paying him to poison the King were lies. I like the doctor. What must he must have gone through? He deserves this moment. He certainly never takes his eyes off Titus, even though the man in question occupies himself with his papers, as if this part of the proceedings has nothing to do with him. Next, we have the pleasure of hearing the perjury charge against Titus in the case of William Parker in Hastings finally read out in full. Truly the season has changed: the wind is all against him now, but I can't bear to look up to where Nat and Anne are sitting. The thought that Henry should be up there with them crushes me all over again.

At last, the clerk calls on me. The court falls silent. I push my way through to the witness box and lift my eyes to stare across at Titus. He raises an eyebrow and cracks his knuckles.

"My Lord," begins a lawyer. "We have heard a great deal of complaint from Mr. Oates that he has been asked to answer these questions and prove his veracity after a lapse of time of several years. The reason that we would like to give Mr. Oates, to the jury and to the wider public, is that we have evidence now of his actions and corruption which, balanced with the overwhelming evidence from St Omer's, creates a damning picture against him. If Mr. Oates had been truthful in the trial of February 5th, 1680, it would be natural to expect that he would call again all the available witnesses who gave evidence of his being in London at the April meeting. Yet he has not. Mr. William Smith, please tell the court what evidence you gave in this regard in the aforementioned trial."

"I gave evidence, My Lord, that Mr. Oates was in London during April and May of the year 1678."

"And was that statement correct and true?"

"It was not."

The reaction around the room is instantaneous, the collective gasp like steam escaping from a giant kettle. I keep my eyes down and bite on my lip to stop its trembling.

Titus's voice rises above the crowd: "My Lord, a point of law! He is a perjurer! The man condemns himself out of his own mouth! Are we to submit to this? To listen to the lies of an admitted criminal?"

The scorn in his voice is like a whip across my face. I lift my eyes long enough to see Judge Jeffreys scowl. He turns and confers with his colleagues on the bench. The Bible rests on the stand in front of me. I finger its leather and pray to be allowed to continue.

Jeffreys finishes his conference and takes a moment resettling himself, adjusting his robes and making sure he has the attention of the whole court. His expression concerns me. Then he speaks.

"The court finds the witness is, by his own admission, unreliable."

This is my nightmare.

Titus slaps the table. The crowd begins to jeer and boo. In the gallery, Southwell frowns and Anne's hands are on her cheeks. Nat is nowhere to be seen.

"We will hear from the Attorney General on this," says Jeffreys. 'If he has any evidence as to this man's perjury, let him explain how this is the responsibility of the accused. But we will not tolerate dishonest men to be heard in a court of law. Criminals, convicted by law or by their own admission, are a disgrace to our good society and the court of our King. Stand down the witness."

I should move. But the judge's words are blows to the head. To be spoken of in such terms with no avenue of redress, is terrible. Failing to bring this evidence against Titus Oates unmans me. I am led away in a daze. People in the crowd shout and complain. They call me a lying make-bait and a sham.

I am all that. And worse.

Chapter Thirty-Nine

Nat

William is as far away from me in the court as it is possible to be. The top of his head disappears from view as he's bustled away. Disappointed, I push my way back up to the balcony to Anne. Her eyes are wide and bright with tears.

"I can't believe it," she whispers.

We sit there, stunned, hoping the Attorney General can salvage something. He's an experienced prosecutor and quickly recovers. "My Lords and gentlemen of the jury, it is a point of fact," he says, "that this man you have seen today, Mr. William Smith, first came to the Crown's attention in 1678, when he was accused by Titus Oates of being a conspirator in the supposed Popish Plot. I refer you to Mr. Oates's own narrative, Article 54."

My lips move in time to the Attorney General's as he reads it; I've gone over Oates's words so often. He reads: "That one Matthew Medbourne, a player in the Duke's Theatre, one Mr. Penny, Mr. Mannock, Mr. Sharpe, and one Mr. William Smith, a schoolteacher, did meet in a club on Thursday nights in the Fuller's Rent near Gray's Inn. And these men did meet there with diverse Jesuits and priests, and with them would vilify the House of Commons and plan to go about the city spreading dissent against our representatives and make further treasonable remarks against the King and the Protestant religion."

That was it. That article had led to both William's and Matthew's arrests. While William spent only days in prison, Matthew died there. No mention of Medbourne's fate is made in court, though. His is just another name in the long list of

Oates's forgotten victims.

"Mr. William Smith was arrested and released in the month of October 1678, due to lack of corroborating evidence, but he lost his licence to teach as a result of his arrest. He next appears on February 5th, 1680 giving evidence in *support* of Mr. Oates. Something of a turnaround, is it not? What love would this schoolteacher have for the man who cost him his career and livelihood? Is it not reasonable to ask what would have induced him to give evidence in support of one who must be considered his enemy?"

Oates is back on his feet. "Perhaps he gave evidence because he was subpoenaed to do so, and he spoke the truth! He stated that he dined with me the day before the priests' meeting – on April 23rd in London – and that was the truth."

"Then why have you not called him to give testimony on your behalf again, Mr. Oates?" Jeffreys folds him arms and peers down at Oates. "You did not call him; the prosecution did. Why would that be?"

"Because he has been got at, of course," squeals Oates. "Because there is a plot to overthrow me and overturn the people's true understanding of the threat these damned Catholics pose to every good Englishman up and down our land!"

"Or," declares the Attorney General, raising his voice to match Oates's. "Or, because he would have foresworn himself – as he did do – though it brings him into great shame and subject to public remark!" He slams his hand on the table. "I have here a paper," he says, his voice steely hard. "This is a certificate, written by Titus Oates, concerning the honesty of Mr. Smith. It is dated just three days before the Jesuits' trial, in February 1680. Have I permission to read it, your Lordship?"

Jeffreys indicates that he has.

"It says, 'These are to certify that William Smith is no Papist, and that he is upon good service at this time for his King and Country, of which, I hope, those that are enquirers after recusants will take notice.' The document is witnessed, My Lord, and signed by Titus Oates."

"Is this your handwriting, Mr. Oates?"

The paper is handed to Oates, who scrunches up his face, peering at it uncertainly.

"I cannot say it is my hand. I do not believe it is," he says.

"He says it is not his hand," says Jeffreys, and glares at Oates.

"Well, I do not say it is *not* my hand. But I do not remember it; not the writing of it, nor what it contains."

"Really? Because many reading this may think it appears remarkably like a bribe." Jeffreys' gaze is withering. 'Mr. Attorney General, have you any further comment?'

"That's not fair," whispers Anne. "He didn't lie in exchange for that piece of paper. He did it for Matthew. And for us."

I squeeze her hand. She is right, and this whole trial disappoints me greatly. I came here for revenge but wish it would come on the wings of truth instead of injustice in a different form.

The prosecution is answering the Judge. "I only wish to add, your Honour, that the jury consider the evidence before them and find the facts that they demonstrate. William Smith was denounced by Mr. Oates, his career ruined. Yet three days before the Jesuit trial, Mr. Smith received a letter from Mr. Oates freeing him from all suspicion. On the 5th of February, Mr. Smith gave material evidence which he now claims was false. I would suggest to the jury that William Smith was pressured into giving evidence in support of Mr. Oates claims, and that this paper was his reward."

"And what do you think, My Lord? Will you suffer this evidence?" splutters Oates. "It is implication and suggestion, not hard evidence against me. I am hardly used, My Lord, hardly used!" He throws himself back into his chair like a child baulking at his dinner.

"Settle yourself, Mr. Oates! Behave in a manner appropriate to my courtroom or I will be obliged to ask you to absent yourself!" calls Jeffreys. "It's not my opinion that is your concern here. My opinion will be given only after our good gentlemen in the jury have drawn their own conclusions. They have heard the prosecution's evidence and attended to your answers. Have you anything further for them? Can you prove by other witnesses that this meeting between you and Mr. Smith did in fact take place? Or perhaps you would like to explain to them why you impugned Mr. Smith in your narrative, yet later issued him with a character reference? Mr. Oates? Anything to add?"

Oates subsides with a wave of one hand and sits for some time supporting his head bent, appearing to pore over his notes.

Anne grabs my arm. "Where is William now? Can you see him?"

"No. Do you think he has gone?"

"I hope so. The way they have insulted him, I would hate for him to hear of it."

She is right. He's been painted as a man weak enough to perjure himself to save his own skin. The greater truth remains hidden.

Suddenly I don't have the stomach for any more of this charade. "I'm going to find him," I say.

Chapter Forty

Anne

I am glad Nat has gone to find poor William. He should not be alone at such a time. As the trial continues, there can be no doubt that it goes badly for Titus Oates. He is asked to produce his final arguments.

"This won't take long," says Southwell, and he is right. Oates has little enough grounds for defence, but nevertheless he tries to turn defence into attack.

"My Lord, to try to convict me of perjury, a whole parcel of witnesses from St Omer's have been brought here. Some came before and were not believed by the jury or by Lord Chief Justice Scroggs. More come now, and I will not remark upon their testimonies but ask the good gentlemen of the jury to consider what manner of men these are. They are all Catholics, every one. All men of the same religion and the same interests. Their testimonies are all the same to me. I object to their evidence as I object to their appearance in this courtroom. I contend that no Papist has any right or should have any expectation to be received as a witness in a court of law. I contend that no Papist should be believed—"

"Have you come here to preach, Mr. Oates?" calls Jeffreys.

"My Lord, I demand to be heard. It is my right to take exception to these witnesses!"

"Your right, Mr. Oates? Your right? Your right is to be heard when you speak properly and to the evidence. Nothing more."

"But, My Lord, I do insist on it!" Oates's chest heaves and his voice rises. "These men's religion is an exception to their testimony—"

"I am warning you, Mr. Oates. You are verging on

impudence if you insist on this."

"But it is a point of law! It is against our laws to be a Jesuit priest or a member of the order of the Romish church!"

"Does the law say they are not good witnesses?"

"It shows that every one of them, trained in St Omer's, has broken the laws of our country."

"And yet they did not own themselves to be Jesuits or priests, or to have taken orders."

"But—"

"But nothing, Mr. Oates. Nothing. You have been heard on this and we will hear no more. If you have nothing more than slander and scandal to offer us, or your bleating refrain that you were believed before, then we can spend no further time in hearing you."

Oates sinks down into his chair. He looks battered.

Southwell and I exchange glances. He puts his hands on his knees. "I believe these matters will conclude to our satisfaction. You will stay and hear the rest?"

I nod.

"Well, you are nothing if not thorough," he says.

Not long afterwards, Oates also leaves the courtroom for a time, pleading illness. The crowd has thinned, the air is clearer, the end in sight. Darkness has fallen outside. When Oates returns, Jeffreys certainly makes sure that the jury knows their judge's opinion of the case. Nat ought to be here for this moment. I hold the Judge's words in my mind in order to repeat them to Nat as faithfully as possible.

"Gentlemen," he says. "When I consider the circumstances of this case now, I do truthfully think it a very strange and wonderful thing that any man should ever have believed in Titus Oates. It is strange to reflect on what popular credit he did have only a short number of years ago. But still, who could have imagined that any man on this earth could have had his impudence, his daring, that he would stand before our King and Parliament and tell such infamous lies, lies which took away the lives of innocent men? Only now have men overcome their fears; only now is there a climate where we

263

can consider these fears more calmly. God forbid that we should have continued any longer in our blindness and delusion. Truly, we must be thankful that this matter is now laid honestly open before us.

"This is a case of perjury before you, but I would ask you to consider it as much, much more. In truth, gentlemen, this is a case of murder. It is murder not done by the hand, but in the form of the Law, and that angers me, as I am sure it angers you and all honest men.

"Indeed, I am angry now. My blood curdles, and my spirits rise when I consider how this man has stood before us, impudent, brazen, without shame or confusion in his face. The monstrous villain has even pretended infirmity so that he could hide from my words and your justice. But it is not his supposed physical infirmity that I ask you to consider. It is the depravity of his mind, the blackness of his soul, and the baseness of his actions that make him unworthy even to tread upon this earth! My words are warm, but you will pardon that. You have the evidence before you. We will wait upon your verdict."

These are the words we've dreamed of hearing. It's the confirmation and vindication of Nat's persistence. Yet I have no sense of jubilation. Instead, I've a rising sense of distaste for the whole affair. For what has really changed, except the season of opinion? And where are the others, to share this moment? Southwell has left, Nat and William have disappeared, and Henry is dead. I want to get out of here. I want to go home. But at the same time, it must be witnessed. We owe it to poor Henry. One of us must see it through.

It is not long until the jury returns the inevitable guilty verdict. Oates looks ill, his face pale and blotchy. Where earlier he blustered, now he cowers in his chair as Jeffreys closes proceedings. "Gentlemen, there has been some talk today of judges and of their opinions of verdicts," he says. "And because of that, I take the liberty now to declare my mind and opinion to you. For my part, I am satisfied, quite satisfied, in my conscience. You have given us today a good and just verdict. And for that, you have my thanks."

It is over. The judges, the jury, the runners, the witnesses, all the crush of spectators, file their way out into the London night. Down below, a glimpse of red hair makes me wonder if Valentine Greatrakes has also wanted to see justice done. For a few moments longer, I stay in my seat. My mind is empty. I'm very tired and hungry.

A story from the schoolroom occurs to me: the story of King Pyrrhus and the great losses he suffered at the hands of the Romans, even though he had been victorious. Nat was dragged away only moments after we lost Martha. Henry died in the fire. And William. William came here today to redeem himself but was shown the door and refused a hearing.

Sudden fear has me leaping to my feet.

Chapter Forty-One

Nat

William is not in the courtroom. I push and twist my way through the crowd three times round until I'm certain. I pass quite near Titus Oates at one point, but I've no more interest in him. When I finally quit the Old Bailey, it's still light. Evening will be with us shortly, however. The clouds are low in the sky, blanketing the city. I stand for a moment and catch my breath, wondering where William has gone.

He is not, like me, a habitué of the coffee shops or a man normally much inclined to drink; but today is a day unlike any other, so I start with the taverns and coffee shops. I draw a blank. I send a boy into the Fuller's Rent, giving him a sketchy picture of my dear friend, but he swears there's no man like that in the place. I go to our home, the print shop, and finally his room across the river – at each place running through the ways to help him through this disastrous testimony.

As I climb up the narrow stairs, I wonder why I didn't come here first. I'm suddenly sure this is where he is, but when I knock, he doesn't answer. I put my ear to the door and hear nothing. Perhaps I've missed him somewhere. Probably he is even now in one of the places I've just left. The idea of starting over again is draining. It has been some time since I left the courtroom. All will be over there by now; Anne should be on her way home. I lean my head against his door to rest it. At my touch, the door swings open.

"William?"

This is the first time I've ever been in his room. His bed is neatly made and his desk is tidy, but paper crunches under my feet. The floor swims with papers and pamphlets, all marked with ink in circles or underscored. There's not a floorboard in sight, just paper everywhere. I'm intruding. Even as I step inside, I imagine how I'll apologise for invading his home.

That's when I see him.

I take in the angle of his neck, his closed eyes, the air between his limp feet and the floor, the hook in the wall, the rope, the fallen stool.

Plunging forward, I grab at his legs to take his weight. Just as I lose hope, a rattle sounds in his throat. I brace myself to support him but won't be able to hold him there for long. He groans, and pain slices my back. I stretch one foot but can't reach the stool. My eyes are wide, my breathing ragged. I don't think I can hold him. I don't think I can. But I'll let my bones crumble and my veins burst before I let him go.

"Nat!"

Anne bursts into the room, a lantern swinging in her hand. She dives at once for the stool and wedges it under William's legs to support his weight.

"Hold him," I say. She pushes him against the wall while I pull up a chair and climb up to untie the rope. Untethered, William's body flails out, but together we catch him. Somehow, we lower him to the floor.

"Is he breathing?" Anne brings the lantern to his face.

"Yes."

"Do we need a doctor? What should we do?"

"Wait!"

William coughs, and slowly one of his hands reaches up. He touches the raw skin on his neck. His eyes open.

"Oh, thank God!" Anne's shoulders drop, and she puts her head in her hands. "I thought I might be too late."

"Too late?" I say. "You knew?"

"Yes. Or no. At least, not for certain. But I suddenly thought of his desperate disappointment and feared the worst. I came straight here." Her eyes are wet with tears.

"We are lucky you did. I couldn't have held him much longer."

"You did wonderfully." She reaches across the bed and takes my left hand. I stretch and hold William's cold fingers in my right.

"Are you sure I shouldn't fetch a doctor?" she says.

"No." It's more of a croak than an answer, but it is William's voice. My shoulders shake. I don't hold back the tears.

It is some time before any of us regain our composure. By then William is propped up in bed and Anne has lit candles so the room looks normal, apart from all the papers now piled up in one corner. I don't look over again at the hook.

"What happened?" William whispers.

"In court?" I ask.

William blinks and nods his head just a fraction.

"I don't know. I didn't care. I was looking for you. We were worried."

Colour rises in William's pale cheek.

"He was found guilty, dear friend,' says Anne. "It is all over. There was no need for this." She slowly waves her arm around the room, taking in William and the mess of papers. William is crying again now. His mouth falls open, and saliva hangs in thin threads between his lips.

But he is alive.

Chapter Forty-Two

Anne

A month later, and for the final time, we go to see Titus Oates in a courtroom. He is brought to hear his sentence wearing heavy iron fetters. He looks genuinely ill now, and his mouth works as though he's chewing on the inside of his cheek. He's unrecognisable as the man I slapped across the face at the Pope-burning procession.

Oates is entitled to plead grounds for clemency or mitigation of his sentence, but he appears unprepared. In a wavering, unsteady voice, he asks for more time before sentencing, but Jeffreys is impatient to see proceedings brought to a close. Nat, William, Sir Robert Southwell, and I peer down from the balcony. There is sweat on Oates's brow and his breathing is laboured. When he stands up, he does so with difficulty, as if he has pains in his legs. He clutches the table for support. There is nothing happening here that the man does not fully deserve. And yet none of us smile.

Jeffreys is bitingly curt. "When a person is convicted of such a foul and malicious perjury as this," he declares, "it is impossible for the court within the laws as they stand, to punish the guilty party in any way proportionally to his offence. Hanging is not open to us, yet it must be said that the law is defective if such a man as this is not to be hanged for his heinous actions. It behoves the court to make an example in this case. Innocent blood has been shed in this land, and all that you have said in your defence is that over forty witnesses should not be listened to simply because they are Roman Catholics. But they have been listened to, and the judgement of the court upon you is as follows:

"First, the court orders that you pay a fine of two thousand marks. Second, that you be stripped of all your Canonical habits."

Next to me, Southwell is nodding.

"Third, the court demands that you stand in the pillory before Westminster Hall upon Monday next between the hours of ten and twelve, with a paper on your head declaring your crime.

"Fourth, upon Tuesday next, you will stand in the pillory at the Royal Exchange between the hours of twelve and two, bearing a similar inscription."

Sir Robert leans forward and he and Nat exchange speaking glances.

"Fifth, you shall next Wednesday be whipped from Aldgate to Newgate." That produces some whispers.

"And sixth, you shall next Friday be whipped from Newgate to Tyburn by the common hangman."

Jeffreys pauses, although it's clear that he has more to say. I hold my breath.

"Your crime, Mr. Oates, which we revile most heartily, is, moreover, a crime that you committed several times, repeatedly swearing falsely about your fellow men. For this reason, we have chosen an annual punishment for you, to best commemorate your repeated offences."

Titus Oates grips the table in front of him as Jeffreys continues.

"Upon the 24th of April every year, for as long as you live, you will stand in the pillory at Tyburn opposite the gallows for one hour.

"Upon the 26th of April every year, you will stand in the pillory in front of Westminster Hall for one hour." Small gasps from around the packed courtroom follow each pronouncement.

"Upon the 28th of April, you will do the same in the pillory at Charing Cross, every year.

"On the 30th of April, you will do the same in the pillory at Temple Gate." Oates sits down heavily in his chair as Jeffreys delivers the final blow.

"And on the 5th of February, in commemoration of the trial in 1680, you will stand in the pillory before the Royal Exchange for one hour. You will do this every year, during your lifetime, and remain a prisoner of the King's Bench for as long as you shall live."

I glance at Nat and William. Both look as shocked as I. Oates's sentence is extraordinary – vindictive even – in its scope.

Jeffreys gets to his feet. "This is the sentence of the court," he says, "and I take leave to tell you that if it had been in my power to carry it further, I would have done so, even to giving the Judgement of death on you, for I am sure that you deserve it. Let him be taken away."

***

A day or two later, we gather in our kitchen. William sits at the table, his long legs sticking out almost to the other side. Nat is teasing me with that look of his, one that always has me reaching for a stray curl to tuck behind one ear. My face is hot. I've just pulled a tray of biscuits from the oven. They steam gently on the table before me. I sip at my cup of bergamot tea and allow myself to hope.

"Will you go and see him pilloried?" I ask Nat.

"Absolutely not. Nor whipped neither. Would you want to?"

"No. It is enough to know that he been dealt with."

"He has been dealt with roughly," Nat says. "Deserved as it is, it gives me no pleasure."

"Did you ever really think it would?" William's face is grave, the scars of the deaths we've suffered still present in the dark shadows under his eyes and the fading burn mark at his neck.

"Once, perhaps," Nat says. "But not now. Now it's the people in this room that give me pleasure. And long may it remain so."

***

We do not look back. Every April, we leave London and go to stay in the country, either with Nat's family in Sussex or, more often, with friends in the Cotswolds. Nat is well rewarded for his pursuit of Oates, as Southwell promised he would be. The knighthood makes a deep and favourable impression on my father and mother. Nat calls the new accord and regular visits between our households the archetypical double-edged sword.

We never go to see Titus Oates suffer his punishments. He was tried and found guilty. He is in prison, that's enough. The manner of his trial unsettled Nat. My husband says he has been left with the abiding sense that nothing has changed in England but the flavour of public opinion; that our inherent bigotry and bias lurk undisturbed. His interest in public life has diminished accordingly. Oh, he hasn't changed his spots completely. He still writes news commentary with a bias towards the Tory rather than Whig line, but the heat for it is gone. He widens his literary interests, and we publish his own translations of Greek and Latin classics. He wins a fine reputation as a reliable reviewer of the theatre.

William and I run the print shop together. Given time and patience, our friend becomes quite adept at the business, and I'm thankful for his help as family obligations come between my new venture and myself.

When our son Henry is born, the memory of what happened with Martha makes me almost afraid to push. But the child squawks his way into the world, and there is never a quiet moment from that day on. The same is true of his sisters, who follow soon after.

We are blessed, Sarah says, and she spends much time with me, helping with her nieces and nephew, although she claims that the calm quiet of her own home is always wonderful after an hour or two with us.

Today, Nat kisses Sarah's cheek as she leaves and then winks at me. I know that look of old. More often than not, he can still tempt me up the stairs with his eyes, but sometimes I like to remember I'm a mature married lady and shake my head at him.

This is not one of those times.

Chapter Forty-Three

William

I go and watch.

It gives me no pleasure, but every April I do it all the same. Anne never mentions Titus Oates, but for the next three years, when they return from the country, Nat asks me if I have watched Titus take his punishment and I tell him that I have. Beyond that, we do not talk of him, although Henry's name is often on our lips as we speak of what he might have said of this or that. As time ticks by, the truth of what we went though seems incredible, and this sensation only increases when Titus is whipped and pilloried every Spring. Each year he grows thinner and weaker, more like the boy he was when I knew him first than that bombastic, vigorous, cursing beast that Nat and I saw dragged from Whitehall in chains. I remind myself of his victims. In their name, I watch him suffer.

When King Charles dies, his brother, James Duke of York, becomes King, but only two years later he is overthrown. Now James's Protestant daughter, Mary, and her husband William of Orange sit on the throne. Titus Oates is pardoned and released from the King's Bench Prison in Southwark.

This I also go and watch.

He shuffles out alone. For a moment, it appears that no-one will meet him. The sycophants and the pleasers that surrounded him in his heady days of fine living in Whitehall are long gone. I'm about to turn away when I notice someone walking toward him. It is Titus's father, Samuel Oates. Samuel does not smile but he does put his arm around his son. It is an everyday gesture. They are two men, father and son, walking down a quiet street; nothing more. Something leaves me in

273

that moment. Some of the bitterness, some of the pain, some of the sorrow, that this man brought into my life.

I would not call the moment happy, but the following year, when there is nothing to watch, my heart is lighter.

Historical Afterword

The Road to Newgate is a work of fiction inspired by real historical events. Most of the characters are based on real people and only a handful are entirely fictional. History books about the Popish Plot show a much more complex picture, with more informers, more trials, and more lies, but the aspects I have focused on – the character of Titus Oates, the mysterious death of St Edmund Berry Godfrey, and the importance of public opinion in bringing Oates to justice – provide a solid representation of this complex period in history.

The man who did most to bring down Titus Oates was Sir Roger L'Estrange. He was the Licenser until his post disappeared in the chaos brought about by Oates's plot revelations. He also wrote *The Observator*, was entrapped by Simpson Tonge, and had a wife called Anne. A man called Nathaniel Thompson wrote in a similar vein, and was involved in efforts to expose Miles Prance's perjury in the murder trial of Green, Berry, and Hill, but little is known about him. My character, Nat, is based on these two men. His personality is invented.

Every story in the novel concerning Titus Oates's upbringing, education, and employment, up until the point he set London on fire with his revelations, is based on the historical record. Where he interacts with my fictional characters, his words and actions are invented, but I believe they are in line with his known character. The storyline of his blackmailing of William Smith is conjecture on my part, but it does account for Smith's various mentions in the historical record. The club that met in Fuller's Rent did exist, and the suggestion of homosexuality in Titus's relationships there, although unproven, is a recurring theme in historical analyses of these events.

Women had a very limited role in public life in the 17th century, but printing was one industry in which a woman could work and gain a level of independence. Although often silent in the historical record, women cannot have been silent in their own lives. This background informed the development of Anne's storyline. Other characters – Henry Broome, Sir Robert Southwell, Valentine Greatrakes, Miles Prance, Mistress Pamphlin, and Henry Moor, for example – were all real people.

The court proceedings in *The Road to Newgate* are based on the historical record. Many of the words – particularly the most extreme and bigoted comments ascribed to Scroggs and Jeffreys – are direct quotes from transcripts of the various trials that took place.

Finally, a note on the timeline. Oates lived the high life in London for several years longer than I allowed him in this novel. Anne, Nat, and William could not wait for the historical chronology of events to play out before they were allowed to move on with their lives. For the record, although his reputation was much diminished from 1681 onwards, Oates was not tried for perjury until after the death of Charles II in 1685. When James II, a Catholic, succeeded to the throne, Oates was tried and convicted as described here. Then, after the Glorious Revolution of 1688 when Protestant rule was re-established under William and Mary, Oates was released from prison. He died in 1705.

For suggestions for further reading and more historical background, please visit my website, **www.kate-braithwaite.com**

Fantastic Books
Great Authors

CROOKED
CAT

Meet our authors and discover
our exciting range:

- Gripping Thrillers
- Cosy Mysteries
- Romantic Chick-Lit
- Fascinating Historicals
- Exciting Fantasy
- Young Adult and Children's
  Adventures
- Non-Fiction

85222011R00168

Made in the USA
Middletown, DE
23 August 2018